LOVE ME

Paul,
thanks for coming!

Enjoy!

Garenne
oo

19/01/..

LOVE ME

Gemma Weekes

Chatto & Windus
LONDON

Published by Chatto & Windus 2009

2 4 6 8 1 0 9 7 5 3 1

Copyright © Gemma Weekes 2009

Gemma Weekes has asserted her right under the Copyright, Designs and
Patents Act 1988 to be identified as the author of this work

First published in Great Britain in 2009 by
Chatto & Windus
Random House, 20 Vauxhall Bridge Road,
London SW1V 2SA
www.rbooks.co.uk

Addresses for companies within The Random House Group
Limited can be found at:
www.randomhouse.co.uk/offices.htm

The Random House Group Limited Reg. No. 954009

A CIP catalogue record for this book
is available from the British Library

ISBN 9780701181154

The Random House Group Limited supports The Forest Stewardship
Council (FSC), the leading international forest certification organisation. All
our titles that are printed on Greenpeace approved FSC certified paper carry
the FSC logo. Our paper procurement policy can be found at
www.rbooks.co.uk/environment

Mixed Sources
Product group from well-managed
forests and other controlled sources
www.fsc.org Cert no. TT-COC-2139
© 1996 Forest Stewardship Council

FSC

Set in Bembo by Palimpsest Book Production Limited,
Grangemouth, Stirlingshire

Printed and bound in Great Britain by
CPI Mackays, Chatham ME5 8TD

Isaiah!

June

heart muscle.

There he is.

There – twinkling like a silver coin amongst the coppers. He hurts brighter than a punch in the face.

What a meal. What a drug. God help me. He's drawn me out like a crack dealer attracts stinking, wild-eyed cats. I'm squeezed blue by love, sweating like a runner, breath shallow, chest a cave full of bats.

It's one of those humid summer nights in London, coloured red with pollution and overflowing with weekend drunks. Neon is loud on the pavement. Girls are out in their strappy clothes and tight shoes and the boys are hair-gelled and over-boozed, yelling up and down the street in their 'look-at-me' tribes. And I wish I loved one of those simple, random boys. A tumble like that would be easy to undo, not like this thing with Zed which is all soaked into the bone and getting rid of it is like trying to scrub off a mud stain with soot.

Look at him. A deep swagger of a man; perfect skin, classic jaw, rocking a letter 'Z' tattoo on his left bicep. He's across the road talking on his mobile, smoking a cigarette in that sly way he does everything. Zed. That's what he calls himself and I wonder who he's talking to 'cause lately he lets my calls go to the beep.

And a first love shouldn't bloom so fierce, you know? It shouldn't be like a fist forever clutched around the heart muscle. You should be able to laugh at pictures of him, only bring him up in conversation as a marker of how far you've come. You should be able to say to your friends without a single twinge:

'If we met now, he wouldn't even get a *hello*, you get me?'

He'd be too stupid, ugly, smelly, skinny, fat . . . whatever it is you wouldn't settle for as a grown-ass woman with standards. Ten years it's been and a first love shouldn't clot the soul. I don't think I even realised how bad I had it until he reappeared.

three months and infinite.

It was around the time the trees regained their spring mojo. Zed sent me an email and I was lightning-struck. He'd been scarce for years and all of a sudden he was saying the unimaginable:

Hey, he wrote in royal blue, Times New Roman. *What's good Brit girl? I've decided to quit sunny Atlanta and come out to London –*

I read that line twice. *London*. I read it three times. He decided *what?*

My crew ain't taking me nowhere right now and I don't think I'm even feeling our material. Plus my mom's leaning on me to suit up and go corporate, the banshee. As you probably know, that's never gonna happen. So I'm swinging over to the UK next week for a while to work on some tracks with this producer called King Scratch – you know him? I didn't. I couldn't move, my fingers sweaty on the keys. *Anyway, type back at me when you get the chance, let me know your location and movements. See you next week.*

Next week. He dropped those words like we saw each other on the regular, like it hadn't been almost ten years since his face. I blinked at the screen and re-read. I'd long thought of my world as being dull and impenetrable, the kick of college a distant memory, just the daily subterranean commute, and the boredom; and the rain and market research job and the odd half-arsed affair. Galaxies away from New York and my teenaged summer of love. I was certain that nothing short of sorcery would break me out.

But there I was the following Wednesday, standing tense and disbelieving in Arrivals at Heathrow Airport, wondering if I'd still recognise him or if he would have shrunk the way places you visited back in childhood always do.

Instead, he'd done the opposite.

Oh. Oh. Oh. My heart stuttered. He'd gone superhero on me. Muscled, opaque, so *tall*. And all his hair was shaved right off, all the lovely cornrows. Something like a monster truck ploughed into me, a near-lethal concoction of old love and new lust. My own pitiful muscles coiled up all over, tight and achy as if yoga had never been invented. It was so good to see him I wished immediately that he hadn't come.

'Wow,' he said when he reached me, eyes grazing my steep curves. 'All grown up, huh?'

My cheek-kiss was awkward. I tried to take his bag and he laughed. I couldn't believe how white his teeth were, how rich his skin. I couldn't remember what I'd been doing since the time I saw him last. A blank decade yawned open behind me.

We sat knee-to-knee on the train into central London. Me stunned, him chatting companionably about this and that, skirting the big lessons, keeping it light. I stared at all his changes, the confidence that had settled down easy into his stance and carriage, filling in all the cracks and wiping any trace of fragility. I was dumb with admiration and grief.

Now, three months and infinite daydreams later, he leans against the wall of the club. Looks at his watch, scratches his face. I'm gonna just tell him straight out: *Zed, let's stop playing stupid games and . . .*

But wait.

Who the fuck is the mystery blonde?

suicide heels.

No!

I'm stopped short, paralysed on the lip of the kerb. All I can see in the evening dim is miles of yellow hair and two white arms wrapped around Zed like a creeper and I think I'm going to vomit. He's laughing at something she said. It chafes me. I want to make him laugh like that, make his cheeks dimple and his eyes narrow. He glances across the street but fails to see me, probably because Blondie's in the way.

I rushed all the way down here with my heart screaming 'I'm late! I'm late!', running for buses and diving for rapidly closing train doors on the choked tube platforms. And all day I've been too nervous to eat and when I've tried, it's gone down like an Irish joke on St Patrick's Day. I've not been feeling very well as a result and I guess that means I'm not being hyperbolical when I conclude that I love him so much he makes me *sick*.

All that just so he can stand over there with some blonde!

Screw it. I'm going home.

'EDEN!' screams the bimbo and this has to be a joke. It can't be. But it is. Even from here that babyish face and ruined voice are unmistakable. It's bloody *her* from work.

'Hey!' She's waving at me like a deranged traffic warden or like I'm hard of hearing. 'Come ON, babes! What are you doing?'

'Max?'

And now I can't go home because they've seen me. So I cross the street and am almost run over by this asshole in a BMW who beeps his horn loud enough to shake me from the heart outwards. For a moment everything stops and all I think about is my blood spread thickly on the glittery black road. I imagine what it would be like to be that big, that *gone*, instead of this little human knot of love and scar tissue and I don't want to die exactly but sometimes I just want to escape my skin. Ball it up and throw it in the wash or something. You know?

'You look fuckin' gorgeous, love!' says Max, pulling me tight in a hug, then giving my mini-dress the once-over. 'She has *legs*! I DON'T believe it!'

'Thanks,' I say, dry-mouthed. She takes my hand and leads me over to Zed.

'Look who's 'ere! She almost got run over just for you! That was close innit, Eden?!' she says with a laugh that's like pinching a kid's cheek too hard.

'Not close enough,' I mumble. But she's already screeched off toward her next victim. Somebody kill me please. I test it out in my head. *Zed. Likes. White. Girls.* Who woulda thunk it? Zed having a penchant for mainstream punani? Billboard punani. Men's mag punani. Bony, blonde punani. So that's his thing these days, is it?

I finally look up at him and his face surrenders nothing. Not even a stray bit of beard or a pimple.

'Oy,' I say in greeting. His eyes are coloured like Pepsi with ice. Glossy eyebrows, full lips.

'Hey,' he says to me, watching Max clatter up the street in her suicide heels. I curdle. I could beat her up in less than a minute even if I had stumps for legs and was sporting a blindfold. Swallowing would burn more calories. But I can't jump ahead. Maybe it's a coincidence. Maybe this is not . . . that.

I go to hug him and for the first time I notice that his left arm is in a sling. Bruises and scratches climb his shoulder, his stance more concave than usual, his face drawn.

'Shit! What happened, Zed?'

He shrugs and pulls me into a brief, one-armed embrace.

'Nothing. I just got in a little accident,' he says. 'How you doing?' I pull away from his firm body, inhaling, memorising. Salt, smoke and musk.

'I'm fine,' I say. 'I wish you could say the same, though. Bloody hell.'

'The fuck you do to your hair?'

'I really don't know. I woke up and it was red. It's a miracle . . .'

'Uh-huh,' he laughs and doesn't mention my dress or even look at it. 'You funny.'

'It was that blasted motorbike, wasn't it?'

Zed sighs. 'Some idiot ran into me and didn't even stop. And of course I have no goddamned insurance,' he shakes his head. 'I got the bike cheap and all but still . . .'

'I bloody told you! I told you!' I say, images flashing through my head. The bike gone one way, and Zed the other. Sun glinting off the collision, helmet split like a nutshell, Zed's perfect face smashed. I come over all hot and shaky just thinking about it. 'I don't know why you bought it in the first place.'

'Well,' he says. I stare at his profile but he won't give me the benefit of his Pepsi-coloured gaze. 'It doesn't matter now.'

'Of course it bloody does, Zed! Were you badly hurt?'

'No more than usual,' he smiles crookedly and scratches the side of his head.

'What do you mean?'

'Look, it ain't nothing serious, ma. I just pulled a ligament in my leg. My arm ain't broken, just bruised real bad.'

I shake my head, vexed beyond words. I'm not sure if my anger is aimed at him or at the fool who ran him over. Just drove off and left him there! What if he'd been dying?

'I can't believe you didn't tell me! Did you go to hospital? I would have come with you! I would have come to visit . . .'

'It's fine. Max was around to help out,' he says. 'But enough about me. What you been up to?'

'This and that. Maybe you'd know that if you took my calls, Evel Knievel.'

'Sorry. You know how it gets . . .'

'Yep,' I reply, fuming. I look down into the concrete, afraid he'll see the addict's gleam I get trapped in my eye whenever he's around. Gratefully, I read the back of a flyer that's been thrust between my fingers, though I might as well try and read a chair leg. I think I've got the title for my next art project: it'll be called *Zed. Likes. White. Girls.* I can write it with a stiletto heel on a chalkboard. In Morse code. Really, really hard. Or I could write it on the back of his stupid head.

He was showing off, I bet. He almost bit the dust showing off for *her.*

'Why you so late getting down here?' he says.

'What?' *How can I be late when you didn't invite me*, I don't say. 'Has it even started yet?'

'I just thought that since you came all this way, you might have wanted to check the rhymes. As unworthy as I am of a discerning audience member like yourself. But I got off stage an hour ago—'

'Zed! You're not going back on?'

'No.'

'That's so typical. I can't believe it. I checked the time on the flyer before I left and I thought that—'

'I'm kidding.'

'What?'

'I was just fuckin' wit you.'

I hit him as hard as I can and then I remember about the accident and say 'Oh God, sorry!' but he just laughs.

'You ain't tough.'

'Whatever,' I say, but he's right. I'm really not. He didn't even flinch. 'So . . . what are you doing out here? Shouldn't you be getting ready for your set?'

He shakes his head, irritation flitting across his features. 'The mics ain't here yet. Can you believe it? Dude says he's on his way.'

'But it's cool though, right? You'll still get to perform?'

'Yeah, it's no problem. They wanted to wait for it to fill up anyway and people are just about getting here now.'

He runs his tongue nervously over his lips and the insane locomotive in my chest picks up speed, rattling the tracks and sending off sparks.

'Since when do you smoke cigarettes?' I blurt.

'What?'

'I *said*, what's with the cancer sticks? That's a new one.'

He fiddles with his lighter. 'What are you? Like, the Health Secretary of Great Britain or something?'

'No, I'm just curious about all these new ways you've been finding lately to put yourself on permanent leave.'

He sneezes, adjusts the leather cuff on his arm. 'Eden . . .'

'Oy, SEXY!' Max is back and hugging my face. 'I still can't believe you're here! I'm so glad you came down.'

And I wish she'd shut up. All over. She has the loudest, most wicked little angel face you've ever seen. And she sounds like a cockney wench who's been on a forty-a-day nicotine habit since Thatcher was prime minister. Heels, bangles, face glitter. So noisy even when her blow-up doll mouth is closed. Which is never.

'I've been trying to call you about this event!' she continues. 'You been bloody avoiding me or somefing?'

'No.' Yes. So that's what the five voicemails were about. Imagine. I've been too depressed about Zed to bother answering all the useless calls that weren't him, while she was calling to invite *me* to *his* gig. The world's gone mad. And the twenty-pack of Marlboro Lights poking out of her designer clutch is another reason to wipe her off the chalkboard. Pretty little coincidence, isn't it? Zed's usually into *herbs*, not chemicals.

'So,' I say, lips tight, voice shaking, 'am I missing something here, kids?'

Zed looks at me quizzically, blows air out between his lips, raises his eyebrows at the ground. Max has the sheer blind complacency to giggle and grab his good hand.

'I don't know *what* you're talking about,' she says conspiratorially. Winking at me. I close my eyes and everything spins for a minute.

wait—

Brooklyn, 23 May

Cherry Pepper,

Had a dream last night you were stuck at the bottom of a well trying to burrow your way out with your fingernails like a little rodent instead of climbing like you should have. Trying to scratch your way through cement! So I thought to myself, putting my hand on my hip just so, I thought, this little creature is my niece? My little warrior woman who belted out a sound like opera when she was born (and that look you gave us, so indignant! As if you were snatched from the unseen right in the middle of an important conversation)? I shouted out. I said, Love, where you going? You gonna get nowhere but dead with them tactics! You didn't answer. I don't know if that's because you couldn't hear me or because you were pretending, but whatever the blockage was in your earholes my voice was dust and you kept on tunnelling. You've always had a head harder than calabash.

Anyway, I woke up from the dream thirsty, with a pen in one hand and a sheet of paper in the other and your mother at my shoulder telling me to tell you to relax. As I write this, she's leaning over and blowing the ink dry. (I'm always telling her how that makes me vexed!) She says you need to let in a breeze, girl. Crack the blinds, throw open the windows, let fresh air sing through the house and smash all the junk on the mantel. The head should always remain cool, you hear me? Cool.

Tell me all about your young life, Cherry Pepper. Write me page upon page. I wonder about you often, whether you're still taking your pictures, whether you're married or have children. Did your father ever drag you into that woman-hating, happy-clappy church of his?

And you know what? In that dream, I should have told you to stand up in that well because if you did I bet you would have been able to see over the side of the damn thing!

Return to us in Brooklyn one day, my dear. Come for J'Ouvert?

Soon,

Aunt K.

kick.

When I reopen my hazel-brights my tormentors are so fresh, so *clean*, while I stand here unravelling. I am a peasant. I do a last-minute check in my compact mirror and my face looks like one of those 'kick me' signs you get stuck on your back in school. Plus my eyeshadow is clearly a mistake. If you should pass me in the street, just give me a box of Kleenex, cab money and tell me to go home right now and stop this. You can even throw in that kick if you like, but it might be useless since I seem to be in love with pain.

'*Cease* with the bimbo act, bitch!' I say.

And Max just thinks I'm kidding, so she laughs.

'Dave!' Zed bellows and shakes his head in relief. 'Where you been, kid?'

I look behind me and there's an irritated little guy with a nose-ring, lugging a bag of equipment. The mics.

'Drama,' Dave says simply. Zed mumbles at the bouncer and Dave scuttles into the club.

'Let's go in,' says Zed.

'Yeah, let's,' I say, wearing a smile faker than a six-pound note.

money.

Can't believe it was only three weeks ago that grown-up
Zed and I were hanging almost daily. I'd appointed myself
his guide and that was my excuse, but the truth is that
within a week of being in the LDN he was already leading
me down streets I'd never heard of. I went quickly from
being a guide to a spy. I wanted to unpick the mystery of
him, how he'd become as powerful and crisp as money.

'Those are hideous,' I said, watching him handle a pair
of black and gold Nikes.

'What?'

'Those,' I said louder, all gnarled up and couldn't help it,
'are so gaudy it's ridiculous. You'd wear those?'

One of the last places we hung out before he became so
hard to reach was a trainer shop in the West End, bright-lit
and teeming with youngsters. He was trying on a pair of the
freshest available and the hem of his carefully cared-for jeans
draped over the clean leather was an eyeful. My digital camera
tickled me from inside my jacket pocket, whirring silently.
My blue metal pet, my most expensive possession. I bought
it as a little consolation prize for myself a year ago, a prize
for non-achievement. But it doesn't know that. It's always full
of *joie de vivre*, winking and blushing, and it has a thing for
Zed almost as bad as I do. I could have sworn it shivered as
I finally freed it from its case and snapped pics of his fingers,
his feet and the perfect line-up at the nape of his neck.

'Maybe,' he said, ignoring the clicker, 'you should be
focusing on your own footwear, sweetie.'

'My kicks are old, that's all. *Those* ones are grotesque right out the box.'

'Old? The Chucks you got on must have been rescued from the Flood!' He paused, looked at the Nikes. 'But maybe you right about these. Damn.'

Eventually he picked out a pair of all-grey sneaks that I had to admit were perfect. *Click, click.* The girl at the till flirted with him as she rang up his purchase, trying to entice him – unsuccessfully – with matching socks and leather protector. He gave her a credit card and I wondered idly if I'd ever qualify to even physically handle a credit card *application* without gloves on.

Finally we walked back out into the muggy blueish day, the Saturday crush of Oxford Street. I had to struggle through all the tourists and budget fashionistas. For him, they moved. I asked if he was Moses and he laughed, oblivious to the women and men who cut eyes at me, coveting him. I suppose they weren't to know that I didn't have him either.

We stopped and walked into the Plaza mall opposite Wardour Street, up to the top floor for eats. I got some fried chicken and chips, he got a sandwich, and we sat at one of those white tables that are probably identical in food courts all over the world.

'I can't believe you spent that much,' I said when we sat down. 'You could probably have got about four pairs of brand-new Chucks for that price.'

'I *could* have,' he replied, 'but that's your style, not mine.'

'What? Not high-end enough for you?'

'I didn't say all o' that. When you get so insecure?'

'Insecure?' I sucked my teeth, felt like I'd been slapped. 'You're the one trying to look like a rap video and I'm the one who's insecure? Please.'

I ate some chicken.

'Yeah, well I know that compared to you I make a lot of effort. But that's probably true of most people.'

'Asshole!'

'You brought it on yourself.'

I gave him the look of death but my hand went to my thick, knotty hair before I could stop it, to the stretched neck of my second-favourite T-shirt.

'What's wrong with the way I dress?' I asked, trying to sound like I didn't care about the answer. Eating more chicken.

'Come on. Look at you . . .' he said, brushing his neat fingers over the jagged holes in my jeans. 'Are you kidding? Why are you so afraid to be pretty? If you ever wore a wedding dress you'd probably have to go jump in a puddle. You couldn't help yourself.'

'At least I'm not some clichéd brand-worshipping B.E.T. lookin' caricature of myself like you! What's the big deal, anyway? Are you saying you've never seen ripped jeans before?'

'Those are not ripped jeans, mama.' He laughed. 'They just given up on life. If denim abuse was a crime you'd be locked up right now.'

'Well you know what? Maybe I don't wanna look like the rest of these hoes!' I told him, and he laughed harder, right into my eyes. 'You can tell me what to wear when you're the one buying it, OK? You can't tell me shit unless you're the one who has to—'

'Fine. I will.'

'What?'

'Let's go.' He wiped his face and hands decisively with a napkin. 'I'll buy you one outfit. If you don't love it, keep the receipt, return it and take the money.'

'Are you serious?' I smirked. 'You're buying me clothes now?'

'No. I'm buying you one outfit.'

I watched him carefully for motives. Went into fight/flight mode thinking about it.

'Why?'

'It'll be fun.'

'Why, Zed?'

'Because you look like hell.'

'Fuck off!'

'But you got potential.'

'For what?'

'Look. Is it a deal or not?'

Slowly I nodded. I wanted to know what would make him like me.

Zed smiled and waggled his eyebrows.

An unfamiliar voice called my name from outside the little half-door. 'Your friend has asked me to ask you if you're gonna be ready soon. He wants to see!'

I stared in the mirror at my big legs and voluminous bosoms, my sudden waist. I couldn't go outside like that. I could barely even stay in the changing room like that. I felt more naked in the tight blue dress he'd given me to try on than I had in my bra and pants. A paradox emerged in my head. Naked, that's how they want you, but flawless. How can they expect both?

I wondered again why he'd done this and felt a sudden jolt of anger.

'Eden?'

Jesus. Didn't she have shelves to stock or something?

'I'll be two seconds.' I breathed deep and tugged at the flimsy hem of the dress. When I got outside his demeanour went from cocky to spontaneous-combustion-level shocked. I don't think he even really knew what nasty tricks a measure of lycra could pull off on my body.

'What?' I said aggressively, like an unprovoked act of violence in the school playground.

His look swept from the picky ends of my hair to the tips of my bare, unpedicured toes. 'Wow . . . Eden! You like it?'

'I suppose.' My face was hot. My hands itched to cover every inch of exposed or over-emphasised flesh. I took an extremely tentative twirl. 'What do you think?'

'Is that a trick question?' he said, cockiness returning. '*Damn*, girl!'

'Thanks, I . . . erm. Thanks.'

'You gonna . . . ?'

'Yeah, I'll take it, definitely.'

I returned swiftly to the changing room to get back into my big, mostly shapeless clothes, but the deal was done and a few moments later my new dress was stuffed in a bag and paid for. The Middle Eastern man who took the money winked at us and made heavily accented jokes about Zed buying an outfit for his woman. Zed didn't even correct him.

I was inspired, walking back up toward Oxford Circus. Wearing something so different made me wonder who else I could be. Tentatively I went into a couple of the big chains and dented my already quite negligible paycheck buying some bangles, earrings and a pair of very skinny jeans. I fantasised about how I was going to feel in my sexed-up wardrobe, with Zed on my arm. I could finally do something about my hair. People would think I was pretty. They'd be envious of us.

'Now all you need is a little facial surgery and you'll be supermodel material.'

I stopped, letting my bags fall on the ground.

'What?' he said. 'I was kidding.'

I said nothing.

'Damn, it was a *joke*.'

salt.

I follow Zed and Max sheep-like into the club, a high-concept affair in blinding white with low ceilings and lighted floors, and booths designed to look like bedrooms. Everywhere there are throw cushions, canopies, fur and feathers. It's not any cooler inside than it was outside in the filthy summer streets and I'm sweat-slicked without taking a single dance step. My Afro is shrinking at a rate that's likely to make my skull implode sometime around three a.m.

All I want to do is run home and sleep deep into Sunday with a duvet pulled over my head, because absolutely no good can come from this night. But that would be an admission of defeat.

Max asks me if I want a drink and I say, like a robot, 'Rum and Coke thanks.'

I don't look at Zed as he introduces me to Lisa, a black girl draped in a nine-foot hair-weave. Shocking. At her scalp you can see the places where kink meets fakery.

'Hey,' she says, cutting me a look. Maybe I'm just sensitive right now, but I could swear it's the same look my mum used to direct at my head Sunday nights before she'd had a chance to attack it with the pressing comb. 'How ya doing?'

'Cool,' I lie. 'Your hair,' I tell her, 'is truly unbelievable.'

When the drink comes, I swallow it so fast it should make my head spin, but it doesn't. I'm introduced to a couple more people but instantly forget their names. When a girl with an enthusiastic ponytail offers to buy drinks,

I have a rum and Coke. And when Nine-Foot Weave offers to buy drinks, I have yet another. The world starts to swim, lengthen and stretch. All the edges stand out: my hand resting on my bare thigh, Max's red mouth and white face, my empty glass dizzy with flashing lights.

My body floats up and my head is a lump of brick.

'Hey Eden, you ready for another one?'

'Yes, please. Whisky and Coke.'

Blondie matches me drink for drink, but she's on vodka.

When it's time for Zed to go on stage I have to muscle my way to the front of the room just to get to him, through a forest of carelessly waving limbs. The DJ fades out the record, and a tiny woman in red introduces the entertainment. She says his name. I grip my drink. There he is, looking even bigger than usual. Shiny. I take down a sip, grateful for the burn.

Zed raps with his chin tilted up, generous lips curled in a faint snarl. His flow is seamless. He doesn't dance. One hand is in its sling and the other lightly cradles the mic. He drops one sharply delivered punch line after another, battle rhymes and boasts, women and money. He's agile in the lips and tongue and brain. There's barely any space to breathe in between lines and no story to speak of and no glimpse of flesh through the cleverness. This is hip-hop for ADD sufferers. But he is a master. Look at all the faces, all the bobbing bodies. They love it and I hate them for putting their greasy gaze all over his talent. Especially Max. By the end of the twenty-minute set she's wearing this proprietary grin like this show was for her personal amusement.

After fierce applause all the vultures turn to each other and begin their appraisals before he's even completely melted from view. *That was alright innit? – Yeah, not bad! – He*

sounds a bit like Rakim . . . ? — You reckon? — Yeah definitely!
— Nah, not at all, mate! Are you deaf? Sounds more like . . . !
A guy in a tilted newsboy cap waves his beer around and
spills half of it on my Chucks.

'Sorry!'

'Fuck off.'

Max goes to the bar. I threaten, cajole and lie my way
to the tiny backstage area with beer-wet feet and when
I get there, Zed's sitting on a wooden chair with his head
cradled by one hand, body shirtless and slick. He's
spotlighted by a single bare lightbulb hanging from the
ceiling.

'Zed.' I have to say it twice before he lifts his face, his
red eyes. He doesn't look surprised to see me. I reach into
my knapsack for my digital and snap him a few times, so
I remember.

'Stop it, Eden. You ever stop doing that?'

I put it away. His irritation excites me. He's so cool usually.
Laughing . . . closed. I instantly soften. I haven't the heart
for banter.

'That was really,' I tell him eventually, trying not to sway,
'really good.'

'Yeah? Well that's odd coming from you.'

'It's not.' I speak quietly and slowly without quite knowing
why, like I'm talking him down from the ledge. 'Nobody
could dispute your talent. Everyone had fun and they
were . . . They were impressed. I watched their faces.'

He nods and smiles opaquely, throwing a white towel
around his neck.

'Didn't you like it?' I ask.

'It was OK,' he says at length, scratching his head. 'But
not good enough.'

'What do you mean? They loved you out there.'

He wipes his face with the towel and says: 'Trust me. The

only thing they really love is fashion, and fashion's a painted whore who sleeps around with everyone and loves nobody but her damned self.'

I don't know what to say so I just stand there blurry-eyed with alcohol and hormones. I thought he was a fan of fashion. He looks so sincere. Maybe all is not lost after all.

'Zed . . .'

But before I can begin the speech I planned in my bedroom mirror, he says he needs a minute and will catch me outside. And then Dave the technician guy comes in.

So I go back out into the club where the music batters my senses and sit back down in the booth with my whisky and Coke. I watch when he emerges with a closed smile and not a single visible trace of his angst. People keep coming up to him, patting his back and slipping him pieces of paper. On comes the mask again and I can't bear it, how flash he is in every line of his body. Women thrust their tits up at him and flick their hair in his face until Max sidles up and that's when I give my drink more attention. She touches him like he's discovered country. They've done it. They've definitely done it.

Suddenly, it reaches me that the hand on my thigh is no longer my own. Instead it belongs to this fool who's been trying to chat me up since I got in here.

'It's *Adrian*, right?'

'Yeah, babes.'

And Zed is dancing. Every movement is packed with irony. He does characters that are never himself. His mouth is open with laughter I can't hear over the music. His face and body say, *look at me* (but not too close)!

'You alright, love?' says Adrian.

'Yeah.'

Zed won't even dance without masks! He jokes around

with the Ponytail and the Nine-Foot Weave, doing The Bump. They adore him.

Is that all he wants – to be adored? Does he prefer that to being a real person? What happened to the backstage Zed? And what about his bad arm – doesn't it hurt too much for him to dance? Maybe it's wrong to think this but I prefer him when the pain shows.

'I work for Sony Records,' says Adrian, wetly into my ear, without any prompting or curiosity on my part. 'Are you a singer?'

'No. I'm tone deaf.'

'Well you look like one,' he says, in a version of Mockney. 'You're fuckin' gorgeous. Love your 'air.'

'Yeah thanks,' I say, and my speech is wobbly. 'I've got to. Um. Gotta say hello to someone.'

I push him off me – realising a few large, uncontrollable steps later that I've also pushed my way onto the dance floor. I can barely feel my legs and the dimness swirls around me. The music is hip-hop. The bass-line goes right through the soles of my All Stars.

I want to be lost between beats, lost in the melodies with my eyes closed. Not here anymore. The ground tips and I feel like a kid in a playground, spinning round and round until she loses her balance.

Max comes up close with her dolly lips and tiny outfit, starts dancing like a stripper. Off-beat. What is it with blondes and the stripper dance? I laugh soggily. I can feel Max's breath on my face, she's trying to rap along with the track but getting it wrong. I do the stripper dance too.

She cracks up, falling about. I catch it like a bug and it shakes me from the ground up. We both scream with it. Max's hair is coming free of the pins, she's sweaty and her cheeks are aflame. She still looks bloody perfect.

I trip over my laces and the view is the pure white ceiling.

'Eden!'

Zed's face is so big all of a sudden! No, it's just close. I can't stop laughing. I shake all the way through. My abdominals hurt, my head pounds, I can't breathe but I can't stop laughing. And I know I can't get up.

I touch my crazy hair and laugh. I think about my trainers and ache with laughter. I think about this man, close enough to kiss. I think about how lonely I am. That's it: lonely! I think the word, *lonely*, and laugh so hard I almost wet my knickers.

'Zed!' I yell back at him, unable to stand. He puts a hand in my left armpit and helps me up. I slump against him and his Cool Water-smelling body. See? He's always there when I need him. He cares about me. Even with his bad arm he's prepared to pick me up.

The DJ announces one more set from an acoustic act, Cody Chesnutt. Everyone is shouting and clapping. I try to clap but miss.

And the problem with alcohol is that after the initial buzz is gone everything starts to get really serious.

Even while your knees still won't support you and you're flopping about like an empty plastic bag in a supermarket car park. Even while your head weighs ten times what your body does and you're still drinking to keep it at bay, it comes down like a Monday morning—

The truth. You're making an ass of yourself in public. You're alone. The truth is your face in the mirror, eyes and lips melted and smearing, your skin with all the blemishes reappearing beneath your make-up.

The truth is that you are *not* having fun.

I started the day with such high expectations, but soon I've made a wobbly dash for the toilets and found myself bowed over some under-disinfected latrine throwing up.

Plop-plop-plop-plop. My body won't tolerate all the crap I've poured into it and has decided to stage a revolt.

Max has turned up like she always does when she's not wanted. She's hovering, trying to smooth my hair back. How dumb is that? I have an *Afro*!

For the whole night he's been touching her all the time. Why does he do it when he's got to know how I feel about—

'Are you OK?'

'Yes!' I tell her. 'Fiiine . . . fine! Go away!'

Then my stomach says a violent 'no' all over again. And again. And again . . .

And fade to black.

funny.

I knocked again. Two weeks ago, a week after Zed's indict-
ment of my dress sense and general level of attractiveness,
I stood outside Zed's flat for an unusually long minute with
all these bombs going off in my chest. *Tick tick, boom. Tick
tick, boom. Tick tick* . . . No answer. It was four twenty-five
in the afternoon. I'd been outside for three-quarters of an
hour.

'Eden?' My friend Dwayne stuck his head out of his car
window, his gaze sticky on my back.

'Yeah.' I looked over at him and then away.

'What do you wanna do? Doesn't look like he's gonna
show up.'

'Of course he is. It's only been twenty minutes!'

'It's been almost an hour! We could go to the cinema . . .'

'No, Dwayne. I told you. He'll be here any second.'

'Are you sure he remembers that you guys were supposed
to meet today?'

'Yes!' I replied. 'Look, you can go now if you like. I'll
just wait outside, no biggie.'

I was an embarrassment to myself, a wasted effort in my
flimsy new tank top. On the front it said,

> *– He who hesitates is last –*
> *Mae West*

which I'd written on with fabric paint and a lip brush. On
the bottom I sported my least mashed-up jeans cut into

shorts and my cleanest pair of Chucks – the green ones. I had on new underwear. I'd shaved all essential areas, scented myself with vanilla and jasmine, blow-dried my hair as straight as I could and pulled it back. While I was putting myself together I kept asking myself what I was getting ready for, but then wouldn't listen to the answer. I'd had my friend Dwayne drive me down to Zed's house, miles out of his way, and then made him wait with me because I was early. Stupid move.

'No, it's cool! I'll wait with you, innit? In case he doesn't come.'

'He *is* gonna come.'

'Well, you might as well get back in the car and sit down. Give those lovely legs of yours a break!'

I cringed but did what he suggested, sped along by an unfriendly look from the woman going into the house next door. Too little space and air inside the car. Too much chat. Dwayne's aftershave and the car freshener fought for dominance. I fought not to gag. I dispensed the odd, canned laugh but his jokes were incomprehensible and all I could hear was the blood behind my eyes, and the name of my beloved buzzing round and around inside my head and then just when all the noise was on the cusp of deafening—

There he was, roaring into sight on a shiny black motorcycle. I knew him even with the helmet on. He parked and jumped off the bike. 'Zed,' I exclaimed quietly, squinting through the buttery summer glare. He pulled off his helmet and started for the flat. I remembered just in time not to open the passenger door blindly into traffic. 'Thanks for the lift, Dwayne . . .'

But before I had a chance to ask what he was doing, Dwayne sprang out of the car and into Zed's path.

'Hey! What's happening!' he exclaimed.

'Uh . . .' Zed was visibly startled. 'Uh. Cool. What's up?'

'I'm alright, ya know!' said Dwayne.

Zed gave him a look of pure bafflement and then he finally saw me sitting there. 'Eden?' I swung my legs out of the car, thighs and palms moist in the heat. 'Damn! We said four, didn't we? Sorry.' I watched his mouth. I was stuck on how he says my name. *Eden*. It sounds different when he says it.

''Salright,' I mumbled, cleared my throat. 'It's fine . . .'

'Whoa! Those are some serious wheels you got there!' screamed Dwayne. I dropped my mobile phone and it went into pieces on the concrete. 'What is that? A sports bike?'

I retrieved the battery about an inch from the toe of Zed's perfect grey trainer. They were a couple of weeks old now and completely without a smudge.

'Yeah it's a Honda CBR one thousand.'

'Kind of flash innit?'

I got back up just in time to see Zed shrug a *whatever* at Dwayne, who remained undeterred.

'I'm not really into bikes to be honest, but if I was I'd definitely be more interested in a road bike. Big old Harley or something. Do you race?'

'Naw . . .' Zed looked about to bust out laughing any minute. Dwayne is one of those slightly chubby brers who looks like he goes down to his local Topman and gets everything he sees in the window. He drops slang like it was a class he took in college. He has big, shiny rims on his tiny hand-me-down car. He's one of those brers who are average height but look short the minute they open their mouth. And next to Zed, he was shrinking by the millisecond. I had to get him out of there.

'I saw you spittin' at Cargo a couple weeks back, actually. I met you after the show,' he said. The time inched toward five. 'I came down with Eden. I'm Dwayne . . . ?'

'Right, right, OK. Cool . . .' Zed nodded his head in obviously faked recognition. 'Dwayne. Thanks for the support.'

'Nah, no problem, mate. I don't get out that much these

days, you know what I mean? I'm studying my *masters degree* at the mo, but I used to dabble a bit here and there back in the day, ya get me? Bit of Djing! I made good money, ya know. But yeah, you should definitely keep it up, blud.' Dwayne was nodding heavily, like he was a hip-hop expert rather than some halfwit who probably thought KRS-one was an industrial cleaning product.

'I hear you,' replied Zed, running a hand over the deep black gloss of his new vehicle. 'Thanks.'

'Yeah, man,' Dwayne added for good measure. 'Definitely keep it up, ya get me?'

'That's the plan.'

'Heavy.' Then Dwayne decided to try and go in for one of those one-armed man-hugs. Zed dodged it and gave him a rather sardonic handshake instead. *At least bloody TRY to act like a threat!* I wanted to shout at Dwayne but instead I just stood there, spare, embarrassed and scowling at my finger-nails. Switching my phone back on.

'So Eden . . .' said Zed eventually.

'Yeah, um, let's go in. Look, Dwayne . . . Thanks for the lift, OK? I'll see you at work,' I said, and gave the Clueless One a chaste peck on the cheek. He went with crab-like reluctance back to his Fiesta.

I didn't look at Zed until the car was moving and when I did I caught him throwing Dwayne deuces, a backwards peace sign. Well, in *America* it means 'peace'.

I tried to stifle a nervous eruption of laughter, but instead some spit went down the wrong way and I choked.

'Eden! You alright?'

'Yeah,' I said when I regained the capacity for speech, wiping my eyes and mouth. 'I'm fine.'

I hesitated near his new motorcycle. It was gorgeous.

'It's OK,' he said, a diamond stud sparkling in his ear. 'You can touch it.'

The bike was smooth as water. I grabbed my camera and took several pictures in quick succession. For the record. My fingers travelled its long curves, nestled in its indentations, hesitated on the seat and the handlebars. Did this mean he was going to stay? For a while at least? The implications of that scrambled me. I saw my wide-open face reflected in the slick black paint. Zed smiled at me indulgently, like I was a child or an eccentric or both, and turned to walk up the front steps. 'Sorry I kept you waiting,' he said.

'You have no idea.'

'Hmmm . . . ?' he glanced at me, struggling with his helmet, the gloves and his bags, trying to open the door. 'What was that?'

'It was no big deal; I wasn't waiting that long. You want some help?'

He told me the keys were in his jeans, voice so close I felt the bass of it right in the seat of my knickers. I journeyed nervous fingers into his pocket, in amongst the warm coins, a biro and the slight damp and the dark.

'OK,' I said. 'Got them.' And then, just to keep talking, I told him he should be careful about carrying pens in his pocket in case of leakages. And he said, 'Riight . . .' and then I couldn't really say anything more because we were touching all the way down the sides of our bodies and it was making me prickle with water. I unlocked the outer door and we were alone in the short, speckless hallway.

'You need the gold one for the front door to the apartment,' he said, brushing my fingers to indicate which one. 'The Yale.'

'Cool.'

'So what's the deal? You got yourself a little personal driver these days, Miss Daisy?'

'What – *Dwayne*? He's just a guy from that market research job I do sometimes! He's not . . .' Zed chuckled, his face

32

amused and unperturbed. 'Fuck you,' I said quietly. Unlocked the door and pushed it open.

The flat stretched and purred before me, ready. Beige walls, dark wooden carvings haunting corners of the living room, cool leather and glass. It belonged to Lewis, a friend of Zed's, and must have cost a fortune to rent. I threw my lightweight jacket on the banister and stood lost and nervous by the stairs, trying to suck some air in. I admitted to myself that I had an agenda. Zed tapped me lightly on the shoulder so I'd move out of his way and I shivered, thinking it was about time he did the same for me.

'You want me to take those?' I asked as he went with his carrier bags to the kitchen.

'No, I'm fine.'

'Sure?'

'Please just go sit your ass down, girl!'

I folded onto the couch, disoriented by his inexplicable purchase. *He's staying?* I kept asking myself, singing the question in rounds. No answers. *What does it mean?* I was drumming relentlessly in the chest and feeling strange in the abdomen. I felt tender and I felt hard. You see, I've had a pattern since I lost him and it's always gone the same way. I've liked people. It's even felt like love sometimes, that particular species of gut-crunching longing. But the minute there's an exchange of fluids . . . *poof!* It goes. Like a blown fuse and all the lights gone black. Every time, *poof!* And there are no more tingles, no more fantasies, no more desire. *It's OK, you can touch it.*

'You want something to drink?' he said. 'Eden?'

'What? What's up?'

'I said, do you want something to drink?'

'Oh yeah. What you got?'

'Coke . . . Ribbenha . . . or water.'

'Ri-what?'

'Ribbenha.'

'I'll have a Coke,' I said.

He went back to the kitchen, then came out and placed my drink on the coffee table, sat next to me on the couch. I told him it was pronounced R*ibeen*a. He shrugged. I asked him about the bike.

'I got it pretty cheap on the net,' he said, opening a small, black tin and reaching over to get a notebook from the coffee table. 'Barely used.' He put the notebook on his knees and tipped out some Mary Jane, picking out seeds; knees pushed delicately together, fingers long and precise. He looked so unexpectedly vulnerable that I couldn't hear anything for a minute except the muscles working easy in his dark forearms and wrists, under the smooth skin; his pink tongue as it slid over the rolling paper. He even made dependency look good.

'Cool. I didn't even know you rode,' I said eventually.

'Yeah, I love it. I love the freedom of it, you know what I mean? You get to a certain speed and it feels like you're flying. It's like you're inside of a vacuum, nothing but you and the air rushing past. Makes me feel close to God, whoever He is.'

'Or She! What kind of speeds are we talking?' I say, breathless. Worried. All I can see is that stick in the road. That car pulling out of an alley right when Zed is at his most religious, racing toward his moment of flight.

He smiles. 'Fast,' he says.

'What, like a hundred miles an hour?'

'At the top of the ride, yeah.'

'You're completely mad!' I exclaim, angry, head crowded with questions and foreboding. Why did he buy the bike? What did it mean for us? And could anybody survive a specimen like the Honda? It had a glint in its fairings. It was too pretty not to hurt him. I could see it.

34

'You want some?' he asked, offering me the spliff.

'No, I don't smoke. You know that.'

'You never used to say that before,' said Zed absently, taking a deep pull, speaking through his nose. I heated. He grinned. 'Remember, I'm the one who taught you.' Memories of us flooded my mind. I sat, pinned by them.

'Please don't tell me you ride that thing when you're buzzing?'

'What you think?' Zed grinned. 'You a rock chick, right? When you gonna get on the back and let me take you for a spin?'

I imagined my arms around his waist, my face in his back. Salt and musk. 'When George W. Bush converts to Islam, mate. Sorry.'

'Wow! It's like *that*?' He re-lit his spliff. 'I really think you could use some of this, ma. You're kind of uptight right now. Lewis has got some connections, man. This haze will make you feel *no* stress.'

'Where *is* Lewis?' I said, hoping he wouldn't be back soon. Lewis was sarcastic, posh and quietly observant enough to make me feel self-conscious. The kind of guy who would notice your earrings or handbag. He had famous parents, I think. He got photographed for magazines.

'Lewis is travelling for a few weeks doing some events,' smiled Zed, picking up on my not-so-subtle dislike. 'It's just me right now.'

'Oh,' I said. 'Right.'

He carefully adjusted his long, solid body and ended up slightly closer than he was before. I really could touch him and no one would walk in on us. I could lay my face in his neck, run my hands over his chest and his smooth head. I could unzip and unbutton him. We could kiss. Oh God. We could *kiss*. And what do you do when you've wanted something for so long and finally here it is, and maybe all you have to do now is not mess up and it can be yours?

'Go on then,' I said.

'What?'

'Pass the dutchie, Rasta.'

He spluttered, coughing and laughing at the same time. 'I was only kidding, E. You can't handle that *Hendrix*, girl . . .'

'Come on!'

'Alright,' he said, with a shrug, smiling again on one side of his mouth. 'But I ain't takin' your ass to no emergency room.'

The first pull made me cough almost hard enough to gag. I looked through my watery eyes at Zed, who was shaking his head and giggling. Actually giggling.

'Wamore!'

'You OK?' he asked, very insincerely, and took back the spliff. 'Drink some Coke, woman. I told you you couldn't handle it.'

'One more!'

'You're crazy . . .'

'Just pass it over.' And this time I managed to hold it down. Smoke seared my throat, fired off a quiet explosion in the back of my head. Suddenly there was s . . . p . . . a . . . c . . . e.

He took a deep inhale of the spliff, held it, then let the smoke out slow and controlled. He held it out to me again with a challenge in his sleepy-lidded eyes. Go on, then. If you're so tough. His lips. My lips.

I did and started to giggle, despite myself. And he smiled, despite himself. We went back and forth for a while, until the room was milky with smoke.

'Here,' he said. 'Not much left.'

'No it's OK. You have it.'

'Hey . . .' he said, 'did you leave an earring last time you were here? And your Pharcyde CD?'

'Is it pink?'

'What?' he asked, leaning his head back.

'The earring.'

'Yeah.'

'Wow! I've been looking for that for ages,' I giggled. 'You've gotta stop stealing my shit, you pervert!'

'What can I say? Pink is my colour, baby.' He stretched over to take my abandoned items from a drawer in a nearby side table. A smooth, deep brown gap appeared between the waistband of his jeans and the hem of his T-shirt and my mouth went dry. He laid the CD and earring on the sofa between us.

'You always leaving your stuff behind,' he said nasally, mid-toke. The roach gleamed and faded. He put it in the ashtray. 'Like Gretel with the breadcrumbs or some shit. Lewis now thinks I'm the biggest player since Barry White.'

My things looked out of place there, next to Zed's thigh. So real! Like, the realest things I'd ever seen, the way they stood out against the cream leather. The air was still as a photo. I twitched toward my digital – my faithful little clicker! – panting like a dog in my jacket pocket but then thought better of it. I didn't want to disturb the moment. I drew my knees up and tucked my pink cotton-covered feet in beside me. And in that hot room, only faint noise and no air came in through the open windows. The big lunch I'd had with Dwayne and the heat and the smoke all put a cat-like ease in my limbs. I burned, and stretched, crossed and uncrossed my legs, unwrapped a lollipop, sucked it, wiped the light sweat off my neck.

I stared at Zed's profile, his elegant eyebrows. He reached over and picked up a bulging blue notebook he'd stashed under the coffee table, opened it and began to read.

'That's a bit anti-social isn't it?' I said.

'Why, you got a better idea about what I should be doing?'

He looked at me. I was silent.

'Cat gotcha tongue?'

'Yeah. No. Course not. Just . . . you know,' I waffled. 'Guess what? I have an idea for an art installation. It would be, like, a bedroom? But everything in it would indicate that someone was missing . . . the bed left unmade, a half-drunk cup of coffee, make-up and clothes everywhere . . .'

A darkness gathered and spilled out between us, clouds of it, thicker than the weed smoke or the humid air. Immediately I wanted to unsay it all and go back to the giggles and the jokes. Stupid me.

Eventually he said, 'Didn't one of your British artists already do that? Tracey-something?'

I floundered, making it up as I went along. Too far in to retreat. 'What she did was different. This would have a projection at the back of the room of a face . . . or if I could have a moving projection, like a ghost? And there'd be poetry being read out over the speakers.'

'What for, Eden? What are you trying to do?' He flicked sightlessly through his notebook, every bone in his face angular with tension. 'Just take your pictures, man. I don't even get all that modern art bullshit.'

'It's a way of challenging reality and what you perceive as reality, that's the point,' I said, drowning. 'It's a way of breaking down all the big ideas about God and man and society and showing how pointless and divisive they are. It shows what our existence really is, that we're all just lost and alienated and . . . um . . . what's the word?' I struggled. 'Autonomous. I mean photos have their place, but they're a craft that you can learn just like anything else. Art goes beyond craft and into the realm of—'

'Sounds to me like you're trying to take the real world and make it,' he struggled, 'cheesy and ridiculous. Life ain't some art installation! It's *real*. Why would you want to put it in a sterile gallery somewhere so folks can pick your life apart?'

'Well one of us has to deal with reality,' I shouted, burning. ''Cause it's certainly not you!'

'What are you talking about?'

'I'm *talking* about you coming over here doing bloody *gangster* rap!' I said, fizzy with adrenaline, running my mouth as fast as I could. 'Are you serious?'

He rose to his feet, jaw set, eyes wild. 'Oh my God.' He paced to the kitchen and back. 'You challenging me on my *rhymes* now? You haven't complained *once* at the shows I've done. I look in the crowd and you out there shaking your ass like it's a box of Tic-Tacs! Now 'cause I think your idea . . . your idea is stupid! You wanna start talking shit?'

'You used to be brave!' I told him, kneeling up on the sofa. 'You used to be a poet and now you're just a rapper. It's embarrassing, mate! Just punchlines and theatre! What's wrong with you? Isn't there a law somewhere against false advertising?' Something in his face went slack. 'That's not you, Zed.'

He sat down, hunched forward, elbows on knees. I started to mumble some wordless apology but he threw a hand up in front of my face. *Stop.*

'So I'm a fake, huh?' he smiled. Shook his head.

'I didn't mean to sound harsh. It's just . . .'

'Well maybe we both are. You acting like you're dealing with shit but you're not. You're still living in the shock of what happened to us. You haven't moved. You ain't breathed. You just hanged some posters on the wall and filled it up with mouldy plates and glasses and called it home.'

I crashed. 'You think that's what my life is?'

He gave a laugh so faint it was merely an exhalation of breath. A corner of his pillowy mouth twitched upward. 'You crack me up, though.'

'Zed.'

'You,' he finally looked up, 'staking out my house with your little boyfriend. What was that? Performance art?'

'He's not my boyfriend.'

'Did you tell your boyfriend you have a crush on me?'

'No . . . no!'

He sat up and leaned toward me, smirking as if rejection were something he had no first-hand experience of. *Crush.* Is that how small he thought it was? His face was flawless and hard. The TV bleated in the background. The weed pounded in my head. I was imploding. He took my chin between his fingers.

'Are you saying that you don't have a crush on me, or are you saying that your boyfriend doesn't know?'

He leaned in further, our faces almost touching. And it was just too easy for him. I could see that. It was *easy.*

'Both!' I yelled, slapping his hand off my chin. 'And I told you that he's not my boyfriend. Shit. How could you push up on me like I'm one of your floozies?'

He recoiled. 'Floozies? This is me you're talking to! After everything . . . Why would you say that?'

''Cause I can't believe you, that's why! You're out of order. I told you that I'm . . . I'm celibate and you still come onto me?'

'You *never* said your ass was celibate.'

'Yes I did.'

'I didn't even touch you. Did I tell you I wanted to fuck? Did I try to fuck you?'

I shivered. 'No but—!'

'Forget it. I don't have time for this. You're such an idiot.'

'I'm an idiot 'cause I won't sleep with you?'

Zed shook his head and got up, took the glasses and the bowl of tortillas back into the kitchen.

'Zed?' He didn't answer. I followed him to the kitchen. 'Zed?'

'Look, I really wanna get some writing done tonight, so let's do this some other time, OK?'

'But I brought that movie I wanted to show you.'

'Yeah well, I'm not even really in the mood for that right now.'

'Alright,' I said, going cold all over. Ruining everything. 'Alright.'

I didn't say anything else and neither did he. Not even goodbye.

I picked up my stuff and left.

I walked by his death toy, up to the main road and round to the bus stop. I sat there for a long time, letting them pass. Thinking about the bed on a platform, the running and the shock. And what do you do when you've wanted something for so long and finally here it is, and maybe all you have to do now is not mess up and it can be yours?

You mess it up, that's what.

And the next time I'd see him, he'd be injured, concave, with bruises and scratches climbing one arm, and Max hanging off the other.

love.

'Mummy!'

Ridley market. Saturday morning. The green and blue print on her long gypsy dress. Her red-painted nails. The sky was blue and very far away. Only slightly closer was her face up there, curls loose and shiny about her cheeks. She carried on talking to a man in brown leather shoes and a woman in trainers.

'Mummy.'

I wanted to pee! Wanted chips and a juice and to sit down and if not I might cry. I might scream. But I was a big girl now. She'd told me I was a big girl and would have to wait for the toilet.

'Mum! Wee-wee!'

'Just a minute, sweetheart.'

'Mum!' I'd forgotten all my other words. 'Mum Mum Mum Mum!'

I hated the market smell. I was out of the buggy and standing low to the wet, slimy ground. It was thousands of legs like a forest, and old, soft fruit and fishy puddles every-where. And I wanted to pee! As usual, we'd spent most of our 'shopping' trip standing around while stupid Mum spoke to stupid people about other stupid people. And sometimes they'd squeak at me and try to touch my head or hold my hands but I didn't like touching people I didn't know.

On and on she went. She was gonna make me wet myself like a baby and then she'd be cross! Why couldn't she just shut up? I kept tugging at her hand but she'd shake me off and not even come down to me with her sweet-smelling hair and smooth face and high voice.

I bit her as hard as I could.

'Ow!'

It was a funny taste, her skin through the green and blue print dress. I didn't stop until she shrieked with pain, dragged me off of her and came down to eye level. She shook me hard, bit me on the arm with her clean, sharp teeth. I screamed.

'You see how that feels? It hurts, Eden!' she said. 'You trying to make me look bad, eh? You don't love your mummy?'

I cried and cried and couldn't answer her.

'Wow, that's a real handful you've got there, Marie!' said the stupid brown-shoed man.

'This chile has a demon, trust me!' she said to him. 'Eden, that's not how nice girls behave, you understand? You don't love your mummy?'

My legs were itchy with urine. I didn't say anything, just screamed louder. I didn't want to love anyone if it meant I had to stand out in the nasty, cold market peeing on myself. I didn't want love.

cheek drool.

I try to stretch my legs out and meet an obstruction. Where am I? Bits of music split and regroup in my mind, Cody Chesnutt singing 'Beautiful Shame'. Open my crusty eyes and I'm instantly rewarded with a headache.

'You OK, darlin'?'

Max. Sitting at the bottom half of the couch so I'm left in an awkward foetal position. She's blindingly pale, in a scrap of white cotton. Her hair is bright enough to stain my retinas. I blink slowly. The scene goes in, out, and finally back into focus.

'No,' I croak, trying to untangle myself from a blue bed sheet. 'I'm very *not* OK.'

'God! Sorry . . . Am I hurtin' ya?' she asks, moving so that my feet and ankles are free.

I sit up and the room hurtles forward, my belly trying to jump through my neck. Flashback to last night's downward spiral, vomit and tears, and a tumble outside the club. A bruise right on the funniest part of my elbow. Zed's dismissive eyes and strong, kind hands guiding me into their cab, making sure I didn't hit my head on the roof. But he should have sent me home. 'What your liver ever do to you, huh?' he joked. It wasn't funny.

'Zed's just gone out to the supermarket and stuff,' Max volunteers. She's watching a cartoon at low volume. I'm horrified to see that her skin looks even better unadorned. I touch my body tentatively and I'm wearing an oversized man's T-shirt, my underwear and cheek drool. Ugh.

'OK,' I answer, trying to keep my words to a minimum. 'How's he gonna manage with his arm?'

Max shrugs. 'He'll be alright.'

I put a hand over my eyes, returning to darkness for a few blissful seconds.

'Feeling pretty rough, innit?' says Max.

'Yeah.'

'A lightweight like you,' she offers, 'you're better off with a little coke or an "E" or something. It's cleaner.'

'Shit, I can barely handle the basics. Like paracetamol.'

She chuckles and shakes her head. 'So young, you are.' In all her twenty-one years on the planet. 'Better for you to be pure, I suppose. If you're into that sort of thing.'

'Aren't you models supposed to live healthy or something?'

'Skinny. Skinny, not healthy,' she laughs. 'Besides, it ain't made no difference to me so far. Thank God for genetics. You want some coffee?'

'Milk and two sugars, please, crack baby.'

She chucks me the middle finger and is gone in a flash of teeth and hair. I need to get out of here.

I rise carefully to go to the bathroom, picking my dress up off the side of the sofa, and everything kaleidoscopes. I go one shaky foot at a time up the narrow stairs and when I turn the shower on it's as loud as an army, but just what I need. I dry off using a towel hanging on the rack and it must be Zed's because it's still very slightly damp and it's probably the closest I'm ever going to come to touching him. I rinse my mouth out with toothpaste and wash the spit off my face. Moisturise with some cream that smells like Zed. I pull my hair with partial success into French braids and two of the hair bands that are on eternal standby on my left wrist.

I need to be awake, sober, alert and tough. And I need to leave right now, before he comes back.

Back on with the dress. Back on with the Converse and bangles. Back on with the eye-bag concealer, deep black kohl and an old lipstick smudged in my cheeks for blush. If ever I needed some kind of mask to wear, today's the day. But in the mirror I still look like the kind of girl it would be easy to resist. I make a mean face and switch the light off, tossing Zed's T-shirt on the floor.

Turns out, I'd be better off locked in the bathroom because when I make it down the stairs Zed is back and they're kissing. Tongue and everything. Their bodies are pure white on pure dark like the husk and the flesh of a coconut. She sits with her bare legs and feet thrown over his loose-fit jeans. Margarine-coloured hair; white, fat-free limbs; pink lips; blue eyes. She's a study in pastels.

By the time their mouths come apart, I'm back upstairs retching into the toilet bowl. Again. The sight of them buried in each other's faces is not the best thing for a weak stomach.

Knock, knock, knock.

'Eden! You alright in there, love?' Max.

'I'm FINE!' I say. 'I'll be down in a minute!'

I wipe my mouth and stare down at the floor tiles, waiting for her footsteps to retreat. I'll go home right now. I'll be fine. I pick up the discarded, oversized T-shirt I slept in and stuff it into my knapsack. A souvenir. I consider pissing on his toothbrush but I'm not sure which one it is and Lewis – as irritating as he is – has done nothing to deserve such treatment. Instead I swipe a couple more keepsakes for the road: Zed's moisturiser and aftershave.

I almost trip down the narrow staircase trying to be fast and sure. My ankle twists on the bottom step. I soldier it. No sprain could hurt as much as I do in the heart muscle. Max flicks a gesture toward my coffee on the table.

'There ya go, love,' she says, turning the volume up on her cartoons. 'You OK, yeah?'

'I'm going home!' I announce to the wall, and set about gathering my things.

'Eden, come here for a minute.' Zed's voice from the kitchen.

'I gotta go!' I yell.

'Just get in here, please.'

I stumble over and lurk mindlessly in the kitchen doorway, watch him begin setting out his ingredients one-handed. He has a gorgeous, broad back. He glances at me while he's whisking eggs in a bowl.

'Yeah, so what do you want?'

'You should eat something, Eden. I'm making breakfast.'

'Well done, chef Wake 'n' Bake,' I say, glancing at the spliff behind his ear, 'but I'll eat at home.'

'You've been throwing up half the night, lush. You go out there without something in your stomach and you're gonna make really good friends with the sidewalk.'

'What the bloody hell do you care?' I say, quietly enough that I hope it won't be heard in the living room.

'Just eat, please. I'll be five minutes.'

'You're not gonna stay and 'ave some breakfast, Eden?' Max pipes up from the next room, lazy cow. 'You ain't even finished that coffee I slaved over!'

'OK,' I hiss at Zed. 'Whatever. Prove whatever it is you want to prove. I like my eggs scrambled.'

'I ain't trying to prove shit. That's your game,' he says, shaking his head. 'I thought you were gonna swallow your tongue last night!'

'You should know what I was trying to do.'

'What? Get alcohol poisoning?'

'Same thing you're gonna do with that thing behind your ear. Relieve some damn stress.'

Five or ten more minutes, and I never have to see either of these fuckers again. I can reclaim myself. Maybe Reiki healing this time, or acupuncture, or something. There must be a special programme out there made especially for serfs like me.

Zed begins throwing things into pans. He doesn't seem like the type of man who'd be so capable. At a glance he might be the type who could burn water and has never done a load of laundry in his life. But he's not. His mum didn't completely fail at raising him. Just mostly. I take my camera out and *snap snap snap*. I feel empty.

'There you go again,' he says. 'I don't know what you intend to do with all those damn pictures.'

When he's done, we all sit down around the coffee table and eat in silence: scrambled eggs, sausages and toast. After the first forkful I stop wanting to retch. Even Max Crack Baby is quiet because her mouth is full. She's really wolfing it down for someone who weighs about the same as a keyring. She takes a breath and turns her blue gaze toward Zed. 'What am I gonna do when you go back to the States, hey?' she pouts. 'The time's coming so quick! I'll starve!'

'That's what cereal is for, my dear.'

'You're so heartless.' Max spots my camera. Takes it. I can't move yet, can't believe what I just heard. The room contracts. He's going back to Atlanta? I thought he'd had enough of life there. Max says to him: 'Will you take a picture of me and Eden, love?'

She leans over and puts her arm around me. She smiles, I don't. Zed takes the picture.

'You're going back?' I ask, before I can stop myself.

'Yeah,' says Zed. 'First week in August.'

'That's just a few weeks away.' I sound destroyed, even to myself.

'So, you can count!'

I push something like a laugh out of my throat. 'So you were just gonna leave without telling me? Nice. Look, thanks for breakfast, OK? It was great.'

He tries to say something but my ears might as well be sewn shut. I tune him out and check I've got my keys, wallet and Oyster card. Good to go. Sometimes I think he does this for fun. On purpose or by accident, he always knows what to do to make me hurt. He's like that evil corner on a coffee table that's fallen in love with your shin-bone.

'Are you going back to Hackney?' says Max suddenly.

'What? Yeah I—'

'Why don't you wait a minute and I'll give you a lift?'

I look at Zed's face and its habitual blankness is disturbed.

'Really, it's no trouble,' babbles Max, 'I'm going in that direction anyway. Going down my nan's in Leyton.'

'OK.'

When she rushes up the stairs to get dressed, Zed stops eating. 'For the record,' he says, 'I'm sorry about what happened last time you came here, Eden. If I gave the wrong impression. No disrespect intended.'

'You're a joker!' I tell him. 'Don't worry. I'm fine. I'm always fine!'

'I mean it, Eden.'

'Just forget it, OK?'

'Why can't you just—'

'Forget it.'

I grab the remote control and turn the volume up loud over his voice and, with a snort of disgust, he begins clearing the table. It takes only a few minutes and a few times watching him wince with pain before I can't watch anymore.

'Zed, let me do it, please.' I don't look at him. 'You have a fucking broken arm!'

'It's not broken . . .'

'Whatever it is! Just get out of the way.'

wait—

Brooklyn, 3 June

You remember Soufriere, Eden? The volcanic springs, black mud, the air hot from above and from below? Well that's where your mother and I were born, in the very place Saint Lucia itself began life. Imagine the power of a whole island being birthed! Big magic! Fire shooting out from the belly of the earth, bubbling, spreading, going cool on the water, exploding with greenery and creatures. We have magma in the blood, Cherry Pepper. It's not easy. We live in the shadow of the Pitons. We are the earthquake. We are the shaded soil.

Your mother and I are so happy you wrote back with questions about your pre-history. These days the past feels very present, and maybe it is. What do any of us know on that score, anyway? Marie says it's not as we think. And she says roots are exactly what you need to settle you, otherwise a good wind could strip you, knock you over and roll you down to the bottom of the hill. And she says you're wrong, Eden. She loved you very, very much.

So. Our childhood . . . Well, I was the first, as you know, and my birth was also considered a miracle, although not a happy one. If I squint, hold my breath and cast my mind back, I can remember Mama's face when she looked at me for the first time. What a look it was! So disappointed and afraid, as if somebody must have done obeah on her and given her a devil baby. I was black, black, black at birth. Like cold volcano fire. I was black as her own father, with the knotty hair that beads at the neck, and she didn't thank me for the memories.

As I grew, the disappointment, revulsion and a strange kind of inside-out wonder would not leave her eyes. I was an accusation in pigtails. I was a blast from the past. She heard chains when she looked at me, she smelled coal-pot fires, pit toilets and heard barefoot workers in the field. For a while I thought my behaviour could make a difference, tried not to do anything wrong to make things worse. I was quiet and obedient. But as time passed I began to realise that I was the very thing that was wrong. I decided to taunt her instead. I oiled my skin well so it shone black in the sun. I let my hair bead in the back. I responded to her endless frowning and cursing and punishments with white, toothy, invincible grins. I turned her upside down. I looked just like her, except blacker. I learned to be angry instead of sad.

It took a full decade for her to conceive again. Probably because she kept her legs crossed at night and faced the wall, looking away from the failed promise of my father's light-brown skin. And that's the only thing she ever really loved about him. But divorce wasn't an option and eventually there was the swelling and the pushing and there was Marie. A child with the soft curls and bright skin Mama had always dreamed of possessing herself. She watched in an agony of pride as Marie's eyes cleared to a bright, transparent hazel. Her daughter, the one she'd always wanted.

Mama watched her sleep. She guarded her jealously from death, so afraid, loading Marie's curly head up with ribbons and berets and bows 'til the child could hardly lift her chin, and in dresses with lace and flowers. How that girl got spoiled! Mama used to open an umbrella on the child's head so she couldn't get dark in the sun on the way to church and she would keep her indoors all the time like a cripple. And 'Katherine!' she would say to me. 'Get out of the house and play!' or 'Get out of the house and hang the clothes to dry!' or just 'Get your black self out of the house!'

Everybody used to say how Marie was so fair and pretty like a doll, and at nights before Marie would go to bed Mama would brush her hair and tell her how she could have anything at all, any man, even the prime minister or Elvis Presley. And then she made Marie pray and tie up her curly hair. Then she would get in bed with my father, whom she hated a little bit less because he went beyond the promise of his light-brown skin and gave her a child yellower than ripe plantain.

She stopped hating me so much. She stopped seeing me. I faded right into the noon shadows and the night-time darkness and I think she managed to convince herself that I hadn't come from her body at all. Me and Marie didn't have a chance then of being close, living as we did in different countries of our mother's mind. She kept us separate. I think she thought that blackness was contagious. And then when I was eleven or twelve she sent me away to live in Castries.

So no, your mother and I weren't close growing up. This is the closest we've ever been.

I guess what I'm trying to say is I know what lonely feels like. I know what unloved feels like, but to me it's like DNA. For you, I think, it's just an outfit you wear. So change it.

Aunt K

eyes forward.

'So . . .' says Max.

'So?' I say.

We're in traffic near Finsbury Park. There are sirens. *Emergency! Emergency!* 'Are you feeling any better?'

'Not really. Think I'm just gonna go home and have a lie-down or something.'

'Good idea,' she says. 'Mind if I smoke?'

'It's your car.'

'Thanks.' She lights one up and sticks it in the corner of her mouth as the sirens speed past and fade. 'Are you pissed off at me?'

I blink. The blood beat does a little two-step. 'Why would I be?'

'You know.' She doesn't look at me. 'About me and Zed?' And because I don't answer right away, she keeps talking and sucking her cigarette in nervy little puffs. 'Because I know he's like family to you, know what I mean? I would have told you about us before, but I s'pose I was waiting 'til there was actually something to tell.'

'Nah it's alright. I don't care,' I say. *I don't. I don't. I don't.*

'You sure? 'Cause it seemed like you might've been having a bit of a row earlier.'

'Yeah. No. Not really,' I tell her, 'more of a disagreement.'

'Disagreement?'

'Stupid stuff, nothing major.' I laugh. 'You know. Like brother and sister.'

'Right . . . Phew!' She grins a glance at me, makes a show

of wiping her dry forehead. 'Just had to check on that one, you know. You're my mate and I wouldn't wanna take the mick. You know that, don't you?'

'Yeah,' I say, feeling muddy and slightly crazed. My mate? We have nothing in common at all, really. I met both her and Dwayne at work. And I'm pretty sure it would depress the hell out of Dwayne to know the only one I had any type of crush on was Max – of the platonic variety of course. She was one of the most extreme-looking people I've ever met, and the Clicker likes that sort of thing.

I was in late for work one day, and my row was already fully populated by the Undead when I arrived. One of the only free seats was next to this living cartoon, this ice-cream blonde who even *sat* mischievously. If beauty had a carica-ture, it would be Max. Improbably large, blue eyes at an improbable distance from each other in her triangular face. A high forehead and narrow, full mouth, cheekbones like razors, white-blonde hair down to her ass. Skinny as a no-fat latte, rocking a shapeless vintage mini-dress over a shrunken jumper. She was shocking to look at. She made the rest of the room look khaki drab. So I took the seat on her left, mainly to see this freakishly pretty thing up close. And then, when I was logging onto my terminal ('terminal' as in 'illness'), she kind of double-taked between phone calls and said:

'Hiya!'

'Hey.'

'Are you new?'

'I wish.'

'Don't we all?' She laughed. I sank a bit in the middle, she was *so* beautiful. I wondered what it must be like.

'I like your dress,' I said.

'Thanks! It was only a tenner!' she replied and went shuffling around in her bag, one of those flimsy jobs you sometimes get free with women's magazines. She had a super-easy manner about her, like she'd never had to worry, ever. She wore leopard-print wedges with ankle straps and purple tights. I stole a photo.

'Are you a photographer or summink?'

'Yeah I . . . well. Sort of. I take pictures.'

'That's bloody brilliant! I'm a model,' she said without self-consciousness. With a promising rustle, she pulled out a packet of Jaffa Cakes and shoved them at me. 'Go on! Be a devil!'

I had one, we introduced ourselves and so began our little mutual appreciation society. I took some pictures of her for free over the next couple of weeks, some of my best. Her portfolio got a boost, and so did my tired routine as I began trailing her around Shoreditch on drinking expeditions.

Well. It was fun while it lasted.

'How did you hook up with him anyway?' I ask now, fighting to be casual.

'Pretty random, really. I bumped into him on Oxford Street a couple of weeks ago and we started talking.'

'You hate Oxford Street.'

'I had a casting.'

'That big one you told me about?'

'Yeah, exactly! For *Gloss* magazine.' Spiteful bastard. I remember that day. Right after what happened with me, he bumped into my friend and gave her his number. 'You've got a bloody good memory. Must be your little puritanical lifestyle.'

'What do you mean, puritanical? I'm a drunk, if you haven't noticed.'

We drive in silence for a while, Max bobbing up and down to the commercial gangsta rap on the radio, singing along.

'You like this shit?' I ask her.

'Not particularly. Just catchy innit?'

'True.'

'I didn't get it, by the way.'

'What?'

'That job in *Gloss* magazine. Bloody bastards. They took this really skinny bitch instead. Properly fucking skinny. Looked like her last meal was breast milk.'

I look out of the window.

'So what,' she says, pushing her hair back and adjusting the mirror, 'is going on with you and Dwayne?'

'Dwayne? What the hell does he have to do with anything?'

'I think he likes you.'

'Well, I don't like him,' I say, then, 'I do . . . but not like that.'

'He's a good bloke, Eden.'

'So? There's a lot of good guys I'm not interested in.'

'Well, you are too pretty for 'im, anyway.'

'Damn right.'

Max taps absently on the steering wheel. 'Well, I like Zed quite a lot,' she says, disjointedly. 'He's got something about him. Mysterious like . . . You know what I mean? Plus, it doesn't hurt that he's so fucking *buff*!' she laughs. 'Bloody 'ell. I told 'im he should try and book some modelling jobs.'

'Yeah,' I say, trying to do something acceptable with my face. Hating her: hating him: hating myself. 'You guys look really happy together.'

Max slides to a halt before a red light, eyes forward.

'We are, I think,' she confirms, and glances over as the light blinks from yellow to green. 'You're so gorgeous with that figure and those lovely eyes . . . You'll find somebody.'

I try to keep the weak curve of my lips intact. 'I'm not looking, actually.'

When we get to Clapton Pond, I ask Max to drop me

off at a corner shop in her beat-up Mini. She says it's no problem, she can wait and then take me home.

'No, it's fine. I don't live far from here . . .' *Parole officer*, I don't say.

'Well, OK.' Max leans over and kisses me on the cheek. 'Be safe, yeah?'

'Thanks for the lift, Max,' I reply, fake-smiling.

'I'll call you later!'

I wait 'til she's out of sight to wipe the bubble-gum-coloured gloss off my face. Walk really fast.

'You alright, princess?' says the Turkish guy in the off-licence, with a wink.

'Give me a bottle of Jack and we'll see,' I tell him, just as a local nut-job walks in for his twentieth can of Special Brew. I leave quickly, before he has a chance to harass me. Take a left into Kenninghall Road where tower blocks dominate the landscape.

My manor isn't as leafy and clean as Zed's upscale, Highgate neighbourhood. It's squashed up, noisy, and full of happenings. The people all seem to be either silent or screaming, barrelling into you or standing in your way. It's all about bald, demoralised patches of grass, stunted trees and a dirty white van parked halfway onto the kerb. It's all about dogshit left to harden. It's all about sweet-faced, hooded boys and running toddlers and silly tarts wearing clubwear at two in the afternoon.

I've not even had a holiday in ten years. This is all it's been for the longest: scummy London with its scarred pavements and faded sky. Oily puddles. Brazen lunatics walking endlessly, repelling gazes like the wrong end of a magnet. And they are the only ones that speak what they're feeling because wherever you are in London, there's no space for big emotions. Swallow it, stifle it, shut up. It's branded into us all at birth or on arrival.

When I look around here sometimes, I kind of understand why my mother felt that she had to leave. But if she'd
made do, if she'd learned to be resigned, all our lives would
be different.

I rub my arms and walk quickly towards home, avoiding
men's gazes.

A cloud's gone over the sun and I feel cold in this dress.

July

get out.

'Brakes, Eden!' Juliet yells, a single eyebrow shooting up. She stops tidying her stall and gives me the look of death.

'What?'

'Repeat, please.'

I sigh. The season is shockingly loyal to us this year. London summers are usually skittish and commitment-phobic. But this year it doesn't budge. The heat hangs over all of us, relentless and heavy as a love affair in the throes of the first fizz. And Juliet is wearing a hoodie.

'Aren't you hot?'

'Nope,' she says. As usual, her tiny frame is kitted out tomboy-ishly in the brightest of clashing primary colours. 'Natural fibres. Ask me if I'm fresh, funky and fly. That, my dear, will be an affirmative.' A girl with short dreads and a poncho saun-ters up and looks over the merchandise. 'Now stop trying to change the subject. Didn't I just ask you a question?'

Quietly I say: 'What part didn't you understand?'

'It's just I thought I heard something really outlandish,' she says loudly. 'Did you say you chucked your job in over *boy* trouble?'

'Juliet . . .'

'How much for these earrings?' the girl asks with a snicker, holding out a pair in the shape of ice-cream cones.

'Fiver.'

'I'll have 'em please.'

Juliet makes the sale in her quick, bird-like way. 'We have the matching medallion . . .'

'Nah thanks.'

She turns to me again. 'You were saying?'

'Come on. Don't start acting stupid now. It's not like market research was my *raison d'être* or some such. It was just pocket-money labour.'

'Your pockets don't need money?'

'Money's not the bloody issue at the moment, J. My heart needs fixing.'

'Your heart!' she grunts. 'Are you light-headed?'

'What?' I fan myself with one of her product flyers. 'No.'

'You have a pain in your chest or in your arm?' she says, eyeing the Portobello market crowds. 'Any shortness of breath?'

'No!'

'Then your heart's fine, bella. You're a strong girl! Look at everything you've been through, everything you've survived!' Sympathy, respect and sadness all fight to dominate her face. 'Lots of people wouldn't have made it. Don't you think you deserve more?'

'I don't know . . .'

'What are you going to do about your income, or lack thereof?'

'I've got my overdraft.'

'Eden!' She shakes her small head and runs an irritated hand over her ever-present cornrows. 'We're supposed to be paying that off, remember? No debts by the end of the year! You may not want to hear this right now, but you need to learn to respect money. It's how you can finally become independent. Plus cold, hard cash will never leave you for a blonde! And if you look after your money . . .'

'. . . then my money will look after me. Yeah, yeah, yeah. Are you even listening to me, or are you watching a repeat of *Oprah* in your head again? You watch it too much as it is!'

'And you don't watch it enough.'

'Look, I had to leave and that's just how it is. I'll get something else. Most people can't avoid it and I'm pretty sure neither can I. But in the meantime, what's the point of rushing to work just so I can wish my time away and comfort myself buying things I don't need? I'm on strike.'

'Fortunate your dad's not on strike as well or else you'd both be living in a cardboard box!'

I grunt.

'Seriously though,' says Juliet, her sharp little dark-brown face contorted with annoyance. 'You need to pick it up and patch it up, miss. I bet you just park your derriere in bed 'til one o'clock in the afternoon, watching mindrot and farting and crying and spending our hard-earned taxes on E. Coli fried chicken! I bet you don't even bother brushing your teeth! Next thing you'll forgo showers and exercise and you'll stop combing your hair and it will turn into one big loc—'

'Come on, J!' I cry out, laughing for the first time in days.

'. . . and you'll weigh five hundred pounds and the remote control will get stuck in your massive crack and they'll have to lower you out of your bedroom window with a crane and—'

'Damn, Juliet! Give your jaw a rest, mate!'

She laughs her throaty laugh and crosses her arms. 'All I'm saying is you need to put Common Sense on the guest list and stop letting Idiocy smash up the party, ya gets?'

'Fair enough.'

'You're my best mate and I love you, Eden.' She pats my shoulder. 'I just don't want to see you hurt.'

'I know.'

'You should go and see her.'

'Who?'

'Your aunt. Maybe she can help you with everything, you know what I mean? And you could go and see your mum. Bring flowers . . .'

I don't say anything.

'Right, it's four o'clock. Let's duck an' sprint, yeah?'

We pack up, load her stuff into the car and she drops me off at the station.

wait—

Brooklyn, 3 July

Yes that's me, you can tell him! I am the daughter of night and the mother of destruction. Why not? Your father is always saying that 'people' say this and 'people' say that, when it's him that say it! How can it be suspicious that a woman of almost ninety years old should die? He tells everyone that I'm the one that killed my mother with obeah and my Rasta ways and drugs and wickedness, but I was a robot before she died. He doesn't even know me, the ignorant fool! She would have deserved it, anyway. Just because she dead now, don't mean she wasn't a wicked woman. So wicked probably she still wicked right now where she lives. Just ash, stuffed in an empty rum bottle on the bookshelf next to the Bible. She always said she wanted to go home to Saint Lucia when the time came but I'm not sure if she even deserves it or if I deserve that painful journey back after all these years.

I'm sorry I never told you when your grandmother passed four years ago, Eden. I didn't want all the hypocrites flocking round the coffin with their long faces and tricky eyes when they don't care! I'm the only one who really cared for her and I'm the only one who'll miss her now she's gone. She was a hard woman to love and her parents are long dead, as are her brothers.

If you want to honour her, make a small plate when you're having dinner. You just put a bit of everything on it, because she was a greedy woman, and a big helping of ketchup on the side. She'll come sit by you. She loved ketchup! Put some white rum in a glass and play her dead behind some Jim Reeves. That's how you say a proper goodbye.

And you can tell your dad that no, I don't worship the devil just because I burn candles and light incense! How people so damn ignorant? And because I have locs that means I must be a Rasta? I have no problem with the Rastas but dreadlocks been around long before they started worshipping Haile Selassie! My hair is a conduit to things unseen, Cherry Pepper, just as yours is. We are women of power. People come from all around for my spiritual guidance and protection, people from all walks of life. Doctors, musicians, lawyers, politicians. I make a better living now than I did at the firm. There's plenty of room for you here. Come whenever you like, don't worry about a thing. Give yourself time to heal and blossom.

You wanted to know why loneliness is my DNA. Well that's because there is a split in my world. My body is almost sixty years old in Brooklyn, but my spirit is still eleven, dark and bony, kneeling outside in the Soufriere sun. Sharp stones cut into my kneecaps. My hands are balled into fists. Sweat and tears sting my eyes. And Angeline is standing over me with eyes that aren't mother's eyes. A little black salope like you can't take the sun? That hard black skin you have there and you think stones can prick it? A knife couldn't prick it!

My mother ruined me for the world. She mellowed in later years, as most do, but it was too late. I spent my childhood being punished for imagined evil glances. I tried not looking at her, but still I was beaten. I was burned with the iron while I pressed and starched my sister's dresses. I was doused in boiling water while I cooked dinner for the house. I was ugly, I was black, I was stupid and I was doomed. Nobody would love a girl like me. I will never get that time back, Eden, it is something I accept. What was taken was taken for good. I flinch at sudden moves; I can't be touched. I sit behind my curtain and blank out the world and laugh at all the chattering people.

I've done it all, Cherry Pepper. I've been the A-grade student, the law graduate, the responsible home owner, and when your grandmother died and there was no love to be had, I became the junkie. I woke up in houses I didn't recognise, with men I didn't recognise. I woke up in the streets with no memory of how I reached there. Now I've come back to the middle and I help others, and that's given a pattern to the cloth. I am at peace. The worst is behind me and ahead is . . . nothing more.

Aunt K

plantain.

Open the front door and my house is spilling over with whingy old-time country music. What a racket. My father's miserable, tuneless wailing doesn't help either. When he sings, it sounds like he's having his arm hair plucked out with tweezers.

'Daaad!' I yell, but no way he can hear me over all the guitar-accompanied drama of Peggy Sue running round town and breaking a cowboy's plaid flannel heart in two. 'You're back!'

The kitchen smells like dinner. My tall and round-bellied father is frying plantain, swaying and singing with fervour. His hair is neatly cut and his beige slacks match his shirt. For the past four days I've had the house to myself while he was away, I'm not sure where. Probably on some team-building trip, learning how to sell televisions with more cultural sensitivity or some such. I'm shocked by my relief at seeing him. I must really be bored. Perhaps Juliet is right that I shouldn't have quit the day job. Now there's nothing to do but watch vapid daytime talk shows and eat and brood.

'Daaad!' I shout over the music. He rears back completely shocked, like I don't live here. 'What if I'd been a BURGLAR?!'

'Hmm? I can't hear you!'

'I'm not surprised.'

'What?'

'I said I'm not SURPRISED you can't HEAR me!' I

scream. 'Are you trying to go DEAF? Please give the country a rest, Dad! I'm losing my will to LIVE.'

'You have no taste in music,' he says, turning down his surprisingly powerful little ghetto blaster. 'You alright?'

'Yeah I'm cool.' I take a seat at the kitchen table. His apron says *What's missing in ch_rch?* I laugh.

'What?'

'Nothing.'

He gives me a suspicious look, then says, 'That's how you went out of the house? Those trousers don't even look clean.'

'But you haven't seen my footwear!' I say, poking one grubby trainer from under the table for his inspection. 'Check me out! Can't get more ladylike than that!'

'You are something else,' he says, shaking his head. 'You should make more of yourself, you know. Why don't you get your hair . . . *done*?'

'Relaxed? That's what you mean, right?'

'Well . . .'

'So I could flick it back over my shoulders like this,' I demonstrate, 'and twirl it daintily around my fingers? I could be a little black Barbie. Doctor Barbie. Or accountant Barbie, perhaps.'

'Oh, don't start with your theatrics! It would be nice and neat, that's all. You'd look pretty, and it would be good for job interviews.'

'Very subtle,' I laugh, getting some cranberry juice from the fridge. Ever since I left the market research job he's been on at me every day to get something else. 'So . . . where've you been?' I ask him, before he can ask me about my latest trip to the job centre. 'I haven't seen you since Thursday.'

'Big people business.'

'Come on, Dad. I *am* big people now!'

'Not in my eyes. You'll always be a dirty-nose chile to me!'

'You been out with old Chanders again?'

'Don't call her that, Eden. I told you already. But . . .' he whispers, 'yes, I have spent some time with the lovely Ms Rose Chanderpaul.'

'Nice.'

'I took her to Paris.'

'Wow,' I say, trying to smile. 'And I thought you were working. How was it? Aren't dirty weekends against your religion?'

'Separate rooms of course, Eden!'

'Oh, you animal! Tell me all about it. Did you have fun?'

He shoots me a look, and decides to treat my enquiry as a sincere one, telling me how lovely and really-a-great-bargain his trip was; frying plantain again and pottering around his yellow kitchen. He painted it last year in a fit of DIY fever so now it's sunny, just like he's been lately with his novelty aprons and trips to Europe. At least the food is familiar. The smell of stewed chicken wafting over from the pots on the stove; rice and peas, and the macaroni cheese in a Pyrex dish on the counter covered in foil. Whatever happens out in the world, the Sunday menu has always been the same in this house. Even if it's just the two of us.

'As it happens, Dad, I've been thinking of making a little trip of my own.'

'Oh yes, where? To work?'

'Ha ha. No, to New York.'

There's a long silence.

'Why?' he asks, although he already knows the answer.

'Aunt K.'

He shakes his head and snorts. 'Humph! I already told you about Katherine! I know she's your family, but that won't protect you from what she's involved in. She's an *obeah* woman. It's better if you have no contact.'

'Oh, please! She's just lonely.'

'There is evil in this world, you know, Eden! There are spirits! Aunt K was always one to try and play with things that a good Christian shouldn't. What have you got in common with her, anyway? It's been ten years since you've seen her. Just let it go.'

'I have *everything* in common with her because she's my family! How would you like it if anyone told me not to talk to your sisters?'

'My sisters are good Christian women! Trust me. Leave that woman alone because she is the last person you need in your life. Look at the way you've been for the past couple of weeks! I thought you were finally getting on your feet lately, but look at you, you've completely lost your sense of direction! You have no job; you leave the place disgusting. All you do is sit in that room. And I'm not saying that she did anything to you, but when you mix with certain people you just don't know . . .'

'I can't believe you! This is my mother's sister we're talking about! How could you even say that? Even if she was some bloody evil witch, why would she want to hurt me?'

'Just be careful. That's all I'm saying.'

'I think she's right, you know, Dad. You have it in for her, don't you?'

'I don't!'

'Yes you do!'

He makes a fed-up noise and goes back to his food. 'Just get a job, Eden,' he says. 'Then maybe you can think about travelling the world.'

stick it.

'What kind of work would you like to get involved in?' says a chirpy little woman in a pink shirt. Her name badge reads 'Margaret'. She's obviously not been here for long enough to fully absorb the profound sense of futility that's sunk into the bones of her colleagues. 'Something else in market research, perhaps?'

'Not sure.' *I'd rather shave my head and stick it in a hot chip fryer.*

'. . . Office admin . . . ?'

'Um . . .' *Are there any lottery winner positions left open? International superstar? Heiress?*

'. . . and there are quite a few retail positions available if that interests you.' *Spy? Assassin? Prime minister? Astronaut?* 'What do you think?'

'I dunno.'

'What skills do you have?'

'Not many.' *I can hold my breath for thirty seconds. I can levitate. I build bombs. I can burp the Old Testament in Latin.*

'You must have some! It looks like you've done a few different kinds of jobs.'

'I know how to use computers.'

'Great! What programs?'

'Mahjong Tiles,' I say. She gives me a confused smile. 'Quite good at that,' I add.

'Mahjong Tiles?' she repeats slowly, drawing out the words in the hope they'll make more sense that way. I look around at all the other unemployed people sitting in chairs, listing the reasons they may be of practical use. To someone. Anyone. Everybody looks bored, including the ones asking the questions. All of them look like they've been asked to play a game in which the winner's already been picked out and it's none of them.

'Yeah, and Pacman.'

'I'm not really sure I understand . . .'

'Minesweeper. Inkball. Solitaire occasionally.'

'Solitaire?' Margaret pushes the fringe out of her face and then, 'Ohhh!' she laughs. 'Funny!'

I don't laugh. 'How much am I gonna get a week?' I ask.

hang up.

There's a woman who guards my dresser from inside her £1.99 clip frame. She's a photo I took once, a few years ago. I call her 'The Woman Who Got Away'. Right now she's hanging out between a calendar and a couple of flyers that I've failed to get rid of from a show Zed did. A lot of the time I don't even notice The Woman, but when I do she speaks to me.

You notice her eyes first, a pale, vacant blue. She's looking up into the air as if the 253 bus – this was taken at the bus stop – may descend from above like a bolt of lightning. But she waits without excitement or dread. She just waits. Soon after the transparent blue eyes, you'll notice the precise, bobbed haircut. You'll notice the fitted denim jacket, buttoned to the neck, her slim jeans and bright flip-flops. You may even notice her painted toenails. Then you'll wonder what's wrong with the photo; why does it have that crazy finish?

But it's not a trick of the light. It will become clear that the woman is, in fact, blasted with dirt from her flip-flops to the precisely cut bob; so dirty that it's very hard to determine the actual shade of anything but the wet blue of those eyes. She's dressed for summer, but if you look into the background of the shot, you'll see several people bundled up in puffa jackets wielding umbrellas against the drizzle. She doesn't belong there, dressed as she is for the summer on a cold, miserable winter day.

I've invented dozens of histories, but the one that sticks

is that she was a perfectly normal girl, doing all those things you do to be normal. And then one day she thought 'enough!' There was no tragic event. Maybe she was on the way to work, looked at her watch and suddenly it all flew apart and she couldn't bear it anymore, all of those things you do just to get back to basic. You fix the bed and then you sleep in it and mess it up and fix it again, drink tea and wash the cup and dirty it drinking tea again, and you feel lonely and phone a friend and talk crap and hang up and feel lonely; and meet someone attractive and have sex and don't get called and meet someone else attractive and have sex and fall in love and meet the family and break up and fall in love and − and − and . . .

But at some point during the course of all this doing, she was done.

Never again would she make her bed, change her clothes, eat Sunday dinner, make a cup of tea, read a magazine, pay a bill, laugh, have sex, fall in love. She would abandon all those mindless cycles and instead wander the indifferent streets of London, acquiring layer after layer of grime.

Sometimes when I look at her, I'm almost broken with sympathy. But mostly I'm just envious.

talking in Kate Bush.

I shake my head. 'I can't believe I agreed to this,' I say to Juliet. 'It's embarrassing.'

'Nothing embarrassing about a wallet full of wonga, mate!' she grins. 'They're only three quid! People are going to *want* to buy them. Trust me!'

We're in the Nice and Friendly, a pub off Portobello, and Juliet's got a sackful of pirated films she's trying to flog to the punters.

'You said you wanted to eat!' I complain.

'Exactly. I'm making some lunch money. DVDs?' she says with quiet intensity to a couple who pass by on the way out.

'Sorry?'

'D,' she whispers loudly, 'V, Ds!'

'You're selling DVDs?' says the guy with ginger dreads and a nose ring.

'Yeah, that's what I said!' They look at her confusedly. 'Oh what, 'cause I'm not Chinese?' laughs Juliet. 'Bit racist, innit?' And then she sells them a copy of the latest Spiderman film.

'Look, I'm not being funny, Juliet, but can we just eat now? This is ridiculous.'

'Alright, alright.' She leads us to the bar and says, 'Don't worry, doss-bunny. I'm paying.'

'Deep and heartfelt thanks, yeah?'

She orders a Guinness. I ask for a rum and Coke.

'You're not serious! Don't you think it's a bit early for the hard stuff?'

'But you're drinking bloody Guinness!'

'First of all, Guinness has a completely different connotation than a rum and Coke. It's got vitamins. Second of all, you and me are very different people. You have self-destructive tendencies. I, on the other hand, am trying to *live*, girl! Ya gets?'

'Whatever, man. Get me what you think I should be drinking, then.'

She orders me half a lager. I give her a look and she says, 'Different connotation.'

'You're mad.'

'Very sane, actually.'

We order two portions of fish and chips and sit by the window to wait.

'So, what you been up to?' she asks.

What should I tell her? Sitting in my room, staring at my mobile, wondering if I should call Zed, deciding not to, then calling him and getting voicemail. Ticking off the days left before he goes home. I say nothing but I'm pretty sure my face says it all.

'Listen, Eden Sweden,' she sighs. 'Maybe this disappointment really is a blessing. You guys are too tangled, it's unhealthy. Just him being around seems to twist your head up. How could you be with him? This is your chance to move on and finally get serious about your future.'

'My future?' I laugh. 'What bloody future?'

'Look, stop pretending that you left your job because of the state of the world, man! You left because that brer hurt your feelings.'

'He's not just some *brer*, Juliet. You know that. Not all of us are cyborgs like you, you know.'

'Yeah, well if having a brain and using it makes me a cyborg, you can start calling me Robocop if ya like.'

'Fish and chips with mushy peas?' The waitress gives the

one with peas to Juliet and I take the one without. She tucks in with gusto, attacking her plate with ketchup, salt and vinegar, knife and fork. She hums with pleasure under her breath. I stare at my dinner with the same feeling I get when I cross a train carriage to pick up a stray newspaper – only to find it's in Dutch.

'Juliet, I'm just . . .' I say, light-headed but too hungry for food. I sip my drink and some of it sloshes over my hand when I replace it on the table. I don't even like beer. 'I'm not built like that. I wish I was.'

She shakes her braided head. 'Stop being such an Ophelia. Get on with your photography or something. Maybe it's never gonna make you rich, but it at least makes you happy.'

'You've never been in love. You don't know what it's like! He won't answer my calls. Can you believe it? I'm not the one who started going out with his friends! Can't believe I punked myself like that. Juliet, I threw my shoes in the lake and they sunk to the bottom, no trace. Had to walk home barefoot through,' I laugh, eyes stinging, 'horse shit.'

'Ah, mate!' She winces. 'You must be in pretty bad shape to start talking in Kate Bush. Didn't get a chance to make any "steps on the water", eh?'

'Nope.'

She rubs my arm awkwardly, probably trying to think of something gentle to say. Gentle isn't really her strong point.

'I know,' she says after a moment, 'that this is really, really hard for you to deal with right now, but you should try and be positive. Concentrate on yourself. Everything happens for a reason. It's the universe at work.'

'Tell the universe it needs a staff assessment, then.'

'Look . . . on a practical note, are you alright? Do you need some copper 'til you get sorted?'

'What?' I'm thinking, as I often do, of that moment in Zed's living room when we were alone all those weeks ago, when it all could have happened, and I messed it up. All those wasted, stillborn moments between us flash through my mind in a never-ending slideshow. 'Sorry?'

'Queen's head. Sterling. Dinero . . . '

'Oh right, yeah . . . yeah I know. No, I'm alright, I've got my overdraft, remember? Plus, I think they're gonna let me sign on the dole.'

'Uh-oh. That's how it starts. Next stop the crane.'

'Shut up, Juliet.'

sunday menu.

Thump, thump, thump! go those heavy feet again, crashing down the stairs. I look over at my dad, but his face only registers affection. There are dimples in his clean-shaven cheeks as he fusses over his table arrangement. New plates, real napkins. *Thump thump thump.* Graceful as a war tank she is. I sit and wait for plaster to shake loose from the ceiling, trying half-heartedly to devise a polite escape. But I've spent so much time in my little airless bedroom that the prospects of either third-wheeling it on my dad's romantic night in or going back up to my cage are equally repugnant.

Ms Chanderpaul finally turns up in the kitchen doorway and I'm perplexed, like always. A massively fat woman of three hundred pounds and imposing height, she is not. She's actually quite tiny. Five feet and round as a little ball. I think that her body must be denser than the average human being's. Maybe she's from Krypton, Superman's planet.

And I'm hearing her loud steps around here more and more often. I keep finding her long curly hairs in the sink, her shoes in the hallway, her handbag on the sofa, her heavy perfume tainting my oxygen.

'Hello sweetheart!' she says, shiny, dark brown face beaming. She's dressed head-to-foot in fuchsia – including eyeshadow. A dark Trinidadian Hindu, with slippery black waves teased and pinned on top of her head. Biggest hair I've ever seen outside Nashville. Well, I've never been to Nashville. But I've seen Dolly Parton on TV.

80

'Hey.'

She smears my cheek with garish lippie, close and away. My senses are drowned in lavender.

'You look . . . well,' she says.

'Thank you,' I tell her, draining the rest of my juice. 'Dad doesn't agree. He thinks I need to do something about my tough, Brillo-pad hair and trampy clothes. I suspect I'm embarrassing him.'

'Eden!' My dad looks frozen with shame. Chanders glances at him with a mildly panicked look, then says, 'I *love* your hair. I think it's wonderful! I'm sure your dad was just trying to be helpful.'

Now she knows better than *I* do what my dad thinks about me.

'Yeah, I'm sure.'

'But I think you're a beautiful girl. I used to dress really *weird* too,' she says, trying to be *down with the kids*, 'when I was a young girl in the seventies.'

I want to say, 'So not much has changed, then?' But I think she might take that the wrong way.

'I have a treat for you all!' she says, bending to take a foil package out of the oven. She brings it over to me and peels back the aluminium to reveal yellow, floury flat breads. She looks at me. 'You like roti?'

'Yeah, I suppose,' I say, and the truth is that roti is lovely, especially made fresh like that, but we never usually have it because my dad can't make it. I feel inexplicably nervous. Don't you need a curry for the roti, anyway? You can't really just have that with stewed chicken. And there's already maca- roni cheese and the rice. Personally I think it's all a bit much. 'My dad told me about your little romantic getaway.'

Ms Chanderpaul is actually blushing. No, she's too brown to blush. I think it's the fuchsia thing. But she looks all happy and coy.

'Your father is a lovely man!' she says.

'Well, not lovely enough,' my dad complains. 'She won't run away with me!'

'Oh, Elliot! Don't be silly.'

'Smart woman,' I manage.

I'm staring at my dad all plump and co-ordinated in neat clothes and his neat smile with his fuchsia girlfriend and the picture shoves me out and backwards. I don't belong in this picture.

'Listen, you two,' I say, 'no offence but I think I'll eat upstairs. Don't want to interrupt.'

My father looks thunderous; Chanders is crestfallen.

Before I can feel guilty, I take my plate and slip away.

knot.

And this is the same house where my mother sat all pointy and pale in the living room, fourteen years ago. She was feline and full of secrets, waiting to pounce on our lives together and shred them to pieces with her slim fingers like the chicken she was eating. My dad did the cooking then, too.

'I can't do this anymore, Elliot.'

I remember that the chicken made her lips shiny. I remember that her lips were shiny because when she began to speak I thought about her shiny lips and how beautiful they made her look even though it was just chicken grease. And even though what she said was scary and sudden. And I wondered if I would grow up to be that beautiful, and about how much easier it would be on my scalp if I had those loose curls like she did. They were silky black and clasped in a romantic knot on top of her head. She was always saying I didn't really take her complexion. *You're red-skinned*, she would say, *but not light like me. My great-grand-father was a white man, you know? Almost.* She'd say it so often, it got on my nerves. *You look like your father.*

I was already taller and broader than her and prayed daily I would stop growing. I remember thinking that her un-motherly clothes were tight in all the right places to make her look like she should be on *Top of the Pops* or on some soap opera, like she wanted to be, instead of in our poorly lit living room.

'I can't do this anymore, Elliot.'

'Sorry, Marie?'

'I can't do this.'

'Do what?'

'This. Sit in this cold room.'

'What? You want to waste the heating?'

'It's not a waste if it stops the cold.'

'What are you talking about?'

'How can the heating be a waste if it STOPS THE COLD!'

'WHY ARE YOU SHOUTING?'

'BECAUSE I AM COLD!'

'Chu! Turn on the heating, then. We'll see when the bill comes.'

'No.'

'No? Woman, you just said you were cold! Turn up the heating.'

'No. I'm not doing this anymore. I'm leaving. I hate it here!'

'I don't understand . . .'

My father temporarily lost his grasp on English, even though it was his only language. My mother kept telling him she was leaving him and he didn't get it until she fled up the stairs with me tight on her heels. I stood in the doorway and watched her begin throwing clothes in one of Dad's ugly, bargain suitcases.

And I knew that she wasn't taking me with her.

blue scream.

So now I'm hanging upside down off the edge of my unmade bed, staring at the damp ceiling and purple paint. At the frameless posters and scribbled Post-its stuck on the walls. Clothes on the floor. CDs, books piled up everywhere. Laptop, pens, pencils, sketchpad strewn over my chequered sheets. And pictures of *him* hiding in a little montage on the wall, pictures of *him* idling in my drawers amongst half-finished packs of paracetamol and lumps of Blu-Tack, pictures of *him* careening through my brain in a never-ending slide show. I don't even know where to begin cleaning up this mess.

Suddenly my feet are vibrating. I lunge for my bag where it's landed at the foot of the bed and dump everything on the floor and it's my mobile screaming its blue scream. Zed.

'Hello?' I say, breathless.

'Oy oy! Sleeping already?'

Pause. It's not Zed.

'Who's this?'

'It's Max! Ain't heard from you in a while.'

'This,' I tell her, 'isn't your phone.'

'Zed gets free calls, innit? A penny saved is a penny earned! Anyway, how are you?'

'Fine.'

'You didn't tell me you were thinking of leaving the job! What happened?'

'Got fed up.'

'You sure you're alright? You sound a bit down and that.'

'Nah, I'm fantastic.'

'Well, you don't sound fantastic. You sound like shit. Listen, you fancy coming out tonight? I'm going to this party down Shoreditch. It's gonna be—'

'I think I'll stick with tea and the telly thanks.'

'Come on! Don't be like that! Have you really got anything better to do? Telly's crap these days. I mean, what are you doing right now?'

'Nothing.' *Jesus*. I shouldn't have said that.

'Well then, nothing is stopping you. If it's about your problems with Zed then talk to him tonight and sort it out since you lot have been friends for so long.'

'Zed's going?'

'Yeah, 'course.'

My face feels really hot and I bang my fist on the side table and it hurts because one of my thick metal bangles is on there. 'Fuck!'

'Whatever he did can't have been that bad . . .'

'Look Max, I've gotta go.'

'What?'

'Bye.'

'Wait! What's got up your arse, girl? You've been acting all weird for ages!'

'No I haven't.'

'You have! We haven't even spoken since you left. Come out and I'll buy you a drink and we can—'

'Piss off.'

'Alright, alright! I'm just trying to help.'

'You're not helping! Just leave it alone. Don't think you can stomp into my life and start telling me what to do! You don't even know me! Why don't you sort yourself out? Bloody anorexic crackhead.'

Silence.

Then she says, 'Why are you being such a penis?'

'I'm not. If I was one, you might try and suck me for a fiver.'

'You know what? You're bang out of fucking order!' she shouts, angry at last. 'What is bloody wrong with you?'

'YOU! Calling me all the time! Can't you take a hint? You get on my nerves and I can't stand you!'

'You're such a . . . ! You know what? I called you 'cos I knew you'd just be moping around on your own like a miserable old fucking cow 'cos you don't even have a life and all you do is run around taking the piss out of anyone who's stupid enough to care about you! It makes me sick, Eden. You're such a—'

Click—

I'm going out. I need air.

candle to Rose.

'Eden? Can I talk to you for a minute?'

Dad's at the bottom of the stairs wearing 'concerned' on his face.

'I'm going out, Dad,' I say, stopping on the middle step, wishing I could fly right through the roof. How would that do for some witchcraft? 'Gotta go.'

'You wait a minute! I'm really worried about the way you're acting!' he says, moving so I'd have to walk through him to get to the door. 'I just heard you screaming down the phone at somebody in your room.'

'I was just chatting to Juliet. You know how we like to catch joke—'

'I really don't understand your attitude these days. All you do is sit in that pigsty watching TV when you should be looking for a job!' He sucks his teeth. 'I can't bear to see you this way, after all this time, just destroying yourself slowly. Drinking too much and dropping out of school and planning trips to New York you can't even afford. Why can't you move on, Eden?' he pleads, as if for his own freedom. 'What's wrong with you?'

'Nothing.'

'This is about my friendship with Ms Chanderpaul, isn't it?' He lowers his voice so Old Chanders won't hear – even though she's singing so loud amid the soap suds I doubt she can hear a thing. She even washes up loudly. *Clang, clang, clang!* go the plates and her voice fits and starts like a dodgy engine. 'Eden, this . . . This is the first time I've felt anything for someone since,' he pauses, 'since your mother. Aren't you happy for me?'

I just look at him.

'Eden? You mustn't think . . .' he sighs. 'I'm not trying to replace her or anything like that.'

'*Course* I'm happy for you, Daddy. Don't I *look* happy? Can't you feel the excitement and joy emanating from my pores?'

'You better come into the living room.'

'I said I'm going out.'

'Eden, don't make me tell you again. Come now!'

So into our old-fashioned living room we go. It has a few touching little modern details these days. An Ikea lamp next to the bookcase, overflowing with modern thrillers and Christian literature. Wooden blinds instead of the old velvet curtains. A stripy rug. But I could be eighteen years old, or thirteen, or ten, sitting here waiting for my lecture. I'm twenty-five years old! My dad tells me to sit down.

'Right!' he says, rubbing his hands together with a business-like air. 'How can we fix your problem with Ms Chanderpaul?'

'I never said I had a problem with her,' I tell him. 'You did.'

'Eden, I see the way you look at her and talk to her. You didn't even sit down and eat your dinner with us! You just ran up to your room. She didn't say anything, but do you know how bad that made Ms Chanderpaul feel? She's always making such a big effort with you! Always trying to be your friend . . .'

'I didn't ask her to do that.'

I know when my dad's angry because his eyes start to bulge out of his head and you could probably drive a train through each nostril. I feel oddly relieved at the familiarity of it, this dance we've done for so long. His contentment is the alien invader, stealing into our home and changing its dimensions, its fragrance, its rate of decay. He's softening around the middle. The laugh lines are deepening around his eyes and mouth. He's growing old.

'Oh my gosh!' he cries, hands thrown in the air, his bottom thrown into the sofa adjacent to mine. His movements are quicker, the bones of his face enhanced. Angry, he's more like the man he was. 'I don't know how you can be so selfish and negative! I've lived my whole life for you and in return, you can't even wish me happiness? For once in my life? You're not a child anymore. You're a big woman!'

For once. In his life.

'You have nothing to say?'

'Dad, I think you're a grown man and you should do whatever you want. And you don't need my approval.'

'You know what your problem is? You've never grown up properly. You got stuck somewhere and you're refusing to move on. I didn't raise such a brat!'

'I'm not a brat.'

'That's exactly what you are. I was so ashamed after the way you acted. Like I taught you no manners. You made me look bad! If you have respect for me, you'll have respect for Ms Chanderpaul because she's who I've chosen to be with and she's treated you with nothing but love and consideration—'

'You *didn't* choose Ms Chanderpaul! She chose you! She's just the first woman who's shown you any real attention. She's not half as good-looking or intelligent as . . . as you are.'

My dad's mouth turns down at the corners and he says in a quiet, dead voice, 'As your mother, you mean? Not as pretty or intelligent as your mother?'

'That's not what I said, Dad. Look, I just want to go out.'

'Go then.'

'Dad . . .'

'Get out! Go if you're going!'

'Dad, what's your problem? I didn't even mention Mum. You did!'

'She's the real reason you're angry though, isn't she? No one can live up to this person you've got built up in your head. Not even you!' he hissed. 'It's pathetic. You dress like you're homeless. You have no passion for life, no direction! Do you know how it feels for me to watch you waste your life?' He shakes his head. 'I don't know how you can live like that. And you want to stand in judgement of Rose? She's a wonderful person . . . why can't you see that? All you're looking at is the outside! Your mother couldn't hold a candle to Rose!'

For a long moment I can't say anything. If I did it might get very hostile in here. 'Whatever, Dad,' I say eventually. 'If you're really set on comparing them, you need to be honest with yourself.'

'It depends on what you value in a person,' he sighs as if he's lost all hope in me. 'If it's kindness, caring, morality and strength then . . . I don't know what went wrong. I did my best with you, but you've grown up to be just as blind and arrogant as she was.'

counterfeit.

CRASH!!!

My mum jumped when the loud noises began down-stairs. That day she left us. She dropped a handful of combs that she'd been holding, all different colours, wide- and fine-toothed. Wooden ones and some that were bright, glittery plastic. They splashed up from the floor and skittered out toward the doorway. My mum didn't move.

I ran down the stairs and eventually I heard her come up behind me outside the open living room.

The china and the crystal lay in shards over everything.

The gentle china.

The crystal goblets and animals.

And my father wasn't done yet for a couple more noisy minutes.

After quiet had restored itself, she didn't yell or cry, but the surest way to make her leave was to take away her refuge. Her beautiful things, her silk cushions, her crystal glasses, her china were the little heaven she'd built away from her ordinary life.

And he ruined them all. Ripped, torn and smashed.

When he was finished, she made her blank way out through the hall and back up the stairs. My dad sat on the floor in the midst of his helplessness, forcing her to leave because he couldn't bear to beg her to stay.

I cut my eleven-year-old foot following her over the debris of her broken refuge, but I kept walking. I knew there were only a few snapshots of her left – blood or no blood.

'Listen,' she said, back upstairs throwing things carelessly into the suitcase, faster and faster, 'don't you ever let a man convince you to give him your soul. You hear me?'

I was watching her take clothes out of her new chest of drawers. She and Dad had decorated the whole place. He hadn't known, but it was her last attempt at making her life liveable.

'Yes, Mum.'

'They're very sneaky.' Now she was crying – over her broken things, not because she was leaving me behind, I thought. 'They say we're the sneaky ones, but it's them.'

Snapshot: a hard green glance my way from her eye corners, her fingers poised behind her left ear tidying a displaced curl, her lips down-turned.

'They tell you all this rubbish about how they'll worship you! They want to plant,' a T-shirt, a pair of trousers, 'your heart in their own chest and water it religiously.' Bras, tights, knickers. 'They don't mean it. They only want to get their hands on it.' An unworn dress. 'Once they've got it, your heart is a dishrag. Your soul is a bonfire in the back yard to burn rubbish. You better hold onto yourself, Eden!'

I didn't know what the hell she was talking about; all I knew was that it sounded stupid and made-up. My dad wouldn't say anything like 'I would like to plant your heart in my own chest.' That was just plain fucking weird. It was all excuses.

'Right. Yeah,' I replied, but I was thinking, *What about me, Mum? Am I your prison too? Am I? Am I a sneaky one?*

'Don't you dare ever let some man come along and spend all of your best years like a handful of counterfeit banknotes.'

If I'm on your side then, 'Why can't I come with you?'

She stopped speaking then, for a moment.

'He's so amazing,' she said eventually, not answering my question. I sank in the middle. She was going to leave me.

'I . . . I met someone else, Eden. I know you don't under-stand things like this yet, but . . .'

'I do.' I swam against the weight of my West Indian training – children don't question adults and any *suggestion* of rudeness is a smackable offence – and I said, 'Are you having an affair?'

My mother looked startled for a minute, as though she'd just noticed I was on the brink of adolescence.

'Affair?' She flickered, confronted by this very hard, tabloid word. I imagine that it didn't sound that way inside her head. 'We're in love. I met him a month ago, when I went to visit your Aunt Katherine in New York.'

I'd so wanted to go. But she wouldn't take me with her then, and she wasn't gonna take me now.

'He's a young actor . . . you know, like me. He's so hand-some.'

I thought of my not bad-looking father downstairs and how much I looked like him and I felt abandoned. I had his nose. Everybody said so.

'Mum, you're not an actress. You're a receptionist.'

'Only part-time! That's not my dream, and he under-stands that. He supports me. He's crazy about me.'

'He must be.'

'What?'

'Crazy.' I wanted to drag her down from her compas-sionless fantasy. She wasn't even thinking about me, not one bit. That man downstairs weeping over all her gentle, destroyed china – that man was my dad. 'Or maybe he just wanted to have sex with you and that's it. At school they said adultery is a sin and you'll go to hell if you do it.'

'Eden!'

'My friends,' I say, breathless with irreverence, 'say it means you're a dirty slapper and you probably have herpes.'

She was speechless, standing there with a pair of tights

dangling over her arm. Really looking at me, like for the first time. I thought about the songs she would play sometimes on the stereo, 'I Can't Stay Away From You' by Gloria Estefan, and how soft her face would look, and whether that was when she was thinking about him, her new man. I wondered if she and I would ever dance again to 'Blue Bayou' and 'Wuthering Heights' with comic abandon. I daydreamed a life in America for short seconds, then got real.

'See you later,' I said, and then left her to pack. Went to my room for my shoes and a jacket, and down the stairs, and out. Nobody stopped me.

I went to Juliet's house and stayed there until I thought my mum was gone, and then I went home and helped my dad clean up.

brick.

There he is. Silhouetted in the window glow like a bug stuck in amber. He doesn't see me. My feet are heavy on the uneven street, pavement cracked by tree roots. A long breath escapes the cage of my chest, my mind empties, a car thunders around the corner. No way I could have avoided this. It was inevitable as the end of childhood, and just as unthinkable.

After the fight with my father, I should have found some easy distraction, let Juliet take me back down to the pub, or have Dwayne tell me some more cross-eyed jokes. I could have gone to watch a film. Stuffed my broken self full of chocolate-covered peanuts, hotdogs and Pepsi. I thought that was where I was going when I walked out of my front door, out into the crouching estate. I was certain in fact. What else was there? I hadn't even thought of the alternative, but still it drew me toward it, pulling me through the deep vein of the city.

On the bus, in the harsh glare of the top deck, I pulled a pencil and paper from my knapsack. *I'm squeezed blue by love, sweating like a runner,* I wrote to him, my handwriting jerky with bus movements, words pouring out like blood from a deep cut, too deep for pain. *Breath shallow, chest a cave full of bats.*

I wrote until there was no more to say, and then I folded my letter and put it carefully in the pocket at the front of my rucksack. I took my phone out, and I began to dial Juliet's number, running through my mind all the things

I should do. But the word, *should*, fell away and down into an abyss. The word *should* has nothing to do with nature. I got off one bus and on to another, going to him, wanting to stay above ground. I walked up the long shallow hill that leads to the road where he lives, leaden except for the maniacal drumming in my chest. This thing I feel, the thing that brought me here, is as indivertible as a change of season. It *is* nature.

I am here. The only question that remains is: what now?

Zed moves away from the window. My mind starts up again, slow thoughts. I could leave the letter in his post box. Or I could knock on his door. But what would I say to him? All I know is that I can't leave this patch of concrete, this moment, until everything is different. I've got to remind him that I exist, remind *myself* that I exist.

I read somewhere that people express thoughts to each other with words, but with art they transmit feelings. Leo Tolstoy, I think. And somewhere else I read that art separates itself from everyday reality, suspended inside a frame and outside time. Like that pile of bricks heaped silently in Zed's neighbour's front garden. That could be art if it wanted to, if it felt like being looked at.

I try to call Zed but he doesn't pick up. I imagine him sitting there, staring at the phone and rolling his eyes—

It starts to rain.

The bricks are flirting with me. The night is wide open. My mind is still.

I crouch and stick my hand through the neighbour's front gate, pick one of the bricks up. Feel the weight and roughness of it. Cool and angular, dusty and absolute. A brick has no questions. It doesn't wish it was a pile of sand or a power drill. A brick is a brick.

My arm is supple, my wrist flicks forward with effortless ease, the brick –

– arcs its way toward Zed's front window and –

– crash! –

The glass shatters and caves and showers down into the street. Sounds like the whole street is exploding! Brain starts up again with a stutter. Quick thoughts. Me. I did that. I did it. Need to run. Can't. Time ticks on so fast it leaves me standing here and sprints back to the bus stop without me.

The light comes back on and Zed is swearing. He emerges at the broken window, jaggedly outlined, bare-chested and furious.

Now he can see me.

Zed disappears from view and I know he must be going to the front door and suddenly my feet have life and the moment crashes down and I'm running. But not fast enough. Not fast at all.

Before I'm even halfway up the road he's hit the pavement in unlaced trainers and unbelted jeans.

'Eden, is that you? Shit! Shit. Oh my GOD! Are you CRAZY? I can't believe . . . Damn!'

I squeeze my eyes shut for a long moment with shame and almost collide with a tree. I stumble but don't fall. I don't think I thought the brick would make an impact in the real world. It was in my head. I thought it would stay in my head. Turn around and he's on the street looking up at the window in jeans and no shirt and one arm on top of his head, swearing to himself. He runs a few steps toward me then stops like he doesn't know what he might do if he catches me. Then he hobbles back to the patch of light outside his busted window. He still has a slight limp and it kills me. He's just a man, after all.

'FUCK!'

'I'm sorry!' I scream at him, balling the letter up in my fist.

'You crazy bitch! Oh my God! I ought to call the police on your ass . . .'

Then I run until I can no longer hear him shouting. I throw my letter in the bin outside the station.

More than anything in the world, I want to paint him. I'd melt down the black vinyl of a Marvin Gaye record, add a measure of dark rum and paint him on raw brick with my fingers. I'd paint him naked. Him naked. Me naked. In a bright room without curtains or carpet, with a mattress in the corner covered in fur and feathers. I'd paint him while he slept, mouth ajar, mind ajar and racing with dreams. His notebooks would be stacked in a pile next to a tin of fountain pens. I'd paint him writing. His eyes hooded and unmoving from the paper, shoulders hunched, fingers urgent. A claw foot bathtub would sit in the corner opposite the mattress and I'd paint him bathing, all his hard and soft parts shiny in the water. I'd take months, years. I'd immortalise him from every angle and then I'd hang all the work in a gallery and then I'd move in and live there. With him—

bella, what?

'Juliet . . . ! I've been trying to get you for ages.'

'Eden, what's wrong?'

'Everything . . . everything. Can I stay at yours tonight?'

'Yeah, 'course girl! No problem. Just calm down, alright? Calm down! How you gonna get here? It's a bit late innit?'

I pull the phone away from my ear and look at the time. It's almost two a.m. I've been knocking back the last three or four hours with ice and no chaser, waiting to get through to her for somewhere to go, someone to tell.

'You had one of your weekend studs round, is it?' I ask her, laughing a dead laugh.

'You sound mashed! Are you alright to even be travelling?'

'I don't care. I can't go home. I think my dad just kicked me out. I'm on the bus coming up to Trafalgar Square.'

'Wait a minute, bella, what exactly did he say? Are you sure you're not misinterpreting. You're good at that, you know!'

'I did some stupid stuff tonight, Juliet. I got back in the house and I tried to apologise,' I struggle with all my words, 'apologise for how I've been acting but he just started again and I exploded!'

'Oh shit! What did you do?'

'It's been a fucking stupid night, Juliet.'

'What happened? You're not saying all of it!'

'Juliet, you know you were saying you could lend me some monies?'

'Yeah?'

'Well, how much?' I ask her, mind spinning yards and yards of new fabric, zig-zag patterns, back and forth. 'How much have you got exactly?'

August

new time and weather.

New York.

There's a taste to it, a scent I forgot I remembered, a dash for my suitcase, a buzzing in my head. La Guardia, bright and crammed with people. Expectant faces and cardboard signs held aloft. Junk food places beckon, plus trains and shuttles, jewellery, clothes. Travellers disperse into their separate lives, temporary companionship forgotten. I'm surrounded by ecstatic reunions in my corner next to the information desk. I'm so awake I can't stand it. I'm terrified. A man — obviously sniffing around for a desperate, ignorant tourist — sidles up. 'You want a cab?' he says, and I say 'No,' and he hears *maybe* so he asks 'Where you going?' and I say, 'It doesn't matter because I don't want a cab!' and he hears *maybe* again. So he hovers. And I'm thinking, is my mouth moving? And I say, 'Piss off!' and he hears, *hang around a bit.*

The language is the same but different. I might need a rifle.

Still so vivid, the first time I flew into the Apple. I was a state. All big-eyed and shaking and couldn't believe I was going to see my mother again. Years were more like centuries back then and it seemed like stars could have formed, super-nova-ed, red-dwarfed and black-holed in the time it had taken her to send me a plane ticket.

And mothers were supposed to cling to their children. What kind of person was she to leave without looking back?

What kind of child was I to inspire a love so thin? Stiffly I went to school and came home, and to the library and home, and ate dinner and watched TV and did my homework and combed my hair. I taught myself not to expect anything, not even a phone call. I accepted that I'd been forgotten.

But she did send for me eventually, when I was fifteen. Perhaps she thought I'd be more interesting by then. First was a short letter saying she'd fly me over for the summer. Yeah right, I thought, folding it up into the smallest square possible and stuffing it in my desk drawer. I read it and refolded it so many times it fell apart, but I didn't believe a word. Not even when the ticket arrived. Not until I was standing at the check-in desk with my bag, passport and scared-looking dad. Even at that point I expected to be turned away. *Ms Eden Jean-Baptiste? I'm afraid there's been a mistake . . .*

But I was wrong. It wasn't a trick. I went through security in a daze. I kept beeping because I forgot to take the change out of my pocket.

The plane ride was somehow both long and quickly over. Announcements came crackling through tiny speakers: new time and weather and I remember thinking how weird it was things like that aren't fixed. What can you rely on if you can't rely on the time to be 6.07 p.m. like it says on your watch?

The city surged up like tears and I plummeted toward her, balled tight in my window seat, my belly bursting into stars. My throat shut. My ears screamed. I tried to conjure her face but it had already begun to go out of focus.

The plane skidded down on the runway and out I came into this new country, blinking and oddly numb. The queues at security went on ceaselessly, so long I almost forgot what I was there for. I heard myself say I was here to spend the summer with my mum. A man so angular he seemed barely human nodded me through immigration, out into the broad and chattering airport. I thought it would be a miracle if I saw her at all. She would have forgotten. Or changed her mind . . .

'EDEN!' she yelled, waving. I saw her instantly. Both of her arms were a-jingle with bracelets. The light was behind her, putting a shine on her black curls and custard-cream skin. Her smile was pure Hollywood. 'EDEN, over here!'

She kissed me loudly on both cheeks and I wasn't sure how to feel. My mind was still on the turning of the world, how 6.07 becomes 1.07 p.m.

'Mum.'

'I can't believe you're here!'

Her soft Caribbean-English accent had now been substituted for an even softer Caribbean-American one. She held me at arm's length, taking in my four years' worth of growth. I shrank from her. I was at the height of my rebellious clashing, and it seemed really cool most of the time but now I just felt stupid in my mismatched clothes. Nothing like Lisa from *The Cosby Show*. I'd really tried with my hair, but it had gone frizzy on the plane. I looked like a baby chicken. She smiled.

'Look at you! Put on a little weight, haven't you?'

'Yeah, and I've also grown tits,' I said.

Mum laughed like it was funny. I hadn't seen her since I was eleven years old and the only thing she could bring herself to say was, *You've put on some weight?*

'The child is hilarious, didn't I tell you?' she said to her new man, Dominic. He was standing off to one side, looking nothing like the husband of a grown woman should. He looked just the right age to play a teenager in films. 'All her life she's been a little comedienne!'

He gave me an empathetic smile, shook his head slightly

like *Don't mind her, she's always like this*. I looked away. 'I'm honoured to finally meet you, Eden,' he said, seeking eye contact. Black hair fell over one eye and he pushed it back.

He pulled my suitcase to the car and loaded it while my mum chatted about New York summers and the great time I was going to have and how sorry she was that I'd have to stay at Aunt K's house but that after all, me and my aunt had always gotten along so well, and Dominic's apartment was tiny. *You know how it is, sweetheart.* Her boy toy offered me a bottle of Coke and a pack of Fritos, asked me if I was tired. He asked me what kind of music I liked so he could play it in his car on the way to Park Slope.

'Eden?'

I jump. Out of nowhere my name is close and in an unfamiliar mouth. A tall, dark-skinned old man is standing next to me, his face very still in all the hubbub. I laugh. 'Sorry,' I say, composing myself. 'Hello.'

'I didn't mean to startle you.'

'It's alright . . .'

'I'm Baba,' he says with a formal air. 'Your aunt sent me to pick you up. Welcome to New York.'

'Thanks,' I say and he takes my bag. His walk is assured and fluid.

'You're more than welcome.'

'How did you recognise me?'

'Ahh,' he smiles, revealing a sparkling gold tooth. 'She described you perfectly.'

brighter and harder.

There is only the singing. Everything else is forgotten. No scuffed stage, no unflattering lights, no stranded chairs or old, mildewed curtains. If you close your eyes, there's no audience in this community hall packed with people. Only a thick, soft voice holding every note perfect.

The singer is no more of a showy specimen than the venue itself. She's round-bodied and of average height, without earrings or lipstick. Her cheap floral dress doesn't match her shoes. Her head is wrapped in a piece of plain black fabric. My camera is heartbroken and sometimes even cynical these days, but I take the picture anyway.

'Where's my aunt?' I whisper to Baba after a few snaps, shaking myself out of the spell cast over the room. 'Is she even here?'

'Of course! Look,' he says, pointing across the small theatre to a slender woman with long locs and immaculate posture.

'But she's fat!' I whisper back. He gives me a strange look. 'No, I don't mean now. She's not fat now. I just mean, she's supposed to be. She's always been fat . . .'

'Well that is your aunt, Eden,' he smiles. 'I suggest you take it up with her.'

I wind my way through the smiling people of all ages and take a seat next to her, which looks to have been left empty for me. I sit for a moment, unable to frame a greeting. She doesn't look round.

'You made it.'

'Yeah.'

'Good,' she says and flashes me a swift grin. I laugh, relieved, a child in the wake of her massive, raw charisma. 'I'm glad.'

'Me too,' I say, helplessly soprano. 'Can't believe I'm here. Everything at home has just been so crap and . . .'

'Wait,' she says, raising a long slender hand, completely serious again. 'Listen.' The singer's voice is sailing effortlessly at what has to be the top of her range, with no hint of strain or breathlessness. No weight. Not even the hackneyed lyrics of the ballad she's singing can disguise her purity. 'That's what hope sounds like, Cherry Pepper. It takes divine strength to be soft when the world is hard. It's just like when, every year, the green shoots push through earth and ice to get to the light. That's the big magic.'

'Magic,' I repeat, liking the sound of the word when she says it. A thing that happens, a thing that *is*. 'I know what you mean . . .'

'Ssshhhh!' says an uptight-looking woman behind me. I throw a slit-eyed look at her and tug at my aunt's arm.

'Speaking of magic though, Aunty, what the hell happened?' I whisper. 'Where's the rest of you? You're skinny!'

'You ever seen a fat crackhead?'

'Aunt K . . . !'

'It's part of me, Eden. It's not who I am now, but there's something liberating about the bottom. Everything is burned away but the very core of you. That's when you know what's real.' Aunt K shakes her head, subtly indicating the singer. She speaks at almost a whisper but still I'm able to hear every spice-scented word. 'Violet's been through it all and I've never met a stronger person.'

'What happened to her?'

'At three years old she was abandoned by her mother to the foster care system, flung rootless from home to home for a decade. She landed somehow with all her wits at an uncle's house when she was thirteen but instead of protecting her,' she lowers her voice further, low and hard, 'he *violated* her. At sixteen years old she decided that even the streets were preferable to the life she had and that's where she ended up, living in alleys and shelters and on dirty floors. In pursuit of the love she'd been missing for so long, she got pregnant at seventeen with her first child and deserted by its father. No place to live, no family, no education, no income.'

The singer deftly scales the bridge of the song, visibly swelling with emotion. Her voice is powerful and sure. A girl sitting in a nearby chair wipes her eyes.

'And she's right there, Eden. She's *singing*,' says Aunt K. 'Nineteen and she's already been through all the seasons of the soul.'

'Nineteen? Bloody hell!' I stare hard; the woman looks about thirty. 'Are you serious?'

'Always.'

'What about now? Where does she live now?'

Aunt K smiles a fierce smile and smoothes her locs down over one shoulder. 'Now she lives in *my* house, Eden. Just like you do.'

The song comes to a soft end, tailed immediately by frantic applause.

'Thank you, Violet!' says the compère, a small man in glasses. The applause continues on and on, punctuated by whistles and shouted compliments. 'She is wonderful, isn't she? Wonderful!' he claps his hands excitedly. 'We're coming to the end of the evening now, ladies and gentlemen, and soon it will be time to go home. Before we do though, I'd like to call up a lady that you saw earlier playing the trumpet. Ms Katherine Montrose, or Umi as we all call her, is the person behind the manhood and womanhood workshops that have given so many of our young people a foundation. Umi, please come up here and make a speech!'

Cheers follow my aunt as she rises from her seat and

walks up the centre aisle to the stage. She kisses the man on both cheeks. 'Good evening, people,' she says. And I just can't square it in my head, the way she was and the way she is. She used to be fat from her gloriously overripe head to her overflowing shoes, with at least two chins and boobs bigger than my head. A proper *matron*. And now look at her, this lean and wiry sorceress with purple in her hair.

'We can be beacons,' she says. 'We can be earth. We can renew the faith of young people when others have failed them over and over.' She takes a breath, and the room takes one with her. 'We can be the light, and help them as we've helped Violet. I'd like to thank you all for coming to this event and helping to raise money for the after-school programme. It's important that our children have an outlet for their creative energy in a society that can be so destructive of their self-esteem and vitality. Already this year, thanks to you all, we've managed to buy computers and recording equipment for the centre, go on several trips, and continue our life-skills, manhood, and womanhood programmes. It takes a village, people. We are that proverbial village. Please speak to Alex,' she indicates the man in glasses standing at the corner of the stage, 'if you're interested in getting involved. He's the head outreach worker here at Bright Prospect Community Centre. I wish you all a safe journey home. Thank you.'

Again there's applause, but I'm so tired my hands barely come together. People approach my aunt with respectful greetings. Business cards, handshakes and hugs are exchanged. Eventually, as the venue begins to empty, she makes it back to my chair and lays a hand on my shoulder. 'Come, niece, it's time to go. You look exhausted.'

'Sorry.' I laugh nervously at her almost unfamiliar face. 'It's just been a long day.'

'Indeed,' she says, and her face is shut so tight that, for a nanosecond, I'm certain that loneliness will kill me.

'Really good event though,' I tell her. 'You're like Oprah Winfrey or Maya Angelou or somebody.'

'Not quite,' she says. 'I've got a few errands, so Baba's going to drop you home.' A flash of that sudden, unexpected grin. 'I'll see you tonight. Violet's cooking.'

Minutes later I'm drowsing in the back seat of a hot car, struck by how different the light is here, brighter and harder, even this close to sunset. I watch the world pass until Baba sends me to sleep with a selection of easy listening favourites on the radio and his profoundly companionable silence.

I awake to increasingly familiar streets. The liquor store and the Caribbean restaurant on the corner. The bodega where Zed and I would buy Lays potato chips and root beers. I'm damp in every fold, fluttery, wide awake. My throat begins to close as I approach the house.

'We're here,' Baba says simply. Outside the window looms the old three-storey family townhouse, looking quietly martyred. Proud of its brick self. I remain motionless and belted to my seat, watching as Baba takes my suitcase out of the boot and rests it by the door. In a few moments he comes back and taps on the window. 'Go inside, someone will let you in,' he says, smiling. I get the impression he smiles a lot. 'I have to go and buy some oil and potatoes for Violet.'

'OK,' I say. And sit there.

'Eden,' he says, with a look of quiet compassion. Just my name. He must know it all.

I drag my heavy body out of the car, trying to remain mindless, and walk through the gate up to the blue front door and knock with a fist that shakes. Can't believe I'm here. 'Hello?' I say. 'Hello?'

I really need to sit down.

'Coming! Wait up!'

And less than a minute later my mother—

113

cloudy mirror.

I almost lose control of my bladder. 'Mum!' I say, before I can stop myself.

She looks all concerned and says, 'No . . . honey . . .'

And of course she isn't. Of course. I'm dazed by her quick form darting outside. In no time she's dragged me and my bags into the house. I mumble at her to hang on while I run for the downstairs toilet, which I still remember is along the hall and just before the kitchen.

The sink with a crack, the tiny shower cubicle, the chipped, cloudy mirror, my face like someone else's. The room smells of bleach and disuse; old but spotlessly clean. I pee for what seems like ages. Wash my hands. Dry them on my T-shirt.

When I return, the stranger makes me jump. She's waiting with a slightly nervous smile in the dim hallway. Pats me on the shoulder, leads me into the living room and fusses me into an armchair.

'Are you OK, sweetheart?' she says in a thick, nasal, Brooklyn accent. 'You look kind of flustered.'

'You . . .' The living room is much brighter than the hall and I see that the woman's resemblance to my mother isn't imagined. Custard cream skin, black curls, light eyes. Although this woman's eyes are grey, not green. 'I'm sorry, you just look like someone I know,' I tell her. She's taller but she's got the same small-boned, narrow body. The same cheekbones. The room does a waltz around me. I wish a room would stay still once in a while. I didn't even really drink much on the plane.

'Right.' She gives me a sharp look. 'You want some water?'
I nod.

When she comes back she sits on a nearby footstool, hands me a glass and watches me take a sip. 'You feel any better?'

Again I move my head, yes.

'Now, I ain't judging you or nothing. But I gotta ask you this. Are you high? 'Cause, girl—'

'What?' This is all too strange. 'Of course not! No!'

'OK. Thank God for that. Probably just the heat then,' she says with a theatrical roll of the eyes. 'It's enough to drive anyone crazy. Anyway, I'm Brandy.' She gives me a dainty handshake. 'It's so good to meet you! Your aunt talks about you all the time. I've never met any of her family but she's been wonderful to me and anyone who is her family is *my* family, you know? That woman is a *saint*.'

'She is,' I say weakly. I feel like if I let go of my knapsack I might just float up to the ceiling like a helium balloon. 'It's really cool what she's been – um – doing at that community centre. I went to the fundraiser straight from the airport.'

'Oh God, I'm so mad I missed it! I had a philosophy class over at Brooklyn College!' she says. 'Doing my degree part-time, you know. Getting that *education*, girl! How was it?!'

'It was . . .' I smile, suddenly thinking of Juliet. She'd have loved it. 'Inspirational.'

'Violet sang?'

'Yeah. She smacked it up.'

Brandy laughs. 'Yep, that's Violet. She gave me some tips for my little show that I do most nights, and now the responses I get are *stupendous*.'

Even her laugh reminds me, the straight white teeth. I grip the side of the chair. 'God, it's so weird . . .'

'What?' She watches my expression and slowly it dawns

on her that, 'Actually, your aunt . . . she always said I remind her of her sister! Which is, like, your mama, right? Maybe that's one of the reasons she took a special interest in me.'

'Yeah . . . you do . . . you do look like her.'

'It's really funny though!' she laughs. 'I'm a boy who looks like somebody's *mama*!'

'Sorry?'

She laughs again, running a hand through her long, dark curls. 'Honey, I'm a *man*! Don't let the pretty fool you. When I met your aunt I was getting beat up on a daily basis and using socks for titties.'

'You're a *man*? Are you taking the piss?'

'Dick, balls an' all, honey dip,' she laughs. 'God, your accent is just adorable!'

'Damn!' The thought slaps me awake. Even knowing the truth, I can barely see it in his . . . her features. 'You're beautiful though!'

'Thank you.' She smiles and tosses her hair. 'Gotta work what you got, right?'

'Damn.'

'When I'm not a chick you can call me Brandon.'

'OK.'

'Right now I'm a "she", and in boxers I'm a "he". You'll pick it up.'

'OK.'

'So,' she says, brushing imaginary dirt off her hands, 'we've gotta get you settled in the basement. I am *so* envious. Your aunt just converted it and it is *creamy*, chica!'

'Cool.' I'm still examining his/her bone structure. He's prettier than me. She. When she's 'Brandy', she's a she. Gosh. My brain.

'Come on,' she says, smiling in encouragement.

We lift the bags and go through a door next to the kitchen, opposite Granny's old bedroom. I glance at the closed door as we go by, trying simultaneously to remember and forget the sound of her pottering around inside, her low radio turned to the news. Somehow it's stranger for someone to be gone when they'd never really made an impact on your life. I don't know how to feel about her being gone, I suppose she always has been. We walk down some steps and emerge somewhere completely removed from the rest of the house. The basement appears to run almost the entire length and breadth of the ground floor, painted in earth tones and furnished with a bed, sofa and mini fridge. The furniture only takes up a small portion of the available space; besides that there's a washer and drier, numerous boxes and bookshelves. Fresh paint scents the air, a smell that calms me for some reason. It's a new world down here, a space where I've never been before. This used to be the most forbidding part of the house and now I think it's the only part where I can bear to spend my time.

'You see how bright it is down here? There's some natural light coming down through this special, um, refractive tube.'

'Wow.'

'Yeah, that's what your aunt said when she heard how much it was gonna cost.' She laughs. 'You got a TV too . . . it's ancient but it works. Plus we got WiFi.'

'A microwave and a canvas and I'd probably never have to leave this room.'

'You don't,' she says. 'You're safe. You're safe with Umi.'

When Brandy leaves, a panic starts in my chest, the full weight of the house pushing down on me. I sink down on the bed and find a note there. Purple handwriting on rough, cream paper.

note.

Cherry Pepper,

Breathe. You are exactly where you need to be.

I hope you enjoy the basement. I thought of you while I decorated it, knowing you'd return to us, so make yourself at home. Brandy's in the ground-floor front bedroom, the one that used to be the dining room. Violet and her baby live on the second floor. Baba lives up there sometimes too, in the front, second-floor bedroom. You go to him if you have any practical problems, if anything breaks or fails or has to get fixed. If he's around, you can ask him for a ride if you need to get somewhere.

For now, you'll find me at the top of the house but don't worry too much if I'm not around. My people are your people. Go to them if you need them.

Take time, niece. I'm glad you're here.

Aunt K.

make believe.

I wake up to light streaming down through the 'refractive tube'. And for a bright, clear second, I have no clue where I am, or when, or even who. The gelatinous heat settles into all my creases, eager to welcome a new victim. I'm a pile of sweaty limbs and a mouth of carpet, heavy as a bucket of water from toenail to split end. I can't believe I made it.

Last night, Violet cooked catfish and fried chicken, rice and greens and banoffee pie for dessert. I got the impression that it was a cherished event to have Aunt K and her niece at the table. She flitted and fussed, smiling her sweet, dimpled smile. I ate every scrap I was given and kept my trap shut. Let others talk. The timbre of Violet's rich voice – even speaking – slumped me in my chair, interweaving as it did with Aunt K's alto and the bass of Baba's untraceable accent. Soon there were no words, only a running harmony of tones and the dark behind my eyelids.

My aunt led me, half-blind with fatigue, down to my bed. She tucked me in like a child, saying she'd be busy today but that Brandy would happily reacquaint me with the city.

Sure enough, this morning there's a note slipped under the door. Brandy tells me in her round, curly handwriting about the muffins on the counter, waffles in the freezer and syrup in the cupboard for breakfast. She had to run out for a beauty appointment but will be back real soon for our 'diva excursion'. *Get fly!* she writes. *Later! Brandy xoxo.*

Get *fly*? I ball up the note and fire it into the nearby

waste basket. Sigh. I stare back at my jet-lagged self from the mirror pasted to the wall. I've come all this way but still, here I am. Just the same as always. I don't think I even know how to be *fly* (pretty, tarted, groomed, slick, exclusive). I feel distinctly un-airborne. Ankle-weighted, in fact.

After an exasperated shower, I dress in my neatest shorts and T-shirt and fight my hair into a ponytail, but by the time I've done that, I'm practically drenched all over again. Feels like I've done a day's worth of manual labour.

'Brandy?'

No sign yet. It's quiet as I climb the stairs up to the kitchen, a silence flavoured by the merest suggestion of a children's television programme wafting down from Violet's floor. A paper bag full of muffins sits on the counter just as Brandy said. The sweet, fresh-baked smell of them is so *America*, a scent that jolts me back to the first time here. I remember the sweetness of being fifteen, even angry as I was then, the sweetness of absolutes and brand-new places. I will never be back there again, at the beginning of that summer. I avert my gaze from the window and its view out into the back yard. I don't have to look out there to know it's crowded with ghosts.

I go out and sit on the sun-blasted front steps to wait for Brandy with my muffin, a book, and my camera. The odd car goes by, light sparking against the metal, music blaring from the speakers. Some kids across the road are embroiled in a raucous tiff. *Click, click, click* goes my clicker. A girl poised inelegantly between childhood and adolescence stands with arms akimbo, hundreds of little braids in her hair, yelling at a boy with a potbelly and cornrows. A shorter girl in pigtails looks on gleefully. *Your mama! – Don't you talk about my mama! – Why? – Whatchoo gonna do about it? – Oooh! Are you gonna let her* talk *to you like that? Are* you?!

A guy comes out of the house next door to the kids and

walks up toward Flatbush Avenue. Not as flash or as tall, but he reminds me of Zed – the New York swagger of him. It makes my heart do the fandango. I remember Zed as a teenager, us walking up this same street, sitting on these steps. Makes me miss him so hard it's an anguish of the bones, blood, muscle – but that's nothing new. I've always missed him, even when we're together, because no amount of belly butterflies or sleepless nights can help a person reach past the limits of the skin, or the boundaries of their mind. No matter how much we wish we could know a loved one's thoughts, we're deaf to them; and no matter how much we love somebody we can't stay with them. If life fails to steal them from us, then death will do it.

What a blind headfuck of a thing it all is.

'It looks,' says Brandy, suddenly in front of me, resplendent in a white summer dress, 'like you got a lot going on inside that brain of yours, girl! Don't hurt yourself!'

'Nothing useful,' I tell her.

'Well, you need to wipe that sour look off your face and smile, honey dip! It's a beautiful summer day in Brooklyn!' She sweeps her arm out like a model on one of those American game shows. *Look at what you've won!!!* 'The question is, what do you wanna do with it?'

I shrug. 'I don't know,' I tell her. 'I'm all yours.'

We walk to Prospect Park station and buy Metrocards from the machines, go through big metal turnstiles, down the steps to the platform. The subway is moody like I remember it, the light a dim yellow, the air blistering hot. A few moments later we get on a cold train full of slightly weird characters you'd be afraid to make eye contact with. Brandy and I ride in near silence, jolting quietly through the underworld. I stare at all the boys staring at her and try not to laugh. She is quaintly oblivious.

We emerge above ground at Atlantic Avenue to electric blue skies and sidewalks thick with noise and people.

'Do you mind if we stop here for a second? I just need to get a couple of things, and then we can go up to Manhattan, do the tourist thing?'

We cross over the street to the mall, push through the double doors into the welcome air-conditioning. All the families are out shopping. Children are yelled at and cuddled, teenagers skulk about looking embarrassed or full of themselves depending on who they're with. The women look mostly harassed, the men unperturbed.

We hang around examining the stalls and going from store to store, Brandy yacking about bargains and body types. I finger stretchy T-shirts and rhinestone-studded jeans and tiny, bright dresses. No wonder Zed thinks I'm a slob. New York girls don't waste a single curve on excess fabric. Or even New York boys dressed as girls.

'I bet London shopping is ten times better, right?'

'I dunno . . . Kind of, maybe.'

'More individual?'

'Yeah, I suppose. But a lot of us are "individual" in exactly the same way though, ya gets? Hand built by robots.'

'Funny!' she laughs.

'But, as you can see,' I say, gesturing at my outfit, 'what I know about fashion could fit inside the average pimple.'

'Nah,' says Brandy with a rapid, surreptitious glance, 'you alright, girl. Nothing wrong with you.'

She goes off to the till point to pay for some dangly earrings and two tank tops. I catch her up at the door.

'Are you serious? There's nothing wrong with me?' I look from her blinding white dress to the ragged thoughtlessness of my outfit and back again. 'You don't have to be nice just because I'm a foreigner, you know. I'm a mess!'

'Damn,' she laughs. 'Why I always gotta end up some-body's fashion guru?'

'I'm sorry.'

'It's OK, it's OK. With talent comes responsibility, right?' she says, waving her dainty hand in dismissal. 'You're not a mess, Eden. People always start talking like that when their mind has changed but their fashion hasn't. What's your problem with how you look? It's not working for you anymore?'

'I just . . .' I say helplessly, dangling like a hooked fish. 'I don't know.'

She smiles. 'Probably all you gotta do is take that look of yours and throw some glitter on it, you know what I'm saying? Your aunt is always complaining that women these days don't know their power.' She taps one long pink nail thoughtfully against her lips. 'Come on, let's go. I'm gonna take you to my favourite store. Maybe we should be tourists some other time.'

We go back out into the faint-worthy, horizon-distorting heat.

'I don't feel like I've got any at all,' I say eventually.

'Any what?'

'Power.'

Brandy sighs and shakes her head. The smell of melted cheese floats out of a pizza place. A group of teenaged boys walk toward us, broad as cowboys, talking animatedly about basketball.

'Everybody's got *absolute* power over themselves, girl,' she says. 'The question is, what do you do with it? You decide what to wear and how to walk and whether or not you accessorise. You do all of that with, like, a goal in mind, either consciously or subconsciously.'

'Really, though?'

'Yep.'

We walk along for a while, her wearing a look of schooled nonchalance on her face and me fighting myself. But eventually I have to ask the obvious. 'Well, what do my clothes say about me, then?'

Brandy stops right in the middle of the street and flips her hair out of her eyes, gives me the head-to-toe. Like every one of her gestures, it's an event in and of itself. 'Turn around,' she commands, ignoring the hard stares people throw her way. I do as requested and she shakes her head. 'You got issues, honey,' she says and starts walking again.

I roll my eyes. 'Oh, well, thanks for that! What are you? Psychic?'

'Just kidding,' she laughs. 'Are you ready for the real?'

I nod.

'Well, from what I can see,' she glances at me, 'you're working an arty, creative look. But it has an edge on it, like you're trying to keep people at a distance, you know what I'm saying? Not bring them in. The shapes aren't that flattering. You play your body down rather than play it up. Your posture is *horrible*, like you're afraid that if you took it up a notch and were sexy and feminine, that you actually wouldn't be able to compete with other women.'

'Damn. OK.'

'But,' she says with a narrow-eyed smile, 'at the same time, I look at your wrinkled, frayed clothes and it's like you *want* somebody to see all the cracks and take care of you. Give you a hug and a glass of milk.'

We stop outside a shop with a naked mannequin in the window. She doesn't ask me if she hit a chord. She has complete confidence.

'Anyway, you have to see this place. It's the best thrift store in Brooklyn and you were born for vintage.'

'I don't even like milk,' I tell her, but she just smiles and waves me through the doors. The bell tinkles and immediately there's a camp roar from the back of the shop.

'MS GORGEOUS!!!'

'JAY!'

A rustle of hangers and a small, pretty man dressed in a slim black shirt, black drainpipes and a white belt darts out from behind the till and air kisses her with gusto.

'How you doing? You look *ridiculous* fine, girl!'

'You too. Working that little Emo look you got going on! You met somebody new, huh?'

'Girl! You like the psychic network in a Wonderbra! Holla!'

They dissolve into giggles. 'So,' Jay says eventually, giving me my second head-to-toe of the day. This one less forgiving. 'Who's your friend?'

'This is Umi's niece over from London. Eden, Jay, Jay, Eden.'

'You're kidding! Oh my God . . . wow! That woman is true royalty. How you doing?' he says, throwing his hand out.

'Hey,' I say and shake it.

'How you like New York?' he says to me, leaning against the cash register. I marvel at his voice and manner; he's like a teenaged black girl trapped in a twenty-something white man's body.

'Cool so far,' I say. 'Well, bloody hot. But cool.'

He laughs. 'How long are you here for?'

'I dunno . . . Three months at least.'

'Wow, that's a long trip.'

I shrug and nod.

Brandy sighs. 'Yada yada yada. Enough small talk, pretty boy! What you got to show me?'

'Weell . . .' Jay smiles. 'It's a very good day in thrift store land! Come on through. I just got these in today . . .' They walk off between the aisles. 'That dress is *hot*, by the way! You tryin' to hurt people's feelings out here or what?'

The store is brightly lit and orderly, not like I expected at all. It doesn't smell of mothballs or the elderly. There's so much stuff I'm momentarily paralysed.

'Hey, Eden!'

'Yeah?'

'What you doing over there, girl?'

'Nothing.'

'That's the problem! Go look at some threads! That's what we here for.'

It seems like just seconds later that Brandy is squealing at me from the back of the store. 'Come see my outfit!'

I follow the squeal and she's stood in front of an antique standing mirror, smoothing a sixties mini-dress down over her narrow hips.

'That's nice,' I say.

'You think so?'

'Yeah, definitely.'

'Hear hear!' yells Jay from the other side of the store where he's arranging the handbags.

'This would look really good for my shows,' she says to herself and then goes back to a colourful rail. 'You gotta try this on,' she says, bundling an eighties prom dress into my limp arms. 'It's gonna look majestic on you!'

'I don't know . . .'

'Try these on too.'

I just stand there.

'Eden, step into my office,' she says, hustling me into a purple-curtained fitting room. 'Now look, I'm not trying to tell you what to do, or how to think. But one thing chicks like *me*,' she places a hand to her padded chest, 'recognise, is that being a chick takes work. That's the problem with you guys. Getting all depressed 'cause you don't look like a supermodel first thing in the morning? Damn! At least ya'll ain't gotta deal with a five o'clock shadow!'

I laugh. 'I'm being serious, chica! To get a little bit deep, you gotta look at femininity as a *construct*, you know what I'm saying? I'm writing a paper on it right now! Femininity takes work and it takes maintenance. And don't waste my time saying you don't care, 'cause it's damn obvious that you do! Otherwise you wouldn't be coming around like, "Oh Brandy! Help me pleeease! Save me from myself!"'

'Shut up! I don't sound like that!'

'I am telling you the damn truth, girl, and you can't take it!'

'Look, I'll try on the bloody things, OK? Are you happy now?'

'I got you smiling, though,' she tickles me. 'I got you smiling!'

The lacy and sequinned prom dress cheers me up despite myself, and I can't help but laugh at the riotous applause from Jay and Brandy when I strike a pose.

'You need to put on a fly pair of sneakers with that and you are good to *go*!' says Jay, looking me up and down. 'Dunks maybe. Or even some Chucks like what you got on.'

'You don't think I need to wear heels?'

'Nah! You ever hear that song by Prince, when he sings,' Jay adopts a startling falsetto, '*I've never seen a pret-ty girl look so tough, baby! You got that LOOK!*'

I laugh. 'Yeah . . .'

'Well that's you, baby. Born to do it!' he snaps his fingers. 'Hey! I'm gonna put that album on right now!'

Brandy tells me to try the peasant dress, all billowy and romantic. She takes a belt and pulls it tight around my waist. 'I love waist belts!' she says. 'Isn't that a sexy feeling?' She takes a step back and studies my body. 'Jay! Come check out this *ridiculous* hourglass figure!'

'Bitch, I am *jealous*!' Jay says, bopping his head to eighties Prince, 'Little Red Corvette'.

'You said you take pictures, right?' she asks me.

'Yeah . . . um . . . I do.'

'Well, I know some of the vainest bitches in the Western hemisphere, so I think I can get you some photography work if you want. Help finance this little fashion injection of yours. What you think, mami?'

I strike a muscle man pose, Jay snaps his fingers again, Brandy giggles and for the first time in ages I feel some distance from all the things that make me sad.

'I think that'd be just fine, actually,' I say.

'And Eden . . .'

'Yeah?'

'Look, I ain't trying to be all up in your business,' she says, lowering her voice, 'but I know a thing or two about getting hurt, how it feels to be in pain.' She takes my shoulder and smiles, shiny-eyed. 'But don't flaunt your scars, girl-friend. OK? You are not your scars.'

real family.

'Hey, Violet.' On my way back from the bodega for snacks, I spot her outside the house with the baby buggy and shopping. 'You need some help?'

'Oh! Yeah. Thanks, girl!' she says. Her skin is the colour of a rich gravy and equally wholesome. She wears a simple baseball cap and beneath it, her eyes and smile are serene. I feel young, lanky and bruised in comparison. 'How you doing?'

'I'm good,' I tell her, wiping sweat off my face. 'What should I grab?'

'If you take the bags,' she says, 'I'll take baby. I can come back for the stroller.'

'No, it's cool, I can manage.'

She unstraps her boy and lifts him out of the buggy. His little sleeping body, clothed in a bright outfit and tiny sandals, moulds itself around her neck.

'Wow. He's cute to the point of physical pain! You do good work!' I say and she laughs. 'What's his name, again?'

'Eko,' she strokes his head. His face is sweet, round and perfectly formed.

'It suits him.'

Once we've finally made it up to her living room, she lays her son down in his play pen and offers me iced tea and banana cake.

'Yes, please. Thanks.'

She goes down the hall to her kitchen and I brace myself against history. Try to be *right now*. It's just a room, after all.

Houses don't have minds, so neither can they have memories. Everything is different from how it was before, back in the days when this room was a library and her bedroom was mine. That summer. The space is now decorated in shades of cream and gold, with shining wooden floors. A toy chest is stored neatly in the corner next to the play pen. There's a bowl of fruit and a stack of magazines on the coffee table. A downy-looking blanket is folded on the arm of the sofa. Doesn't seem like anything bad could happen here.

Outside the door is the staircase that goes right the way to the top. Aunt K is either sick or mad to live there. I don't know which.

'Here.' She places a generous slice of cake and my drink on the coffee table. 'Hope you like it! Just tried a new recipe.'

We sit for a moment enjoying her latest creation. It deserves, and gets, a moment of silence.

'This is really bloody good,' I say as enthusiastically as I can manage. 'Don't want to be cheeky, but I think you're gonna have to give me some for later.'

She mutters something about my 'cute' accent and laughs. 'I'll see what I can do,' she says. Then she gives me a look that somehow manages to be both shy and accusatory. 'I like your hair.'

'Thanks.'

'Is it all yours?'

'Yeah, 'course!' I exclaim, and pat my Afro, softened by mysterious oils and manoeuvred into a cascade of shining twists. 'Brandy took me to this salon in Harlem. I think I'm her little project at the moment.'

Violet's eyes flicker down at the wooden floor and up. 'I know the place. Hair and Now, right? You guys go down the street to the soul food restaurant after?'

'Yeah,' I say, feeling a bit cheap. 'Yeah we did. She must do this with all the girls.' I laugh. 'Maybe one day we should all hang out or something.'

'Yeah. Yeah we should,' she says. Pause. 'You look really pretty. I wish some oils could do that to *my* hair.'

I cough. This is an alien feeling. 'Nah, trust me! My hair is a pain in the ass. I can barely get a comb through it! It was magic what they did.'

'That's what chicks with good hair always say.'

'Good hair? What are you talking about?'

Violet smiles sadly, tugging at the peak of her baseball cap. 'Don't worry about it, girl. Just say thank you. It's a compliment.'

'Have you been there? I'm telling you they can take any hair texture and . . .'

'They said I should cut it all off.'

For a moment we say nothing.

'Why?'

She shrugs. 'It's too damaged. I mean . . . I wanted to grow out my relaxer gradually but they said the best thing I could do was to just shave it off.'

'Maybe you should. You've definitely got the face for it.'

'That's what Brandy said. But hell. I need my hair! I just want to look pretty, you know? Like a girl,' she says, and I'm undone by her simplicity. She's not afraid to want what she wants. 'But anyway,' she lets loose a smile, and I really want to tell her how she doesn't even need hair with a smile like that, but the moment has passed. 'You want some more cake? I'll still pack you some up for later too.'

'Yes, please. Thanks.'

I'm too full for the cake she brings me but I eat it anyway, for something to do. 'How do you know my aunt?'

'Well, I met her a couple years ago at Bright Prospects, back when I was pregnant with Eko,' Violet says, seeming relieved at the change of subject. 'She taught a workshop in life skills and really helped me out, you know? Helped me see things different. Like I had a future.' She pours me out some more iced tea. 'I started doing singing workshops with the kids and stuff. I was living in a hostel at the time, and they were gonna house me. But when Umi saw the apartment, she said she couldn't let me live somewhere like that so she gave me a roof. She's a true blessing to me, the closest thing I've ever really had to a real family.' She takes a sip of her tea. 'I'm gonna miss her while she's away!'

'Away?' I pause mid-bite. Put the cake back down on my plate. 'Where?'

'She's going to Saint Lucia tomorrow!'

I'm not sure I heard right.

'Excuse me?'

Violet looks at me. 'Damn, she hasn't told you yet? That's so like her! Always just doing her own thing, you know?'

'But I just got here! I thought I was coming here to spend time with her. It felt like,' I can barely get the words out, 'she needed me!'

'Honey, there's one thing you need to know about Umi. She don't need *no* one! We need her! If she's decided to leave you here for a while, then that's 'cause she thinks you'll do better without her.'

'I can't bloody believe it.'

'Don't worry, you got us! You need anything, you just let me know. Or Brandy, or Baba if he's around . . .'

'Yeah. Thanks.'

I take my cake and go, purposely not seeking out Aunt K for more information. Who does she think she is, anyway? With all these people stacked around her like weird disciples in the Church of Katherine! I remember the first night going up to dinner with Violet. I faltered at the base of the steps, steps I'd thought I could never climb again. We weren't going all the way to the top but still, we were close enough. She gave me this hard, unforgiving look, and she said, 'Eden. We are *not* the weak! We persevere, we survive. *Get* up those steps and stop making a fool of yourself!'

I was stunned, humiliated standing there. She had no right to judge me for being damaged. I'd earned it. I almost told her as much, but she was gone before I could open my mouth to say a word, leaving me to climb the stairs on my own.

And I'll make it through this summer on my own as well. I'm bloody used to it.

traffic on film.

It's very dark. My dream is slippery. Gone. Sweaty sheets are tangled around my legs and something woke me up but I don't know what it was. It's a week now since Aunt K left for Saint Lucia, giving me a big, nonchalant hug as if inviting someone to stay and then going off without them is something she does as a matter of course. The house feels different without her in it, more dangerous by far. Before she left, I was living with Aunt K. Now I just live in Flatbush with a house full of near-strangers.

I'll lie here, very still and quiet. It will come back to me. There are snatches of conversation from passers-by on the street outside. Police sirens. Next door a radio playing tinny hip-hop. Cats are fighting. But none of those noises are what woke me up. I think there's someone upstairs, on the ground floor. And Brandy's gone for the weekend. I saw her pack up and leave for a pageant she's doing in Washington DC. That sound again.

Footsteps.

Blood is beating loud in my head and I don't know if I should get up because if it's a burglar he might hear me. But I would have known if something big woke me up, like shattering glass or a door being bashed in, wouldn't I? A door opens. Closes. Something is wheeled across the floor. I should go up there. If it's Brandy, if she's back early, or if it's Violet suffering from insomnia, or Baba on some inexplicable night-time mission, then I want to know right now so I can stop being scared.

In the dark my feet land silently. I leave the light off, sneak up the basement stairs without creaking, and push out into the hall. The light is on in the kitchen and there's a rustling sound. It has to be Brandy having a go at the tortilla chips. I could use a chat right now anyway, about ordinary things. About haircuts and celebrities and the weather. Anything.

'Brandy? I'm *so* happy you—'

Then everything sticks in my throat because it's not her. It's not a *her* all. It's a *him* − a really big him, and I rear back and I'm listening to this loud, shrill sound that I realise is me screaming and who is this guy and how did he get in and why is he here?

Then the man jumps and spins around in shock and my body is shot through with fear, like sped-up traffic on film when you can only see the coloured lights streaking through the black and even if the sound is off the images are noisy and . . .

'Zed?'

I keep trying to flick this hallucination out of my eyes because that's what this has to be.

'What the . . . ?' he stares at me. 'Eden? Jesus Christ, girl! Stop screaming.'

'No way!' I shout, still hopped up on adrenaline. Shock claws blackly at the edges of my vision. 'Zed? Oh my God.'

He closes his eyes and takes measured breaths for a moment, lashes thick against his cheeks. 'So Juliet wasn't yanking my chain. What, are you stalking me now?'

'I'm not stalking you. How could I be stalking you when I was here first? Damn, Zed. Damn. What are you *doing* here?' I say, but it's taking me a while to get all of this out because I'm starting to hyperventilate. Aunt K must have done this! What is she bloody playing at? 'Shit . . . I thought you were . . .' breathe, 'a burglar! I thought . . . What are you doing here? You said you were going home!'

'What?'

'Atlanta!'

'I never said anything about Atlanta, Eden. You know I've about had enough of living with my mother. It was going to be New York after London.'

I gasp for air.

'Sit down. You are such a drama queen!' His forehead glistens. He drags first the front and then the back of his hand across it. 'Sit!'

I sink down into a chair and he – none too gently – empties some junk food on the kitchen table and then stuffs the paper bag over my face. He's wearing a black T-shirt over a white one and there's sweat in the hollow of his neck. He's always what I've just been thinking about, even if I was thinking about something else. And now he's here. In the corner is a massive black holdall with the airport tags still stuck on it. That must be what I heard being dragged across the floor.

'Zed, I'm sorry . . .'

'Where's Aunt K?'

I avoid the question, keep my head down, breathe in, out, in, out. 'How the hell did you get in here?'

'She sent me a key.'

He begins walking off in the direction of the living room. I get up and follow.

'Zed!'

He stops to turn around and I crash into him.

'I honestly didn't know you were coming here. How could I?' I tell him, pushing into the front room. He sits down, I don't. 'Seems like you must be the one doing the stalking! And why did you get in touch with Juliet anyway? Were you thinking of hooking up with her too?'

'Please!' he says, sending an evil look my way. 'Be serious! After what happened, I didn't know what you were capable of. You better be glad I managed to track her down because your dad was about to report you missing to the cops. How could you leave without telling him? Are you out of your mind?'

'Shit! The police?' The adrenaline starts up again. 'So *now* he cares what happens to me, right?'

'Grow up, Eden. He's your dad.' He sighs. 'I really just don't understand you.' He leans back in his armchair. 'Why are you here?'

I stare at him. The question grows fat between us. I don't really know. 'Aunt K started writing me letters at the beginning of the year,' I tell him eventually. 'It just felt right to come here. I was worried about her. Everybody was saying she'd gone bonkers.'

'Has she?'

'Maybe. I arrived here and about two days later she went to Saint Lucia.'

'Are you serious? She said she wanted to hang out and hear my new music. Play some trumpet on it.'

I shake my head. 'Well, she's gone to spread my grandmother's ashes. She was keeping them in a rum bottle, if you can believe it.'

'Damn. Maybe the old lady did lose her mind!' The irreverence of it surprises me with a giggle. People around here don't ever talk about her like she's a regular person. 'Ms Katherine . . .' He shakes his head and laughs. 'That woman always does her own thing, man. For two years after your grandmother died, she wouldn't let me come round here. I could barely get in touch with her at all. And then I get this letter saying "Where have you been? Come on over whenever you want!" Then I come and find you here.'

He peels off his damp-looking T-shirts to reveal a white tank underneath, the tufts of black hair in his armpits. I swallow.

'It's good,' I say before I can stop myself. 'It's good to see you though, Zed. How long are you staying?'

'Thanks,' he says without reciprocating. 'I don't know. Not long. I need to find an apartment.' He digs a packet of Zig-Zags and a dime bag out of his pocket and starts rolling a spliff on the coffee table, filling the air with that earthy, pungent smell. He is so sure in all of his movements, so complete. 'Max says hello.'

'Right. Yeah. OK,' I say, my face heating up. 'Do you think you should be smoking in here, Zed? It's kind of disrespectful,' I tell him. In this dull room, his skin boasts a rude shine. The scent of his aftershave, sweat and drugs cuts through the dust. I imagine that if furniture could feel emotion, the old-fashioned chair he's sitting on would shiver with indignation. This is still an old woman's haunt, from the days when my grandmother lived here. Dark wood, knick-knacks and doilies. Sepia photographs. He's too big for this room. 'Where did you get that from? Don't tell me you smuggled it on the plane.'

'Uh . . . yeah, Eden. That's exactly what I did. 'Cause they don't sell weed in New York.' He makes a fed-up noise. 'Let's just stop talking now, alright? I'm tired.'

'Why is it always *you* who decides when we stop talking?'

'Somebody has to.'

There he goes, smoking like he wants not a single wisp of marijuana lost to the air. He only looks at his two careful fingers and the spliff clutched snug between them. I draw my knees up to my chest, feeling locked in a room outside a room.

'When Aunt K comes back, her house is gonna stink.'

He blows smoke out of his nose.

'Zed?'

Nothing. Just his deep inhale, his small exhale. I've been dismissed.

I go back to the basement.

sudden red.

When I met Zed for the first time, I was fighting down the massive realisation that just because my mum had invited me to New York, didn't mean she wanted to spend time with me. She'd pretty much abandoned me to the care of chubby, quiet Aunt K, only dropping in for the occasional condescending visit. I hadn't expected Zed. I came back from a listless walk to the corner store and found Uncle Paul in the hallway talking to my aunt. I greeted them both but they were pretty irrelevant to me at that point because they were, after all, old.

And then in the next moment, walking into the living room, my heart had reset itself, rebooted.

I didn't curse much back then, aged fifteen, but—

Who the *fudge* was this work of art, this shiny-sexy boy perched nonchalantly in my spot on the couch? He looked just like a condensation-beaded glass of lemonade on a steaming hot day. And it was a steaming hot day. He was sitting there, all *finished* . . . like there'd be no space for anyone else, not even on the chair that was empty. I stood all hot and squirmy in the hallway. I stared. *Ba-doomp, ba-doomp.* My heart was louder than the TV.

He was skinnier then, less distinct, but he was still more of a man than any of the other boys I'd met who were his age. Neat, intricate cornrows hugged his scalp, while his clothes were so oversized that we could probably both fit inside them, no problem. And I wouldn't have minded that at all.

'Hi,' I said eventually.

'Whassup?' he replied, and his accent did things to me. The afternoon sun was coming in warm from the street and I had a vision of the summer holidays coloured deep with romance and tragedy.

I had no idea.

'What?'

'What,' he enunciated, 'is going on?'

Pause. 'Um, not much. You?'

'I'm cool,' he said, letting his eyes drift back to the TV. He wasn't mean, necessarily. But the look said, *She's just a kid*. If I'd set those words to music, it would have been the soundtrack to my life back then. I wasn't a sexy fifteen-year-old.

'Aaron! Stand up in the presence of a lady,' Uncle Paul barked at his son, stepping abruptly into the room. It wasn't hard to see where Zed got his looks from. Paul – a childhood friend of my aunt's – was a very symmetrical man, upright and handsome. He had an old-school nobility about him, none of his son's wily twinkle. The boy popped right out of his seat, and me almost out of my skin. I wiped my hands on my shorts, struggling to regain my composure.

'Eden, this is my son Aaron. Aaron, this is Aunt Katherine's niece, Eden. You guys are a similar age, so I thought it would be a good idea for you to meet each other.' He gave his boy a hard look. 'It would be nice for Aaron to make some *new* friends. He can show you around New York the way I used to do for your auntie. Be useful for a change.'

Aaron said, 'Nice to meet you,' and pulled his oversized jeans up, something that would turn out to be an endearing little tic of his. Uncle Paul looked at his son like he needed either a hard slap or Jesus Christ and he wasn't sure which one. Maybe both.

When Paul left again, Aaron said that he went by the name Zed these days.

'Zed.' I tested it. What a weird nickname. 'Aunt K kept talking like . . . talking like you were,' I stuttered, 'gonna be a little boy.'

The not-so-small boy grinned. 'No, not little,' he said. He already had an air of worldliness about him, of cheerful, wolfish corruption. He sat down, spreading his legs as wide as they could go. 'I'm sixteen. Why you still standing in the door? You scared of me or what?'

''Course I'm not scared,' I said, sitting next to him, sweating, inspired, inexplicably different. I was thinking that he probably only messed with teen princesses; mini-women with tight clothes and inked-in lips. I decided not to get my hopes up. Just looking at him, my hair felt more messed up, my kicks felt more beat down, my chest felt less breast-y.

I asked him what it was like to be a teenager in New York, and was it true there were shootings every day and that everyone was in gangs. He said yeah, there are shootings, and yeah, there are gangs. But there were other things too and that it wasn't like the movies. 'Does everyone,' he asked, 'in England drink tea with their little finger poked out?'

'No.'

'Exactly. What's it like living in London?'

'I dunno,' I said. 'It's weird. English people hate young people and then some of us have the nerve to be black too.' He laughed, surprised. Disappointment had made me precociously cynical. It's ironic really, because these days I think that disappointment is what's keeping me teenaged.

He turned slightly in his seat to pound fists with me and it made our knees touch. I missed the first time and almost punched him in the neck. I went hollow. It was the beginning of the lesson I was going to learn about all the ways your body can betray you when you're in love.

I told him I was going to the bathroom and fled upstairs to my room, trying to work out what had just happened to me, shaken at my sudden and violent bout of emotional indigestion. The rap star sag of his jeans. The nonchalance of his posture.

I threw myself across the bed and thought of him, this boy as sudden as a knife-cut to your fingers whilst peeling fruit. The pain. The instant red. He made me want to know what my mother knew, do things I didn't know anything about (yet).

chasm.

My fist on Zed's bedroom door is the loudest thing I've ever heard. *Tap, tap, tap.*

'Zed?' I say, then a bit louder, 'Zed? Hey. Are you awake?'

Tap, tap, tap. He's taken the room that used to be my grandmother's: the small, box-shaped one next to the kitchen.

I push the door ajar and he's passed out horizontally across the disordered mattress, light slanting across his face from the hall behind me. There are pages of his heavy, angular handwriting scattered over the bed and the floor. I stand in the purgatory of the open doorway feeling like an intruder. Which I suppose I am.

'Zed?' I say again, so quietly that he probably wouldn't be able to hear me even if he was up. Instead of leaving, like I should, I sit gingerly on his bed and examine the planes of his face. Sweat is shining on his neck and gathering in tiny beads on his forehead. The heat is almost unbearable. I'm close enough to feel it radiate from his skin but there might as well be light years between my body and his. The space is infinite. Every time I look at him, I stand teetering on the edge of the chasm where my obsession ends and his indifference begins, stretching away and away and away. His face is relentlessly peaceful.

'Could you turn the light off?' he says suddenly, eyes closed, and I think I just had a stroke.

'Shit! You're awake?'

'Yeah. I'd prefer to be called Zed, though.'

'Ha. Ha.'

'Go on.'

'What?'

'The light,' he says. 'I'm getting a headache.'

When I return, he's turned over onto his back and moved closer to the wall. I try not to stare at his chest.

'So what's up? Are you here to put a pillow over my head? Finish the job?'

'Come on! No, Zed.' I pause. 'Look, I want to pay for the window.'

'I already did.'

'Then what can I do?'

'Nothing, Eden. Just let it go.'

'But I want to make things better,' I tell him, 'I wasn't . . . myself. I didn't mean to do it. There was just so much going on in my head . . .'

'Look, you're creeping me out standing there. Sit down or go away.'

For a moment, we listen to what sounds like a drunken fight somewhere outside. Then I slowly begin to collect his writing into a pile so there's room for me to sit, but he grabs it from me and jams it haphazard on the bedside table. I take a seat.

'Listen,' he says eventually. Faint light from the window colouring his face blue. 'If you think that we're gonna somehow be instantly cool after what you did, that's not gonna happen.'

'Fair enough.'

'I'm just being straight with you.'

'That's it for us, isn't it? You don't even want to be friends anymore.'

'What did you really expect? Did you think I was gonna buy you a thank-you card?'

'I can understand that,' I say, exhausted. 'I can understand that. It's just a shame after everything we've been through, after all of this time.' He scratches the top of his head, adjusts his position. 'So,' I say with masochistic abandon, desperate to numb myself. 'So. What about Max? What happened with her?'

Shrug. 'Well, I guess we're still kind of seeing each other.'

'Wow. Didn't know it was serious like that. So you guys are long-distance now?'

'Well, I like her a lot. Plus seeing how her career is going, she'll prob'ly get work over here at some point.'

'Right. Well. That's nice. That's nice.' Picture a broken elevator speeding down the shaft, crashing at the bottom. That's my belly. After several moments I ask him, dying: 'Do you ever think, like, what's the point of all this?'

'Of what?'

'Everything. I mean, sometimes I just don't understand any of it.'

'Here we go.'

'I just think that dissatisfaction is the one constant in the human condition. It makes practically everything you do meaningless.'

'You know what I think?'

'What?'

'I think you should go to sleep.'

'Good idea,' I say. 'Zed . . . do you hate me?'

'Hate is a strong word.'

'I've been having nightmares about my mother and then it all just keeps leaking into my awake time. You know, the mood, and the colours. They stain me all day. Does that ever happen to you? Do your dreams leak?'

'They used to. I don't dream anymore.'

'Everybody dreams.'

'Not me,' he says. 'I just . . . Look, I'm tired. Let's talk tomorrow or something. Close the door on your way out.'

'What were you gonna say?'

'Good night.'

I get up and go two steps toward the door before he stops me.

'Eden,' he says softly, with that particular inflection of his that makes me a brand-new thing. 'Why did you do it?'

'What?' I ask, knowing.

'The brick.'

It seems to me that my answer could change everything, past as well as present as well as future. I'm swallowed by fear. 'I don't know.'

He lies back down. 'Good night,' he says, colder this time.

turn around.

I have these dreams lately where I'm on a staircase grab-
bing handfuls of my mother's gypsy skirt and the staircase
ends in darkness and I can't even see the landing and I
can't even see the steps all I can see is my mother's skirt
and she won't slow down no matter how hard I pull and
her feet are bare hitting my tiny face and shoulders and
my little fists are straining trying to stop her walking up
the steps and no matter how hard I shout we are both
enveloped in silence not even her steps are audible and
then the delicate fabric keeps tearing off in my fists and I
leap and grab hold again and she's almost at the top and
the fabric keeps tearing and I can't hold on and it's like
she doesn't even know I'm there and she won't turn around
she just keeps kicking me with every step and the fabric
tears and I fall down the steps all the way to the bottom
head over foot over head over foot and it hurts and I cry
silently and scream at my mother but there is no sound
and she's already completely disappeared into the thick
darkness at the top of the steps—

gone sunset.

Around eight in the morning I give up on oblivion and stand in the shower for a while. The temperature is lukewarm. Trying to sleep with Zed in the house is a trial. I'm spent. Every time I start to drift off, I remember he's here and my mind is like a drop of water in hot oil. Carefully I shave my legs and armpits. When I'm clean, I put on a really nice lotion I stole from the Body Shop on a day I felt particularly invincible, file my feet smooth, paint my toenails orange. Peasant dress. Waist belt. Flip-flops. I painstakingly shape my brows the way Brandy taught me to and tug my hair into French braids with a handful of shine gel, praying no one lights a match within ten yards of my flammable head.

But when I get upstairs, Zed's room is empty.

The bed is made with barely a wrinkle. All his poetry is gone. No shoes beside the bed. No bags. It's only nine thirty. He didn't even say goodbye.

I sit on his bed for a moment to collect myself. It still smells like him in here. I feel ridiculous and bereft. I'm all dressed up with no one to show.

'Hey,' he says, appearing in the doorway.

I jump to my feet.

A white T-shirt is stark against his skin; a duffel bag hangs off one shoulder.

He says: 'What are you doing in here?'

'Zed!' I tug at my clothes, tell him I thought he left.

'No,' he says, 'not yet. I was out on the front steps wakin' and bakin'.'

'Oh.'

'I thought it was good manners to knock first.'

'I did knock.'

'Did I answer?' He raises an eyebrow. I laugh, defeated, face gone sunset.

'Where you off to so early?'

'I've got a session.'

'Right,' I say, trying not to sound distraught. 'Like, in the studio?'

'Yep.'

'Cool.'

He hesitates. 'You?'

'I. Uh. I don't know, really. I was just gonna drift around a little bit. See the sights or something.'

'Alright.' He gives my little makeover a subtle exploration with his eyes. I tingle.

'Well, see ya,' he says, heading for the front door. 'I'm out.'

'Zed . . . wait,' I say to his back. 'You going to the subway?'

He turns around, flickers momentarily. 'Yeah,' he says and I try not to look desperate. 'Yeah,' he repeats. 'Come on.'

here and go.

'Omega!' A grizzly bear of a man dressed head-to-toe in oversized, heavily branded clothing pulls the door open. He grins, one gold tooth catching the light. 'What's good, alphabet geek?'

'Everything! You know I'm a contented son of a bitch,' says Zed. The bear laughs high-pitched like a girl or a velvet-wearing pimp. 'Hey, Bleak, this is Eden. She'll just be here loitering 'cause her time is obviously pretty cheap right now.'

'What's good, ma?'

'Not much.'

The bear laughs again. He and Zed smack palms and we're ushered into a low-lit, messy apartment with black leather sofas and black heroes framed on the walls, from Mohammed Ali to a big-haired Angela Davis. It smells like years of daily marijuana abuse and the musky odour of people sleeping in their street clothes. A widescreen TV displays mute booty-shaking.

'Omega?' I enquire.

'I go by many names, precious,' Zed replies and his manner is slippery. I wonder what I've gotten myself into. We didn't talk much on the way here, too close for small talk and too guarded for anything else. On the subway, he gave me directions for some good art galleries in Manhattan and Harlem, and for the Statue of Liberty in case I was feeling mainstream. After he'd finished his tour guide impression, I asked him where the studio was.

'Queens,' he said.

'I've never,' I struggled, 'I've never been to Queens.' Zed smiled and shook his head almost imperceptibly. I was like a gambler hoping that eventually my luck would change if I just stayed in the game. I should have fought myself harder, but maybe I'd managed to convince myself, as we took our silent trip under New York, that if we didn't speak, he wouldn't notice that we'd failed to part ways.

And now, apparently, my 'time is cheap'. I don't know if that's a bad reflection on him or on me.

Bleak offers me some Koolaid. I decide that drinking anything unsealed in this apartment is probably a bad idea.

'No thanks.'

'Suit yourself,' he grins knowingly. 'Well, come on through and listen to some of these beats.'

He leads us into an even dimmer room, which likely housed a bed in a former life but now is rigged up with a computer, mixing desk, and countless other unknown gadgets. Zed takes a seat in the leather swivel chair furthest from the computer. Bleak lets me sit in the one directly in front of it.

'Just for a hot minute though, ma. Only the captain gets to sit at the helm, you feel me?'

Bleak flicks a switch and the apartment is flooded with repetitive, beat-heavy music, dark and discordant. Zed magicks a spliff out into the open and lights it, head nodding in time.

'You feelin' that, son?'

'It's marvellous.'

'You got something for it?'

'Any second now.'

'Alright, I'm gonna let you hear some of the other shit I've been working on.' Bleak looks at me. 'So now you gonna have to scoot over onto the amateur's chair, baby girl!' he says, pointing one giant finger at a worn little two-seater sofa in the corner of the room. I go over there and perch like a canary. 'Perfect.'

'What time is Nami coming through?' Zed asks, mid-toke.

'You know how she's always late, man! It was supposed to be an hour ago, but who knows?'

They smoke so hard that after forty minutes or so I'm starting to lose any little cognitive ability I had to begin with. They don't speak to me. Bleak plays some different beats and Zed scribbles intensely in a tiny notebook, mumbling. He carries himself differently here and it's like he's a stranger.

'London girl! What you doing?'

I lower the clicker. 'I was, um, just taking a couple of pictures. Is that OK?'

'You a narc?'

'No.'

'CIA? FBI? SWV?'

I laugh. 'No!'

'Then you good, ma. You cool. You got skills?'

'I suppose.'

'Well, let me see them photos when you done. We need some shit for the site.'

In five minutes I've captured it all. The heat and the smoke wring every ounce of will out of my body and I lay my head on the arm of the sofa, giving in to the inevitable. I wake up when a door slams and there's suddenly a very loud woman's voice in the room.

'Zed! Damn you are one good-looking motherfucker! Make me scared to look in a mirror.' They both laugh. I open my eyes and the girl's bum is at eye-level in jeans so tight that the little flesh she has spills over the top. I try to press back into the wall, terrified that any moment she'll sit on my head. 'Shit, Bleak, what you lookin' at? You know your ass *always* has been and *always* will be ugly. Can't have everything, huh, playa?'

'Shut your pie-hole, fish face.'

I figure the only way to avoid being crushed by denim-butt is to stand. She jumps and turns, gives me a brazen look head-to-toe.

'Hey! Didn't see you back there!' she says and she's pretty enough. A Demerara brown girl with big sleepy eyelids, a long fake ponytail and equally fake nails.

'Yeah. Nice to meet you.'

'Nami.'

'Eden.'

'What kinda accent you . . . ?'

'I'm from London.'

'London, England?' She flicks her ponytail.

'Yep.'

'Oh snap!' she says, laughing. 'They got sisters over there now?'

'A few.'

'OK. Welcome to Queens then, Ms Black Princess Di-an-a.'

'She's dead.'

Nami smiles and winks at me, turns back to her banter with the guys. I sit back down. Bleak plays her the first beat he put on when I came in.

'We think you should put one of your dirty hooks on this one, fish face.'

She nods her head, begins humming a melody. Bleak gets her a stool to sit on from another room. I guess he was serious about my chair being for outsiders only.

Nine p.m. and I've been here all day long sitting in this funky chair falling in and out of consciousness. Zed and the crew have recorded three tracks or so and lit up constantly. I'm higher than a plane mid-Atlantic and queasy from a couple of slices of sweaty-looking pizza I had hours ago. And still hungry. Not a good combination. I wish I could leave myself here and go.

'Hey, princess!' says Bleak, snapping his fingers in front of my face. 'Princess?' he turns to Zed. 'Dude! This chick has gone into a trance.'

'What?' I say.

'You wanna do a little skit for the album?' he says. 'That accent of yours is delightful.'

'You mean like, be on Zed's album?'

'No,' says Zed, 'I don't do gimmicks.'

'It would be for a side project me and Nami are doing,' says Bleak.

'Oh.'

'Don't keel over from excitement or anything,' the bear laughs.

'What would I have to do?'

'Pretend like you're a stern schoolteacher.'

'Are you serious?'

'I'm gonna be your naughty student,' he swigs his massive bottle of beer, 'and you gotta tell me to behave otherwise I get a spanking.'

I look at Zed.

'I can't do that!'

'You just gotta pretend, ma. I ain't really gonna make you punish me with a ruler.'

Nami almost falls over. 'Bleak, you are a hot mess.'

'Unless you *want* to . . .' the bear continues, twirling his untwirlable moustache. 'Do you?'

'Fuck off!'

'Oooh! Cool it, Princess. I was just kidding. Seriously, you gonna help us out with this thing?'

I look at Zed but he's talking to Nami, laughing at us.

One of her slim, heavily ringed hands is on his arm.

'Yeah. Alright,' I say. 'I'll do it.'

Bleak sets me up in a box room next door that's been soundproofed and converted into a booth. I've been here all day so I might as well make it count for something. I put the headphones on and Bleak tells me what to say.

'Just start with that little script I gave you, then go with it. Do what you wanna do! I'll be talking back to you through the cans; that'll help keep it natural, know what I'm sayin'?'

When he's gone I switch the light off.

'I'm just gonna set some levels. Say something to me, ma.'

'One, two. One, two,' I say into the mic. Cough. My voice is so loud. The silence around it is velvet. 'One, two.'

'OK, just freestyle it. Have fun. I'm gonna put in my parts later . . . You ready?'

'Um. Yeah.'

Couple of beats go by in the dark. 'When you're ready,' he says.

'Cease your insolence, boy!' I say, imagining Zed in school uniform. 'If you speak one more time while I'm speaking, you are going to be a very, very sorry young man! Very sorry. I've had enough of your back chat!' I pretend that I'm powerful and sexy. Rocking a skin-tight pencil skirt and wire-rimmed spectacles. I fear no man. 'I run this class-room, not you, you snivelling little worm!' I imagine having a whip in my drawer. I don't follow boys around begging for scraps of attention. They sweat when they see me and put apples on my desk. 'Say it! I'm pathetic and stupid and I deserve a spanking.'

I'm pathetic, and stupid . . .

'Write it on the blackboard immediately! I want two hundred lines!'

Please ma'am!

'That's not good enough! You are a stupid boy. Lick the blackboard clean and start again. You are going to have detention every day until you learn to do it right! Lick it,' I say, enjoying myself, 'clean!'

There's a moment of silence and then the bear says: 'Goddamn!' He coughs. 'I think that's a wrap. You better get out the booth before you make me have an accident, ma!'

'Yuk,' I laugh. 'That's disgusting.'

'You know you love me.'

When I get back in the room, Zed is writing in his note-book and doesn't look up.

'That shit was hilarious!' says Nami. 'Damn girl!'

'Thanks.'

Bleak slaps me on the palm. 'Looks like you're part of the fam now, Little Red.' He grins. 'You down with High Jinks!'

'High Jinks?'

'Yeah, High Jinks is the team. Me, Ms Tsunami over there and another dude you ain't met yet. He was *s'posed* to be here today actually but he's a busy guy.'

'Jimi Hendrix-type motherfucker,' says Nami, chewing her words like a true New Yorker. 'Mad talented.'

'You know what? You should come through Fort Greene park Sunday afternoon.'

'Why? What's happening?'

'A cool little outdoors shindig, you know what I mean? I'll be spinning some old-school hip-hop and soul music for man, woman and child. Doing my thing. You know.'

'Cool . . .'

'Hey,' says Zed, standing up, 'you ready to get out of here, Eden?'

'Um . . .' I've been waiting for those words all day and he says them just when I'm starting to have some fun. Typical. 'Yeah, I suppose so. If we're finished.'

Bleak looks at Zed. 'Yeah. We done with the skit. Might need to have Little Red come back here one of these days though, put a hook on one of these joints.'

'Serious?'

'Three things I don't kid about, English girl. My food . . .'

'I can tell, fattie!' laughs Nami.

'My ganja, and my beats.'

'Cool . . .'

'Take my card.'

He whips one out of his back pocket. The print is white on black. His name, cell, and MySpace address.

I go to the loo. Then when I come back I say my good-byes and we're out.

'So you don't do gimmicks, huh?' I say when we walk out of the communal doors into the street. It's just as warm outside as it was in the apartment. I look at the starless sky and the people walking up and down about their night-time business.

'I know you don't think much of my style, but I'm trying to get back to basics.'

'When did I ever say that?'

'That interlude you did was funny, though.'

'Thanks.'

We stop outside a bodega. 'You want anything?' he says. 'I'm 'bout to get myself some Zig-Zags.'

'A Coke, please. And an Almond Joy.'

'Come get it yourself then.' He seems to have all but healed from the accident. No limp. His swagger is back.

'Asshole.'

'Yep.'

It's about a ten-minute walk to the station. We talk about music all the way there, the tracks he did and what he wants to add to them or do differently next time. I don't understand most of what he says. By the time we go underground I've stopped trying. My mind is consumed with the thought that we're alone again, finally. But it seems to me sometimes like he's locked away from himself, locked away from us. I want to say something but don't know what. Something to destroy the distance.

'Do you think,' I say, mouth dry as dust, 'about your dad a lot?'

'He's gone, Eden,' he says, walking ahead.

'I know that, but do you think about him often? That's all I'm asking . . . I mean. How do you feel . . . ?'

'I feel like thinking about him,' he glances at me, 'or *talking* about him is not gonna bring him back.'

We reach the yellow platform and there's a pale teen with body piercings and a man with heavy dreadlocks. It must be thirty degrees and his coat is padded.

'New York is so crazy,' I say quietly.

'It is,' says Zed. 'Here's your train.'

'My train?'

'Yeah.'

I turn to look at him. 'Aren't you coming with me?'

'I wasn't planning to.'

I step on the train and lean against the doors before they close. I feel so stupid. I try not to look surprised or hurt.

'But I don't even know how to get back,' I say. 'Zed, it's almost midnight.'

'There's a map on the train.'

'This is New York! I can't believe—'

'You'll be cool,' he says.

The doors close.

wait—

It's been so long, Cherry Pepper. So long. I'd forgotten this was home, the intensity of the blue and the green, the palms and the banana trees and the sea. Oh Lord God. I was crying when I stepped off the plane and no one asked if I was OK because each one of them, white and black, young and old, was struck through with awe at the beauty of the landscape. Land like this forgives you when you stand on it. It enfolds you in the scent of growing things. It lives! This land is my mother too, and I've missed her.

I carried Angeline to our village, something like the way she carried me before she knew how deeply I would disappoint her. I showed her the house we lived in all those years ago, and how it's changed.

I feel young, like I have another chance at being twelve, but without the pain. This time I play in the river and the sunshine and eat local bread on the front steps with corned beef and sorrel. I rub coconut oil into my skin until it gleams and this time I am beautiful, just like my older mother, the one that still lives, lush with trees and rain. I swim in the sea and go to the market for spices. I roast breadfruit and share it with my baby cousins. In the evening I sit with strangers in the rum shop and talk about family and music and magic. And I listen to the stories of my great aunt, who's survived the best part of a century.

Butterscotch like Angeline, wrinkled and delicately boned.
Even without teeth she smiles. She reminds me how to
survive with grace.

Soon,

Aunt K.

armour or strategy.

I knew I was going to end up here.

The sun is king in Fort Greene park, high and searing. The colours are acid trip-intense. Ice-cream melting into puddles. Children scampering brown-limbed all over the parched grass. Couples and careless knots of friends lay squinting at each other and up into the blue. So many smiles. Barbecue, pollution, trees and flowers scent the air.

In my knapsack I have a bag of tortilla chips and a bottle of fruit punch laced with Jack. I sample a little of each at the gates for strength and Dutch courage because I'm not sure what's more scary to me: if Zed is here – or if he isn't. I've only seen glimpses of him since the studio, and he's always curt and en route somewhere fast.

Maybe Bleak will have forgotten he even asked me to come. People are always saying that Americans are more expansive but less sincere than us Brits. And if he's on the decks he might not be free to socialise. And maybe this isn't even the right place anyway, because house music is on instead of the vintage soul Bleak said he'd be spinning and I can't see him anywhere and let's face it – he'd be a difficult guy to miss.

I sit on the nearest park bench for a little while to orient myself, feeling exposed. The barbecue smell is coming from the far side of the park. I see the stall. Going over there will give me something to do. I don't have to eat; I could just buy it and stand around.

A new song starts and a few people whoop and cheer in their various groups. A girl in a velour playsuit falls into me dancing, gives a giggly apology but doesn't sound particularly sorry. Not rude. Just not sorry. Barrelling into strangers halfway through doing the 'running man' or some insane variation thereof shows just what a crazy fun gal she really is. Her friends roll their eyes affectionately. I continue straight on toward the barbecue.

'Hey, sis,' says the healthily rounded woman serving the food. 'Chicken? Fish?'

'Just chicken, please.'

'You want coleslaw or potato salad?'

'Coleslaw . . . how much is this?'

'Five dollars. Pay over there.' She points to a tall, skinny guy at the end of the long table.

'I got it, Makita.' A familiar voice behind me. 'Put it on my tab.'

The well-fed woman laughs. 'Hey, Bleak,' she says.

I turn around and he looks even bigger and blacker than he did before. 'Oi! There you are!' I say, relieved.

'Little Red,' he grins, 'you made it. What's good, ma?'

'Barbecue. Punk rock. Jack Daniel's.'

He smiles, exposing a mouth full of gold. 'You're funny. I'm 'bout to jump on the decks, sis . . .'

'Yeah, no problem. No problem. That's what I thought anyway. I'll just—'

'. . . so why don't you go over and meet my peeps? They're all sitting under that tree over there, that freaky-looking collection of no-hopers.'

I laugh.

'Go on over when you got your food and introduce yourself. Tell 'em Bleak sent you.'

'OK.'

'Alright. Later.'

'Thanks,' I say to Makita.

'You're welcome.' She smiles.

I watch Bleak amble over to the decks about one hundred yards away. He acknowledges several people on the way, stopping to dispense hugs and pounds on the fist. He exchanges greetings with the present DJ, sets up, puts his headphones on and starts digging around in some crates. A few moments later gentle strains of Marvin Gaye are drifting through the park.

Under the tree there is an array of people spread out on a checked tablecloth, some West African print fabric, and a piece of tarp. They're engaged in various conversations, rocking fashions that range from conservative to crazy, wearing their skin in shades milky to blue-black.

I sit carefully on the edge of the group where the conversations seem the least involved, on the tarp.

'Wow, it is so hot today!' says a girl wearing long micro-braids in her hair and a tongue ring. 'The air is like pudding.'

'You are *not* kidding,' says a bald girl with thick lashes. She spies me. 'Hey.'

'Hey,' I say, 'I'm a friend of Bleak's.'

'Cool,' she smiles, a gap between her two front teeth. 'What's your name?'

'Eden.'

'Nice to meet you, girl. I'm Zahara.'

Then the girl with braids introduces herself. 'Rosemary.'

'Hey.'

'So,' says Zahara, leaning back on the tarp, 'you're from the UK, right?'

'Yeah, London actually.'

'Cool. So you're staying at Bleak's place?'

'No . . . I just met him this week through a friend.' I try to look bonelessly indolent like they do. 'Zed? You know him?'

'Yeah I do . . .'

'Tall, black guy,' I say unnecessarily, 'bald head . . .'

'Yeah.' Zahara yawns.

'Have you seen him?'

'Who?'

'Zed,' I say. I'm reaching for nonchalance. I think I missed, though. 'My mate.'

'Yeah, I'm sure I've seen him.' Rosemary reaches over and taps a guy who's lying next to her, staring at the sky. 'Hey.' The guy lifts his head. 'Eden's looking for her boyfriend, Zed.'

'No . . . no . . . !' I say, just around the same time he passes the message to someone else.

'I'm going over there, anyway,' says a female with long Afro-twists and short shorts as she gets to her feet. 'If I see him, I'll tell him wifey's missing him. Gotta stick together, huh?' she winks at me.

'No . . . No! I'm not . . . he uh . . .' I say limply. This is one of those moments where, no matter what I do, I'm going to look like an idiot. She's up and gone before my tired mind can concoct a solution. 'I didn't say *boy*friend.'

I have a swig of spiked fruit punch. And another. Lie back on the tarp. There's pretty much nothing I can do to make the situation with Zed better anyway. No point panicking. None whatsoever. Concentrate on the clouds. Pretend I am one. Just vapour.

'So we're dating now?'

Right by my ear. My belly flips. I daren't turn my head.

'What?' I reply. When in doubt, play dumb. 'We are?'

'Melanie said my *girlfriend* Eden was looking for me.'

'Oh,' I manage an anaemic laugh, 'that's funny. She must have heard wrong.'

'Right.'

I can smell his skin. Salt, detergent, cologne, weed.

Stare at the clouds. Be vapour.

'So what's this?' he says, trying to tug the bottle out of my hand. 'Fruit punch got you laid out like that?'

'Yeah . . . no . . .' I almost head-butt him trying to get up. He's laying next to me. His teeth are white, his head gleams, his body is solid in a tank top, long shorts and a pair of Nikes I haven't seen before. His arms are folded under his head. I thought he'd be angry. His contradictions leave me without armour or strategy. 'I mean it's just juice and I'm not laid out, just catching a breeze. Trying to relax.'

He shakes his head, face unreadable.

'So these are your friends?' I say.

'Some of them,' he replies. I look around at all the eclectic people, so colourful and pretty and languid. There are funksters and hippies, rockers and earthy types; all coded by their garments and hairstyles and they are so pleased with themselves. I think that sensible people in London tend to find that embarrassing. British people who *don't* find self-satisfaction embarrassing are usually either obnoxious or dim, which makes this kind of tableau extremely rare back home. I'm refreshed and threatened in equal parts.

'Hey Zed, is this you right here?' a Mohawk-wearing guy says, nodding at me, sitting beside us with two friends. I didn't notice when Zahara and Rosemary moved, but now they're over on the checked tablecloth. 'This your wifey?'

'No she's—' Zed starts.

'I'm a free agent,' I say, louder than I intended, like I've got Tourette's or some such. 'This fool ain't my type.'

'Oooh snap!' The stranger laughs, turns back to Zed. 'Well then, may I have the pleasure of an introduction with this young goddess? She doesn't look native.'

'This,' Zed says, with a slightly ironic flourish, 'is Eden. Eden, this corny asshole is Joe. The funny-looking one is Mikey . . .'

'Hey!' Mikey and Joe protest simultaneously.

'And that's Devon. Over there is Zahara, Rosemary, Melanie and Miguel.'

'Hi,' I say. People wave or tell Zed they've already met me.

'Are you British?' asks Joe.

'Yeah. From London.'

'Damn, I love that accent.' He pushes out his lips and nods in approval. 'So, you're not the girl to finally civilise this guy?'

'Nah. We homies,' says Zed. And damn it! Wasn't that pretty clear already? Why he have to say it so fast like the idea of us being together isn't even a distant relation – five times removed – to being a possibility? And you know, Mohican Joe is actually quite presentable. He has this rakish thing going on and he's so trendy it's got to hurt (the boy has *pointy shoes* on for God's sake). But then I look at Zed and he makes other boys disappear. Always.

Zed gets up and walks off.

'. . . for a living?'

'Sorry?'

'I was just asking,' says Joe, 'what you did for a living.'

'For a living? Um . . . Breathe oxygen. That's about it. I don't do anything for a wage at the moment. I'm here care of Barclays Bank. And my mate Juliet.'

He and Devon laugh.

'Well, what do you do when you do what you do, pretty girl?'

'You know . . .' *Pretty girl.* It's been a while since I've been called anything but crazy by a man. Brandy doesn't count unless she's in boxers. 'All the stuff that doesn't pay. Photography mainly,' I say, brandishing my camera.

'Are you having your work shown anywhere?'

'No.'

'Right, well, you're around the right crowd. Everybody here's involved in some kind of art or another. A lot of actors, musicians . . . you should circulate at some point. You could take some portraits. Make some change that way?'

'Yeah . . . cool! Thank you. I'll definitely give that a try.'

'No problem, sweetie. I know how it is with the suffering for one's art. I'm a film-maker—'

'Here we go. Spike Lee on crack.'

'Shut up, Devon . . .'

'So what brings you to our fair shores, young lady?' says Devon, ignoring his friend's request.

I shrug. 'Just hanging out.'

'How long,' says Joe, giving his friend a dirty look, 'you in town for?'

'A couple of months.'

'You're here for a while then. Old Barclay must have given you the hook-up!'

'I'm just cheap. I intend to make those dollars stretch like spandex.'

Joe laughs. 'Hey, take my number. You gotta let me give you the, uh, guided tour sometime.'

'Right. Yeah. OK.'

'Man, she ain't feeling you, Joe! Just leave the girl alone!' says Devon, laughing.

'Don't be mad, chump. One day life'll treat you better,' twinkles Joe, obviously the one who's luckier with women. 'Hey, look who it is. The big chief.'

A new boy comes over and sits nearby on the African print fabric. Skinny, pale brown, with an unshaven face and fistfuls of little black curls; ripped jeans and a faded Hendrix T-shirt. He's playing with a blade of grass. A few people seem to know him, give gentle smiles and nods, like he's a soft-eyed animal they're wary of scaring away. On his right is a guitar case with a worn-looking book on top of it. He must be the musician Bleak was talking about. I just feel it. He's a 'Hendrix-type motherfucker' if there ever was one. Zed goes over and gives him a pound on the fist.

'Young genius!' he says by way of a greeting.

167

'Gifted black! What's up?' The new boy's voice is deep and raspy, an unexpected counterpoint to his childlike grin. Zed knows so many people. Sometimes I feel like I know almost no one. I have no crew, no team back in London. Just Juliet, and a disparate bunch of people who don't know each other and who can mostly tolerate me. And I guess nowadays I have Brandy, but she's not around that much. Less and less, in fact.

'So how did you get interested in film?' I ask Mohican Joe.

'Well, you know, ever since I was a kid, really. It always fascinated me. I got a camcorder for my birthday when I was ten, and there's been no stopping me since . . .'

But then the guitar is singing under the new boy's fingers, one melancholy riff, round and round. And although he plays it quiet like he doesn't want to disturb anyone, it changes the atmosphere.

'Beautiful, huh?' says Mohican Joe.

'Yeah.'

Zed sits smaller than usual at the edge of the tablecloth, curved, with his arms balanced on his knees. He's gone somewhere on the sad chords.

'Spanish is one seriously talented dude,' says Mohican Joe, playing with the stud beneath his lip. 'Kid is sick. Between me and you? One time the guy brought me to tears. I was down at the Knitting Factory blubbing like a little girl whose Barbie doll fell down the waste disposal.'

'Don't worry,' I tell him, smiling, 'I won't tell anybody.'

'Too late. I told everybody,' says Devon.

'Come on, lady,' says Mohican Joe, 'I'll introduce you.'

The boy called Spanish has his hairy shins crossed under him, and on closer inspection I realise I've got exactly the same pair of Converse All Stars he's wearing, except his are even more worn than mine. Mohican Joe has to say his name a couple of times to get his attention.

'Hey Joe!' Spanish says eventually, breaking off from his riff and playing the Hendrix song of the same name.

They laugh.

'I'll never get tired of that!' says Joe with his wily smile. 'I have a lovely young lady from London you need to meet. Photographer, artist, thinker and fulltime goddess. Spanish, this is Eden. Eden, Spanish.'

'Hi,' he says. His gaze is intense, and I get the weird impression it's because he refuses to do the standard full-body evaluation. The almost golden eyes and dark irises stay resolutely north of my neck.

'Hey. Nice to meet you! That's beautiful, what you're playing.'

'It's for your boy over here.' He indicates Zed, who's rooting around in his knapsack. 'He's got an idea for it.'

'Cool,' I say, but I'm thinking, *your boy*? How does he even know we know each other when he just got here? News travels fast, I suppose.

'So we gonna get a preview of this masterpiece?' Joe says to Zed.

'No,' Zed replies.

'I've heard a lot about you. I'm a friend of Bleak's,' I tell Spanish. He's so skinny. His sharp bones and wild hair make him look like an old man, but everything else about his face is painfully young and cinematic.

'Cool.'

'I went down to his studio on Wednesday.'

'OK.'

'So, why do they call you Spanish?' I ask him.

'Long story,' he says. 'But no, I don't speak-a the language.'

I laugh. I didn't expect a joke from him. He looks so solemn.

He stops playing for a moment, laying his fingers over the strings to stop the vibration. His nails are clipped right down, his hands angular and strong.

'You sing, don't you?'

'No.'

'Yes you do.'

'Uh . . . no I don't. Joe just told you what I'm into.'

'Yes you do. I can tell by the quality of your speaking voice.'

Is he crazy? I look around for some non-verbal back-up from Joe or Zed, but neither are looking my way. Joe's talking to some girl about an event going on tonight. Zed's staring into his notebook.

Spanish goes back to playing his guitar.

'Listen, I can't sing to save my life, OK? Plus you've barely even heard me speak!'

'It's not that you can't sing, it's that you *don't* sing,' he says, somehow managing to look other than smug. 'Only reason you don't is 'cause it would probably make you feel too vulnerable and you don't like that. There's almost nothing more exposing than singing in public.'

'Right. Whatever. A photographer *afraid* of exposure? That sounds kinda negative to me.' I laugh. 'Pun intended, of course.'

He shrugs. 'With photography you have your lens to hide behind.'

'You don't know me from a box of fried chicken, Spanish.'

'I know you about as well as anybody else.' He smiles. 'And if you don't sing, what the hell were you doing in the studio? Forgive me, but you don't look much like a rapper.' He turns away, conversation done. I decide not to tell him about the schoolteacher skit. 'Hey, Zed?' he says. 'You wanna run this through one more time, man? I'm gonna bounce soon. I was just passing through.'

'Hey, does this mean we can all hear it?' says Mohican Joe.

'I said no,' says Zed. 'Damn, Joe! How you even know I've got something finished?'

'Are you kidding? You're the most prolific guy I know! I ain't never seen you without a pen in one hand and a spliff in the other. You got a new track on that MySpace website every ten minutes!'

'Look, ain't shit for free out here but air and grass! You wanna hear my rhymes, buy the album.'

'But the sun's going down and the evening is ripe for the beauty of a soul exposed . . .'

'Get the fuck out of here, man. I'm serious.'

'Alright, alright . . .' Joe shrugs and grins at me, unfazed. Walks off to talk to the others.

Spanish and Zed take their guitar and notebook respectively and start moving off a short distance from the rest of the group.

'Can I come?' I say.

'Sure,' says Spanish. I get up.

'Eden, stay here,' says Zed. Voice hard, face closed.

'I said she could come.' Spanish doesn't even raise his voice. He's quiet and impossible to contradict. 'No need to get all aggressive, homie. Seems like she'd be a sympathetic audience. It's good to test it.'

'Fuck it. Whatever,' says Zed, sloping off. I smile at Spanish. I've never heard anyone stand up to Zed like that, and he just met me.

'Come on,' he says.

When we find a quieter spot, Spanish starts playing his guitar again, louder than before. More resonant. He adds little flourishes to the chords, humming along with the melody. The sound tweaks my heart muscle. Even with all his mad talk, I didn't expect him to be a singer. And so good at it. I feel all of this hope and despair swilling around inside me.

Then Zed begins to speak and the first line makes me shiver.

'*Mama – if I climb inside myself can I take you with me?*' he asks the grass in front of him. He's never sounded so like himself.

broken.

I offer no applause. Just breathe hard.

Avoiding my eyes, Zed closes his notebook. 'So what you think, dog? You think it's a good marriage?'

Spanish nods. 'I think it's getting there.'

'It needs a bridge, right? Some kind of break down . . .'

I want to reach out, but I can't. The chasm is still there, stretching away and away. His body is real, solid, sweating, only a few feet from my own, but I'm in prison. Something just happened to me.

'Yeah . . . yeah. Maybe. Although I like it simple too, you know? Sincere.'

'Right. I feel you.'

Spanish zips the guitar into its case and they both stand up so I do the same. Zed keeps talking about the track and the studio and a bunch of other stuff I can't put together in my head. I'm thinking about what I just heard.

'It's been a pleasure,' Spanish says politely, nodding his head at me. 'Take care of yourself.'

'Yeah, thank you,' I say. 'Thank you.'

'You ain't got time to chill for a minute?' Zed says to him. 'I got some more ideas . . .'

'Band rehearsal, man. I gotta dust.'

'Right right.' They both start walking toward the group. Spanish raises his hand at everyone and keeps going, guitar slung over his back, off into the sun. Zed sits on the tarp. I sit next to him. He speaks to Rosemary about the weather. I don't understand. I tap him on the shoulder.

'Zed,' I say, 'Zed . . .'

'What?' he replies.

'That was beautiful . . . I mean, I liked it a lot. It was more like a poem, right? Than a rap, I mean.'

'Yeah it was,' he says, face bland, voice limp. 'Glad you liked it.' He's acting like I'm some tramp who just walked over to ask him for money.

Zahara is back. She sits behind me. 'So . . . Eden! I went to London a couple of years ago—'

'Sorry,' I tell her.

I walk away and don't say goodbye to anyone.

call me lucky.

On the other end of a subway ride is City Hall and the river. The Brooklyn Bridge arcs majestically toward Manhattan in a haze of car fumes. I stand at the railings and watch the East River, sparkling with sun. In the shadows, the water looks implausibly deep. Lovers kiss on a park bench. I move as far away as I can, irritated by their arrogance. Nobody wants to see that shit.

The heat won't let up. I wipe sweat from my face and neck, dry my hands on my shorts. I'm flaccid with weariness, sick with hope. Something about that poem Zed just recited, it sent me back to the beginning. It was the exact texture of those early sparks, feet touching under the table, fingers finding each other in half-empty movie theatres. He must be talking about me. But is he? Does he still feel it? I don't know. I can't know. Right now, it seems to me that a slim chance is a tougher deal than none at all.

Or the lyrics might mean that he's moved on. In love with somebody else.

'HEY!' shouts a sudden voice nearby and my thoughts break out and scatter like a flock of pigeons. A young man walks up and stands next to me. 'Good afternoon. Or is it a good afternoon for you? Mine is so-so. Definitely not fantastic. But maybe it will be now you're here.' He's olive-skinned, with deep-set blue eyes, a shaved head and all the barely tangible signs of a broken mind. Or heart. Or both. 'What's your name? They call me Lucky. I come here to think too . . . you know, when I'm not at my job. It's really nice here. The river and the lights. It's really peaceful even though we're right in the middle of the city. It feels like you're far away from it all, the noise and cars and stuff, you know what I mean? Really far away, like in Europe or somewhere.'

'Yeah,' I reply, and I'm thinking that cracked people are the most dangerous. Pain leaves them blind, deaf and drunk behind the wheel, driving in the wrong lane. And that's why most are afraid of people like this boy, including me.

'Really nice. I like the water. I like the sky . . . sometimes I write things about them in my little book.' He lifts up a small leatherbound notepad. 'I write about a lot of things. Stuff that affects me and makes me feel sad or angry or when I'm really scared and can't do anything about it I write it all down and I feel better.'

'OK . . .'

'Yeah. Sometimes I write to my mom and dad, but I don't send it though because I never really knew them and they're bad, they're not like you and me. I don't know you really well, but I can tell that you're a nice person and that you don't try to hurt people. My parents aren't like you. They're empty. Bad people always are. They're like, hollow. You know what I mean? Hollow. That's why they do things that are wrong, because they're trying to fill themselves up or something, I guess. My parents are in jail for things they did, but sometimes I still miss them. Human beings are like that. When we love people we still miss them even if they hurt us . . .'

'I'm sorry but I'm,' I say, feeling chained and ill, 'I'm late. I've got to go.'

'Where are you going? Can I come?'

'No. I don't know you.' I have to get away from him.

'Can I take your number then? Maybe we can hang out sometime? Girls like the movies, right? Or to go to restaurants? We could do whatever you want . . .'

Quickly I walk away. I keep my face blank and unresponsive, refusing to acknowledge looks of sympathetic amusement from the lovers on the park bench and from a man walking his dog.

They may be laughing at the kid, but it feels as if they're laughing at me too. And I can't help but wonder how many times people have walked away from him.

wait—

Cherry Pepper,

Castries never used to be so small or so achingly poor or rich or pretty. I walked by the deep harbour today, a steep drop from the road. There was still no kind of fence or barrier. I imagined that a person might jump without planning to, just for the oblivion of it. The market is a mountain of fresh produce. Music flows together seamlessly from a dozen sources, distilled by the sweet air. The children are neat and shiny, just like I was at eleven. This is where the first half of my childhood ended and the second one began, in the little toy-like house on Coral Street. Flaking pink and green paint.

I was sent here alone, with a light bag full of my belongings. I came up the front steps and stood in the doorway, gave my shy greetings. I had all the reserve of a child made aware of herself too early. Paul's mother embraced me with a hard species of warmth. She was strong, fair, a real mother. I thanked her for having me and she shushed me with vigour, hinting at favours that had gone back and forth between our families for longer than anyone cared to remember. She took my bag away and replaced it with a bowl of soup.

I absorbed my new world. Hotter, dustier and smellier. The Hippolytes' house was half the size of what I was used to. Cockroaches stalked the wooden floors like kings and only thin walls separated family from family, and nothing could ever be hidden. The sound of creaking beds, loud arguments, fights and laughter would provide nightly entertainment from the neighbouring houses. But it wouldn't take long for me to realise I was happier here than in my mother's silent, immaculate home. I felt alive for the first time, electrified by the newness of it, by the freedom I suddenly had to be myself.

Paul and his two brothers bounced in the door at sunset with airy excuses for their mother and wide, happy grins. He was the one closest to me in age, although a couple of years younger, so we became fast friends. The games we used to play! Ticky tock with stones out on the sidewalks, and marbles, and tag. We'd race each other to the end of Coral St and back, laughing all the way.

Paul's niece lives here now, with her husband and children. It's changed less than I thought possible. The smell is the same, of wood expanding, of the drains, of food cooking, of time rolling out slow and fragrant. Enough time here for almost anything. Seems like there's an hour for every minute in America. The walls must be thinner between people. I can't help but wonder if Paul visits sometimes, now that he has no need of a plane ticket. Out of the corner of my eye, I almost see him standing at the window, looking out.

Being back here is another knot unpicked. I remember how strong I was, how determined to shed my eleven-year-old wounds and start fresh. Be something new. And here I am now, a grown woman, half a century later with my friend gone. But I'm not old, I realise that now. Youth is not in the age of a body, but in a person's willingness to start! And start again. And again. And again . . .

Soon,

Aunt K

every shot, flawless.

I wake up to a guitar and the hot, dry sound of a man singing
'Redemption Song'. A fancy cushion is rough under my damp
face, my legs are thrown over the side of the living room couch.
I feel far from rested. For three days I've knocked around
this barren house and these bare neighbouring streets. Bare
of Zed. Falling in and out of blue-black naps all day long,
up at night watching game shows and porn. The basement
oppressed me today. I felt all the weight of the house pressing
down. I came up to the living room needing a change of
scene, up to where my grandmother would sit at the window
and watch the world before she died. The patch of world I
could see through the glass was uneventful. I fell asleep again.

Cautiously I open one eye and Spanish is sitting cross-
legged on the floor. He's wearing a velvet jacket in the
eighty-degree heat but looks, if anything, as if he might be
cold. He stops when he sees me looking at him, guitar
cradled like a pet in his lap. I fuss with my rumpled clothes.

'Aren't you hot?' I ask him. My voice is hoarse.

'No,' he says, scratching his head through the wild curls.

'But it's boiling in here.'

He shrugs. 'I've been fasting. Everything changes when you
fast for long enough. It's like the body gets quieter and quieter.'

'Well that explains why you're so skinny.' His face: with
all its starved, tortured angles. His lips are flushed, his eyes
golden syrup against the beige skin. His hair is dirty, jeans
cut haphazardly at the shin, exposing bony knees. His All
Stars make my oldest, most disgusting pair look brand new.

'What have you got against your body, anyway,' I say, pulling myself into a sitting position, 'that you're trying to make it shut up?'

'Nothing,' he says. 'I just want to hear what my soul has to say.'

'Right.'

'Yours is like rock music,' he says.

'Huh?'

'Your body.'

I say nothing to that because I'm not sure if it's a compliment or an accusation. There's a chuckle. 'Thrash metal.' Zed's voice from a deep corner of the room jerks me utterly awake. I didn't know he was here. Was half-convinced I was dreaming Spanish. They look impossibly staged. Zed almost invisible, sitting on the floor in the crevice between a sofa and the bookcase. Spanish sitting closer, pale brown washed gold by the sun through old curtains. I pull a cushion to my chest. 'She's like thrash metal, dog.'

'No, not thrash. Psychedelic rock, like in the seventies, man! Flowers and LSD,' says Spanish, slowly.

'What time is it?'

''Bout three thirty.'

It's still light, so that means it's the afternoon. I wouldn't be sure if it wasn't for the windows.

Spanish starts singing again, softly this time.

'What's your real name, anyway?' I ask.

He says, 'That don't mean shit. A real name is an oxymoron. A name isn't real. It's just a symbol.'

'Is that why you're fasting? Is your body just a symbol too?'

'I'm fasting because freedom isn't free.'

'Freedom,' I repeat. It's a word that always seems to swell and hover when you say it. And today the meaning eludes me completely. I chase it around my mind as if it's a helium balloon with the air escaping.

'Freedom?' Zed's laugh is very slightly vicious. 'You need to liberate your damn stomach, man. It ain't right. A free man doesn't choose to starve. Crazy-ass . . .'

'You're only saying that shit 'cause you're a slave. That's exactly what I'm talking about! Too many of us these days are a slave to our nuts or our stomachs. Usually both. You're just too close-minded to see that.'

Zed laughs again and then we're all silent. Spanish lightly plays his tune, round and round. So natural he may not even know he's playing. His fingers are quick on the frets.

'So when did you get back?' I ask Zed.

'About half an hour ago. I went to a party that just kept on going.'

'Right,' I say, anger leaden in my stomach. I can barely look at him. 'Good, was it?'

'Bananas.'

I spent a lot of my time awake today looking at Zed's website. I don't know what I was looking for. Clues? The URL should be www.needlesstorture.com.

There were images in his 'gallery' from performances he's done, face shiny black and swirling with coloured lights. Mic clutched tight in his hand. I kept thinking about all the people who were looking at him that moment. Anyone could. They could be using him as a screensaver, waking up to his face every morning. Printing him on T-shirts. Jerking off. There were so many girls with their little soft-porny thumbnail pics and vapid comments that I had to leave the site or risk submitting to my darker urges. I felt like leaving a comment of my own: *Zed, please stop rapping, you're terrible at it and ugly and how's your herpes, by the way?*

I didn't, though.

And just for the extra kicks, I found Max on her model agency website. She had an online portfolio and was unblemished in every picture, unassailable. In this one, a femme fatale. In that one, an ingénue. A leggy alien. Every shot, flawless. She can be anything she wants, to anybody. I dared not Google my own name in case it just came back as Bible stories. Eden who? Indeed.

'What? Did you miss me?' laughs Zed. 'Looks like you been sucking on limes.'

'Why don't you,' I say, evenly, 'go suck an exhaust pipe?'

I swing my legs off the couch and almost catch Spanish in the head. He barely flinches. I think that odd word – freedom – again. I look at his clothes, wonder idly if he's had a shower today.

'My band's playing at a bar downtown tonight,' he says to me quietly, his voice husky and sincere. Zed's phone rings and he answers it and I wonder who it is but I don't really care. Spanish says: 'We gotta go do a sound check, get ready for our set.'

'Cool,' I say. 'Let's go.'

'What?'

'I said, let's go.'

Glance over at Zed, grinning into the phone, the long shadows of his eyes. Bastard.

Spanish smiles. 'OK,' he says. 'Yeah. Good. You know . . . I think it's gonna matter what you think of us. The guys are gonna drive down there in the van so we gotta take the subway.'

I go to the small shower a few rooms down, next to the one Zed sleeps in, and wash off my all-day funk. My head is full of plots.

In my towel, I go to the living room and say, pointlessly, 'I won't be long.'

'K,' says Spanish. Zed smokes and stretches.

In the basement I pick my short shorts up off the floor. They need a wash and I don't usually wear them outdoors, but whatever. Braid my hair sternly away from my face. The colour is washing out again, back to the sandy brown it was before I dyed it. I go back to the living room and Spanish is alone. He's moved from the floor to the armchair and looks me over carefully. I wish I'd put on more fabric.

'Ready?' he says.

'Yep.'

We sit close on the subway, en route to Spanish's sound check. I feel liberated! Zed-less on purpose. Spanish idly strokes his battered guitar case and looks perfectly happy with our lack of conversation. Personally, I think that's a luxury of the properly acquainted.

'You know what?' I say to the side of his face. My clicker likes him, squealing in excitement at the play of light on his cheekbones and jaw, at his careful way with the world, his lovely hands.

'What, Ms Photo Obsessive Soul-stealer?' he says to the row of empty seats opposite. I snap them too, and then his eyelashes, his moist, translucent gaze.

'I think the subway is where sinners go when they die.' He gives me a quizzical glance. 'Seriously. It's like corporal punishment down here. The platforms are one hundred degrees and you're cooking like a pig on a spit, then on the train they freeze your ass off.'

'I guess you wish you had on a velvet jacket right now too, huh?'

'Very funny,' I laugh.

'You guys don't have air-conditioning on the trains in London in summer?'

'No.'

'And you prefer that?'

'No. I complain about that too.'

Spanish shakes his head and laughs.

'What?'

'I think you like being unhappy.'

rock and roll.

Spanish lugs his instruments out of the van and up to the front door of his building, a two-family house in Bed-Stuy. I watch his walk from the back: straight-backed but loose. His jeans drag in the dirt. All around is New York at full volume, full of happenings outside every store-front, on every street corner, shouts of hostility and laughter. Sirens. Music. Just like the movies. The moon gives us only one cool half of its face, an eternity away from these dark, hot streets.

We pour single file into the musty communal hallway. His two band-mates bring up the rear with their languorous, giggling banter. Neither Spanish nor I say very much at all. I feel stiff all over and uncoordinated, tripping up on a bicycle that's leaning against the wall. It clatters to the ground.

'Shit!'

'You OK?' asks Spanish, whipping round, steadying me. I can feel the warmth of his fingers through my T-shirt.

'Yeah,' I say, trying to lift the bike back into place but making it worse. 'Crap. I'm such an idiot . . .'

'You're not. Accidents happen. Nobody died.' Quickly, he restores order. 'See?' he smiles. 'Good as new.'

I nod. And finally, when he's reassured of my good spirits, we go upstairs and round on the landing to where he lives on the second floor. The walls are purple, the floors stripped and bright. There are achingly vivid paintings leaned up against the walls that can't seem to make up their minds if they're abstract or not. Twisted perspectives. I feel excited and a little bit ill looking at them. An upturned wooden crate serves as a coffee table and old sofas are covered in faded, once-colourful throws and cushions. Scattered around the room are various instruments including several guitars, bongo drums, a keyboard and some funky world music-y looking ones I don't know the names of. There are books stacked in a corner next to a small television poised on yet another upturned crate. The windows are dressed in long swathes of velvet.

Despite the Bohemian styling, nothing appears out of place or dusty. Not a stray cup, CD, or discarded item of clothing can be seen anywhere. I follow everyone else's example and take my shoes off.

'You shouldn't wear sneakers without socks,' says Spanish.

'Right,' I reply.

We sit in near silence while the bassist and the drummer recline on beanbags, rolling their zoots. Spanish remains standing, staring at us all with a thoughtful look on his face. It occurs to me that I really don't know these guys. Especially not Spanish. He wafted, alert and critical, through his sound checks at that little bar in Tribeca. But the minute he launched into his set two hours later, I realised that nothing I'd seen of him so far was represented, none of that gentleness. Fronting his band he was a different animal entirely. He was violent, strutting, hoarse, cruel. His music was by turns ethereal and hellish. I almost ran away. And I've known his band members for exactly four hours.

'Why so blue, Spanish?' says Rasta Jesus. The drummer.

'Ain't shit.'

'Whatever, man. You got that look on your face.'

'I wish ya'll wouldn't smoke that garbage in my house.'

Sub and Rasta Jesus just look at each other and keep smoking. I think they catch my bemused look 'cause the drummer, who has this sweet, pore-less face like the nickname suggests, says,

'Don't worry. He always says that. Forgets it was the green gave him the first seeds of his inspiration.'

I sit alone on the couch wondering where Zed is and thinking that maybe I made my point back at the house. I'll just wait for a good opportunity to drop it in the conversation that I'm leaving. I should have gone back after the show. Don't know why I didn't.

'I'm past that. Ya'll fuckers are still locked in the beginner's class,' he says, shaking his head. 'You smoke, Eden?'

'No,' I lie. Well, sort of lie. It's not like I've ever bought any.

'Me neither.' He glances at his band members. 'Weed is poison. It's a lie. It's been promoted in hip-hop like it's our culture. But really, it's just a *trick* to start kids off smoking so young they're completely numb.'

'What's up with you, amigo? The show was pretty perfect today.'

'You,' Spanish jabs the air with his finger, 'were playing too fast.'

Rasta Jesus shakes his head and shrugs.

'I think the shit was immaculate,' Sub comments, rubbing an almost black hand over his bleached blond hair.

'You want anything to drink, Eden?' Spanish asks me.

'What you got?'

'Water.'

I laugh; he doesn't. 'OK.'

He jumps up with sudden force and disappears out of the room. Rasta Jesus and Sub both sort of shrug at me with their eyes and keep smoking. There's a funny unpredictable feeling to everything here. I wish someone would put on some music or the TV or something.

Spanish returns with a bottle of water, two glasses, and a look on his face, like he just tasted something bad. He pours it out for us and puts the bottle on the table.

'I'm mad we don't see more black people at the gigs,' he says to the others, waving his water around so it spills over the sides of the glass. Some lands on my leg and I watch as a single drop races down my thigh. 'Sorry!' he says, and wipes it away without thinking.

'It's OK.'

'Sorry!' he says again, snatching his fingers away from my flesh.

'I'm just happy we have anyone come and see us,' says Rasta Jesus.

The bassist is examining his fingernails like he's heard it all before.

'But this is our shit, RJ,' says Spanish with quiet intensity. 'It's ours. I hate the way we act like we can't be nothing but rappers and RnB androids . . .'

'You just gotta give it time. Life is all about seasons and cycles.'

'It's a plan to lock us into tiny boxes where we can't breathe like free men.' Spanish wipes his mouth. 'They've made it out like blackness is this *small* thing. Some kind of fashion statement. It's a crime . . .'

'But Spanish—'

'It makes me so mad 'cause people come up to me and they like the music but they act like it's some kind of weird alternative to the bullshit mainstream.' His face has actually gone a bit pink. 'You know what I mean?'

'Not really,' I say, feeling contrary. The others snigger. Spanish stops for a moment.

'It's not alternative, Eden. It's *ours*,' he repeats, sitting beside me. 'The first beat of the drum in Africa. The shamanic out-of-body experience. Inter-dimensional music. Experimentation, improvisation, the fucking blues. That's ours. How'd we get so small?' He's nodding, staring at all our faces. 'A clown, a whore or a savage,' he says, and I wonder if he's being general or

187

specific. 'That's all we're supposed to be. You know what I say?'

'What do you say?' I murmur. His face is close and beautiful, his breath scentless.

'Suck my biro, cracker.'

I choke with laughter. Sub shakes his head and smiles. Rasta Jesus blows out smoke and says, 'Crazy half-white motherfucker.'

'No such thing as half-white, RJ.'

'God!' Sub exclaims languidly. 'Shut up for a minute, Malcolm Mohammed Martin Luther Farrakhan. Let the girl relax.'

I laugh, but Spanish continues to glow with evangelical fervour. 'I like you,' he says to me suddenly. 'Do you need anything? Are you hungry? I don't have much food here, but I think there's pasta . . . or I could go and get you something . . .'

'No, I'm fine.'

'Be right back,' says Spanish, gone again.

'Interesting,' observes Rasta Jesus with a puff and an arched eyebrow.

'It was a good show,' I say for want of something coherent to say.

Sub wanders over to the stereo and puts some music on, then he and RJ talk about its technical proficiency and whether or not it lacks soul. It becomes clear to them quite quickly that I don't have an opinion.

'Here.' Spanish shoves a tall glass full of pink in front of me. 'I had some, uh, organic berries in the freezer so I made you a smoothie. I put some honey and wheatgerm in there for you as well.'

'Thank you,' I say.

'You're welcome. It's,' he scratches his curly head, 'really good for you. You know. Just in case you were hungry.'

He watches while I take a sip. 'It's lovely,' I tell him earnestly.

'You're sure? It's sweet enough?'

'It's perfect.'

Spanish nods, as if he suspected as much. I lied, though. It's too sour.

'You should check out this film called *Waking Life*,' Sub tells me. 'I haven't seen it in a while, actually; it's really good. You seen it?'

'No.'

'You should. It's a classic.'

'Yeah, she should,' says Rasta Jesus with a laugh and a surreptitious glance my way. 'Why don't you put it in, Spanish?'

Spanish smiles beatifically, seeming to miss the double entendre, and kneels down beside a pile of DVDs next to the little television. He finds the box and fingers it gently. 'This is a beautiful film. You'll like it, Eden.'

'Well actually . . .' I mumble, 'I need to get back. See if Zed's still around.'

'Sorry, what did you say?'

'Nothing.'

He stretches over to switch everything on from the mains and as he's setting up the DVD player I stare at the back of his neck and all the tiny curls.

The movie starts, a wash of colour animated over real footage. Nothing is ever still. Hair, eyes, piano keys. A bed bobs just like a boat. Spanish peels off his jacket to reveal a New York Dolls T-shirt and his body surprises me with its warmth. He sits close against my side while I watch the TV, joyfully examining his hands, smiling at me, patting my hair.

'It's just amazing,' he says.

'What?'

He places a finger in the dimple on my chin. 'It's amazing. Your design, you know? That you could be made like that. Born like that. It's amazing. It's proof you come from God.' He palms the side of my face softly, without intent. Like a child would.

I look round and Rasta Jesus is sitting there with a subtle curve on his lips and an 'I know something you don't know!' expression. I give him a 'what on earth is going on with your boy?' face in return.

'Flesh of the gods, man,' he says to me in explanation.

'What are you talking about?'

'Young Spanish likes to dabble in fungi of the psyche-delic persuasion.'

'Huh?'

'Magic mushrooms, lady.'

'Are you serious?'

Spanish isn't listening. Instead he's gently examining my hair. 'I thought he was against drugs. Spanish, I thought you were against drugs.'

'What?'

'Drugs! I thought you were against drugs.'

'I'm not on drugs,' he says and then, with a smile, 'Shrooms aren't drugs. They're a . . . gateway . . . to reality. You know what I mean? Like you. Rasta and Sub. I can see you all so clearly I can't bear it. You're all so fucking real, you know? So real.'

His eyes are shiny and I suspect he might cry.

'Don't worry. He's harmless,' Rasta Jesus says, smiling, as if all my thoughts are appearing in a bubble over my head. 'Chill and finish watching the movie. By the time it's over he'll probably be on his way back from outer space.'

So that's what we do. And the film is almost as trippy as Spanish's behaviour. This is the most surreal experience of my life. My mind is scattered. Maybe I should leave, but

I don't even know where the nearest subway station is and by all accounts, this isn't the safest part of town. And who'll look after him if I leave? I try to relax, but the nerves keep building. I don't know whether it's down to fear of a text-book dangerous situation or because his head is heavy on my shoulder and I don't know how to get it off and it's the first time in a very long time that anyone's sat so close to me.

'Right, missy, we gotta go,' says RJ a few moments after the end of the film. 'It was good to meet you! You enjoyed the movie?'

'Yeah. Yeah, I did.'

'Cool. Make sure you come out and see us play again sometime, girl! Spanish . . .' He taps the high boy's curls. 'Hey buddy, we're leaving.'

Spanish strokes my arm and says nothing, hums the theme from a sitcom.

'Later, friends,' says Sub with a grin. 'We still on for rehearsal tomorrow, right Spanish?'

'Come on, Sub,' laughs Rasta Jesus. 'He ain't even in our dimension right now.'

As if in confirmation of that fact, Spanish gets up quietly and leaves the room.

'Where's he gone?'

Sub just shakes his head. They don't suggest that I catch a ride with them and neither do I. I just can't frame the words. I watch them file out of the door. I hear them walk down the stairs. It's still not too late! I could catch them up and ask them to give me a ride to the subway at least.

I watch them from the window as they get in the van and drive away. Then I carefully search the apartment until I find Spanish crouching in the bottom of his built-in wardrobe.

I don't say anything. Get in and sit with him.

no dreams.

Zed has disappeared again. It might be nothing and of course he's OK, but I can't shake my irritation, my fear, my disappointment. I don't know why, but I thought he'd be here when I returned, just because I'd been away. I dreamed it all the way back on the subway, how his face would look at the door. I imagined him smoking a nervous zoot in the living room, checking his watch. I imagined something delicious and smoky cooking in his head. But no. It's been another quiet, empty procession of days without incident. Every day I've checked his room. The bed is made without a crease. Nothing is moved.

Finally I can't help myself any longer and rap hard on Brandy's bedroom door.

'Hey! Are you in?' *Knock, knock, knock.* 'Brandy?'

Pause.

Knock, knock, knock.

'Yeah, come on in.'

'Brandy! I . . .' I push the door open, and for a moment I don't know who I'm looking at. Pause. 'Brandon.'

'Eden,' he replies, and gives me a clouded smile.

'I . . . um. Nice to meet you,' I say, completely lost, failing at a friendly chuckle. His voice is different, his posture, his presence. 'Wow.'

'You can say it.'

'Say what?'

'I'm not as cute as a boy, huh?'

His face looks slimmer and shaded, longer, harder. His

eyes are weary. His hair is a cap of short, black waves that start further back on his head than the lace front wig. He wears a T-shirt and a pair of long shorts. There is no theatre to him. He's not an event. 'You . . .' I struggle, 'you're just a different person. I'd have to look at you for a while.'

He smiles, nods. He looks more like Brandy when he smiles.

I look around his room. It's simple and neat in shades of pale green and white. The bed is made. There's barely a sign of girlhood anywhere, aside from his make-up bag and the wig on a stand, his big, fake hair. There's a picture on his dresser of Violet, laughing. I didn't even know they were close like that. I've barely even seen them together at all.

'What's up,' he says. 'You look a few layers' worth of freaked out right now.'

'Um. Have you seen Zed at all? I'm just wondering, you know, because I haven't seen him for a few days.'

'Sorry, I haven't,' he says. And I feel stranded between panic at Zed's disappearance and the shock of Brandon's bare face. They intertwine. 'Not since Monday I don't think.'

'Alright. OK. Cool. So . . . you're alright, though, yeah?'

'I'm good,' he says quietly. 'I'm gonna go visit some family in New Jersey for a couple days.' Even his legs are crossed the mannish way, with one calf crossed over his knee. It makes me feel lonely, like he's a stranger. 'Are you?'

'What, going to New Jersey?'

'No,' he laughs. 'I meant are you good?'

'Yeah. I'm . . . yeah. I'm gonna go. I'll see you later.'

Another day and still no sign. Not a single shiny blink from my mobile phone either. From anybody. And I thought Spanish and I would be allies. The bond seemed almost blood-thick between us, sitting in the closet together, singing the theme from *M.A.S.H.*

But then it's not simple. I don't even know if Spanish wants to see me again. Everything was different when I woke up the morning after. He was staring into my face with those uncanny golden eyes of his, unblinking as a cat's. Before he'd said a word I could see he'd dried up sober as a Monday morning.

'Hey,' he said huskily, then cleared his throat. Despite the heat, he'd pulled a sheet right up to my neck and was lying as far away from me as he possibly could without falling off the bed.

'Morning, Spanish,' I said, careful to direct my morning breath away from him.

'I'm sorry if . . . if I scared you or anything. You know, last night?'

'It's alright.'

'Eight o'clock. I gotta get my day started.'

A couple of cars blasted hip-hop outside.

'Right.' I stretched out. The bed was comfortable and the day ahead was uninviting.

'Eden, you gotta go. I don't really do this.'

'What?' I asked, my body sparking with all manner of impulses. He was trying to kill something between us. But him trying to kill it meant it existed.

'This.'

'I don't understand.'

Spanish closed his eyes and opened them. 'Thanks for staying with me last night.'

I shrugged, pretending not to be tense. 'I was stranded,' I told him. It felt like a confession. How long had I been stranded? For much longer than a night, I think.

'Thanks anyway. It was nice you being here. I usually like to be alone.'

'Look, it's not even a big deal, Spanish.'

'That's what you think?' Our gazes collided and ricocheted. His honesty disarmed me, his unfashionable gravity.

'Nothing even happened.'

'What? Sex? That's the only thing that can happen, right?'

'Spanish . . .'

'Really, Eden,' he jumped up in that sudden way he has, gave me a towel and pointed me to the bathroom. 'When you're ready I'll take you to the subway, alright?'

We walked to the station in complete silence. A force-field had sprung up around him but I pressed my phone number on him anyway. I shouldn't have bothered. Now he's yet another man who won't use it.

I unpack The Woman from my bag, safe in her little clip frame. 'You have it all figured out, don't you?' I say to her and wish she could talk back, though I'm pretty sure that even if she could, she wouldn't. Sigh.

Our lives are so tenuous, built around other people who may or may not have even built their lives around us. These random blood sacs poised to spill any moment and be lost to the earth.

I remember when I was a little kid in primary school, we'd make papier maché balloons. We'd blow up real ones and paste them over with dollops of thick glue and newspaper. When they'd dried and hardened, we'd paint them in bright colours and we'd pop the balloon inside with a pin. It reminds me of all the layers we paste onto the people we love, the memories and expectations. Those things last longer than people do and go on for ever, holding the shape of a ghost.

'Hey . . . Violet!' Me on the second floor, gripping the banister.

'Eden.' She comes out of her living room with a giggling Eko on her hip. 'You alright? What's up?'

'I'm fine. You know I just wondered if, um, you've seen Zed at all in the past couple of days?'

'Zed? You mean that dude who moved in downstairs?'

'Right.'

'No, sorry, I ain't seen him, girl. Actually I was gon' ask you to bring him up for dinner one of these nights! I've barely had a chance to talk to him.'

'Yeah, definitely. I'll tell him.'

no dice.

Outside the New York sun is a yellow shout. I can't see until I put my shades on. I walk up Flatbush Avenue, lazily in search of Zed's stride, not really expecting to see it. The sky is scummy; there's a veil of wispy cloud and smog muddying the blue. And I'm sick of sunshine. I'm sick of heat. What I wouldn't do for a cool and gentle grey day in London. I feel like I'm melting, fusing. I'm hungry, but I walk past the Chinese and the Mexican and the Italian and the West Indian buffet and even Papa's Fried Chicken. I walk into clothes shops and listlessly finger the clothes. I ignore the shop assistants. I don't like my face in the mirror.

I imagine how it would feel to smash the sky with a gargantuan hammer or to blow the trees over, or to sweep buildings away with one fist. I wish I was that powerful. I wish I had any power.

I don't catch the eyes of the hungry men on the street corners; they look at my legs and at my breasts and they make corny overtures. But right now I'm fed up of all that. I want to be a tree. I want to be a bowl of water, or a length of fabric or a bar of soap or a fucking bedside lamp. Not anything they can look at in that way.

They're all the same. If they had a chance to mean something to me, they'd either stick me on some pedestal so high it gives me a nosebleed or they'd use me like toilet paper. And that's all I see in every one of those gazes, from the skinny boys and the buff ones, and the tall ones and the munchkins and the ones older than God; I see only two tribes.

Wolves and lambs.

I walk up past Prospect Park, over Atlantic Avenue and near that big Target Mall I went to with Brandy, take a right on Hanson Place. It's a long, long walk. He has to be somewhere, I think.

Inside Fort Greene Park, I look around for Zed's friends, but that was a Sunday thing. They're probably at work now. I don't know what I expected to see. There's no one but a few strangers with their dogs, and a few smaller strangers playing football. I finally crack and try his mobile again.

And it's always like the first time, calling him. Fifteen-year-old me sitting at the telephone, deaf with nerves, full of a pleasant terror like just before a really big plunge on a rollercoaster when time itself seems to pause. The phone rang in his dad's apartment and I wondered what the sound would catch him doing and if he'd be thinking about me. That first time I called he answered 'Hello?' and my gut flipped. 'It's Eden,' I managed without a waver. In my pocket were three folded twenty-dollar notes from the pawn shop. I was quite victoriously without jewellery. 'Let's go out,' I said, feeling liberated and wicked. 'I've got money.' He laughed. 'Whoa . . . it's like that? I'm on my way, girl!'

But that was then. Now my call goes through to voicemail. No dice.

I consume my pizza and Snapple. I do a circuit of the park. I try the mobile. I stare at the clouds. I try the mobile.

I sit down on the dry grass and cry. I'm exhausted.

Then I ignore a concerned look on a passing face and go home.

empty glass.

And I know right away that he's back. I click the door open and smell weed. Plus there's an open box of juice and his keys sitting on the coffee table.

So after a very short time wondering if I should just play it cool and go down to the basement I decide against it and take the few steps it takes to get to his bedroom. The door is slightly ajar. There are sounds.

I push his room open and Zed is thrusting languidly into some jiggle-breasted stranger. Dark-haired, red-cheeked, making dents in his skin with her stubby fingers. His face is turned away so I can't see, but hers is un-remarkable. Not stunning like Max. She's not Max. She's just anyone and you shouldn't be able to fuck in a room like this. Under the weed and the body fluids it still smells faintly of old lady. He's almost fully dressed, the skin of his ass barely visible between his tank top and the waist-band of his jeans.

'Zed!' she screeches, making a pathetic attempt to cover herself. 'Zed!' I watch his uninspired moves while the stranger keeps yelling his name until eventually he realises that it's not a reaction to his prowess. She pushes him off of her.

'Fuck,' he says.

'Zed! There's someone here. Stop.'

When he finally turns around I'm suddenly mobilised. I don't wait for anything to register in his eyes but walk blindly through the dark house, face hot, head full of white noise. A sound like speaker interference. I can hear them really tinny through all the buzzing.

'Oh shit!'

'Is that your girlfriend or something?' Squeak, squeak her little voice goes.

'Oh shit.'

'You didn't tell me you had a girlfriend! You didn't fucking—'

Movement, cloth, zippers.

'Look, I can't deal with this right now.'

'You want me to leave?'

'Yes.'

'I can't believe—'

'I'll call you.'

'Zed!'

'I'll call you, OK?'

I make it to the basement door underwater, and I lock it behind me.

I put my headphones in as loud as they can go and lay there with a pillow over my head until Zed has given up knocking on the door.

Behind my eyelids, Zed has armies marching through me unchecked, burning and pillaging. Zed in a million and one poses. Zed the first time I saw him, shining clean and boxfresh in his new gear, Zed quiet in black, eyes leaking softly, Zed tickling me when I was fifteen to make me let go of the TV remote, Zed cooking me breakfast that time I got drunk, Zed in jeans, Zed in a suit, Zed in Hackney, Zed in Notting Hill, Zed in New York, Zed's mouth and spiky lashes and fuzzy chin and smooth body and firm bum and voice and laugh and smile and sigh and all those half-cut looks and all that anger and fakeness and pain and arrogance. Zed kissing his white girl and his slim fingers and big feet, his favourite songs, his cologne, his limp hugs, his tight grins, his weed, his style, his elusive soul.

Decolonisation will require an act of violence against myself comparable to the revolutions of France and Haiti. I'll cut him away like the tumour he is.

So eventually the severe need of a drink finally drives me upstairs into a house quiet enough that I assume he's left again. But I was wrong. I can hear the TV on in the living room.

I go straight into the kitchen where I know I have a bottle of something hot that's not coffee. I drink it straight – no ice – at the crooked table, nibbling dejectedly at a packet of crisps. I pour out some more Jack and pretend I don't hear when Zed walks up and stands in the doorway.

'What's up?' he says.

'You tell me, Casanova.'

'Eden, I . . .'

'I guess it's kind of serious with her too, hey Zed? Nice to see you have no problem getting serious with girls. Max is lucky you get so much practice.'

Without answering, he pours himself a bowl of Cap'n Crunch and sits at the table. I refill. 'I just . . .' He shakes his head. 'It was just a thing. You know what I mean?'

'Not really. Why don't you explain?'

'What's the point? Would anything I say make a difference to you, right now?' I shrug. He takes a bite of cereal. 'So how was that show the other night?' I hate when people speak with their mouths full. It's disgusting. 'Spanish and his guys?'

'He's a genius.'

'Indubitably.'

'We didn't fuck.'

He stops chewing for a second and I look up from my glass. He stares.

'I didn't ask you that.'

So I put the empty glass in the sink and take the bottle with me.

'Good night, Zed,' I say.

the biggest leap.

Harlem, ten years ago.

Zed didn't look at me while he unlocked the door to his dad's apartment. I listened to the breath stop in his throat. I watched the warm, salty curve of his neck. He was just a boy then, sweet and unfinished. His ears were still slightly too large for his head, his neck too skinny, his cornrows beginning to unravel at the temples. But he was already towering and broad in stature, with quick slanted eyes and hard cheekbones. He thought he might be handsome. He wasn't sure yet.

He jiggled the keys once more in the lock and it seemed to me that the door gave – finally – with a sigh. I felt as if I were hurtling toward a precipice. I can't remember if we spoke or not. I can't remember breathing, but I know that I must have. Every part of my body was chiming like a bell. We laughed to mask the tension, walked into the small, neat living room, sat on the forest-green couch that yielded to us with a leather squeak. We were very young and dwarfed by the event that lay before us. I knew I'd never be the same again. I'd already begun to change irrevocably, and now the only way to move was forward. The inevitability of it seemed tangible. It made everything from the couch to the remote control complicit in our inelegant mating ritual. The TV only thickened the silence. Then he said: 'You wanna see my room?'

'OK,' I replied, half-strangled, embarrassed for us. We were not smooth.

I remember that it was a small room, and that it was opposite the bathroom. The carpet and curtains were dark blue. There was a bookshelf and no TV and a Wu Tang Clan poster on the wall.

'Dominic said you write poetry,' I ventured, thinking back to a conversation me and my step-dad had weeks before in a diner.

'Yeah . . . sometimes,' he said bashfully. I liquefied. 'You wanna, uhm. You wanna hear some?'

He reached down under his bed and his arm brushed mine. He pulled out a Nike box full of notebooks. He began reading to me. The blood roared in my eardrums. I heard nothing. I felt tremendous weight pushing down from all around me, toward him.

He stopped reading. Looked at me. 'What do you think?'

'Beautiful,' I said, but I think he knew I'd not been listening to his poem. 'Zed, what I said the other day. I wasn't kidding.'
I'm ready.

'I know,' he said, putting his long fingers to my cheek. It seemed to take days for him to reach my face with his own. A kiss is the biggest leap you can take to reach another person; the space is interminable. And I'd been so far away from everybody for so long. When his lips touched mine I felt like I was part of the world, and like a woman, and like I had another chance to be worth something to somebody.

His tongue soft in my mouth, his arms around me. We fell back into his bed and he hit his head on the wall. We laughed at each other then, and the moment was infinitely more tender. I pushed the notebooks to the floor.

'Are you sure about this?'

'Yes.'

We undressed. His body was dark and firm and covered me completely. I reached down and touched him through his shorts, feeling electrified, a thousand little shocks from every place he kissed me. He took off the shorts and was heavy in my hands, and warm. I was scared. He told me not to be afraid, as if my thinking was loud enough for him to hear.

'I've never done this before either,' he whispered.

'You're a . . . !'

'Yeah.'

'But you said—'

'I lied,' he told me. 'Sorry.'

'It's OK,' I said, feeling even softer for him. 'It's OK.'

And he pulled the sheet over us, struggled into the rubber that had probably been sitting in his wallet for a few years. It was really going to happen. I clutched at his neck and shoulders, ran my hands over his hair.

'Ouch!' I cried. 'OUCH!' And it really hurt.

'It'll be cool, just let me . . .'

'Ouch!' My insides. Everything opening out to receive him . . . reluctantly. It felt different from the way I thought it was going to feel. An entire universe of nerve-endings came awake.

'OK . . . OK.'

'No don't stop . . .'

'I thought you said—'

'No. Keep going,' I said. 'Keep going.'

After the pain ended, mostly my mind was empty. For the first time, I had no mind – only a body. But in a moment of laughing self-consciousness, I thought about everyone waiting for us at the house, Marie and Paul and Aunt K, and us over here in Harlem.

I smiled, Zed smiled and some of his sweat dripped in my eye.

these dreams.

Mama — if I climb inside myself
Can I take you with me?
Mama — I can't breathe, I can't speak
Mama — I can't sleep through these dreams —

She like a tight-rope —
being shaken at both ends like —
Drop, sucker!
It's a knot
I been picking at lately
Love supposed to be this soft descent
like snow, like confetti like —
But what if it's more like falling off the back of a moving
*   truck?*
Getting up 100 yards away
With a concussion
All the skin scraped off your left side?
And did he fall or
Was he pushed?

She want artery blood
She want
I can't hear myself through her handwriting
Is such an inky mess
She a garden full of weeds.
A garden full of overripe
Flowers, thorns and bugs;

Roots tunnelling under ground.
Everything edible, everything poison.
She a garden humming with too much.

Mama – if I climb inside myself
Can I take you with me?
Mama – I can't breathe, I can't speak
Mama – I can't sleep through these dreams –

She got eyes like church shoes on a beggar
Collecting tears
Fat mouth spilling with poem
Overripe body
Black lashes
Red-coloured and not yellow
Bright and sharp as summer concrete
Sharp in the knees and in the elbows.

A kiss would be like drinking pepper sauce
Through a straw, mama
Her sweet-sweet garden smells
Her bubble-gum breath,
Her incessant talk.
She never shuts up,
Even when she's silent.
Even when she's gone.
But she's never gone and
And look.

Here she comes
A blind tourist walking
My dark alleys armed with
A flashlight and a fruit basket
Like she fully intent on saving the world

And I'm it —
Crazy, beautiful girl

Mama — if I climb inside myself
Can I take you with me?
Mama — I can't breathe, I can't speak
Mama — I can't sleep through these dreams —

I can't sleep, I can't sleep
Through these dreams
I can't sleep
I can't sleep
I can't sleep —

September

hungry.

Five sunsets 'til Labor Day and September hasn't taken the heat down one degree.

The basement is an oven that tips me half-baked out into the Brooklyn streets. No cooler out here, but there's light and people, air, movement; some terrain outside the blasted landscape of my own mind.

Out on Fenimore Street I give my clicker an assignment, twisting it this way and that in my damp palms. I want to steal pictures of summer's official last days, the kids doing their best to pack every second to bursting with mischief as the new school year approaches. I snatch pictures of high-heeled, Technicolor sandals and contrasting toenails. Of men profiling in convertibles. Tree on sky, sneaker on pavement, summer in the city. I capture covert images of women sitting outside in their mas camps, laughing together and hand-stitching bright costumes for the Labor Day parade.

I creep closer. The costumes are fabulous. Feathered, glittered and shiny. All colours, all shapes. I'm starting to wish I had a costume too. An excitement has begun inside me that I can't name . . .

'Hey!'

I've been caught.

'Sorry! Sorry . . .' I lower my camera.

'What you doing?' says a big woman with hair a bright, sewn-in myriad of colours. She stands up. 'You taking pictures of us?'

'Erm . . .'

'What are you? A spy or a photographer?'

'A . . . a photographer,' I tell her. 'I'm visiting from London. I'm sorry, I should have asked first.'

'Yeah you should have!' says peacock head, then she flashes a smile for the first time. 'But it's cool. You just gotta send us a copy of the photos, OK?'

'Yeah! Yeah. Thanks!' I say, relieved. 'No problem!'

The four women all huddle together, smiling big and clutching their fantastic creations. All of their faces have that particular quality I've seen everywhere lately as we head toward a change of season. Every moment aware of its imminent death, every moment electric.

'Are you going to J'Ouvert morning before the parade as well?'

'Of course!' they say and, 'You best believe it!' and 'Hell yeah, I'm going!'

'What's it like?'

'Every year,' says a woman in a bright headwrap and chunky jewellery, 'I can feel my ancestors at J'Ouvert. I imagine how it must have looked, that first sunrise after slavery finally ended. A new beginning. You make sure you experience it while you're here, even if you don't make it to the actual parade.'

'I will,' I tell them, making myself a promise. I'm going even if it's a solo expedition – a scenario that seems more than likely at this point.

Aunt K still isn't back. Brandy doesn't want to go out much. She's either at work, or upstairs with Violet helping out with Eko. And Zed, for what it's worth, got a job in a bar near Prospect Park. *What about your music?* I asked him, angling the question sharp, to wound. He laughed. *What about it? You think I'm Jay-Z or somebody? I blew all my savings in London and there ain't much I can do with a microphone if I'm dead from hunger,* he shrugged.

Now we avoid each other even more, if that's possible. And there's no sign of Spanish, either.

In fact, the only man who calls me is my dad, who tracked me down through Juliet. He's doing the 'come back, all is forgiven' routine, but it's probably just because he thinks it will look un-Christian if there's a rift between us. Plus he wanted to break the news of his engagement to Old Chanders, who wants to put me in God knows what kind of fuchsia atrocity of a bridesmaid's dress. I may have to stay in New York for ever just to avoid the indignity of it.

'Thanks, ladies! Enjoy the parade,' I say, wishing I could stay with them. They all tell me I should do the same, and one of the women writes down her email address and hands it to me with a flourish. 'I'll send the pictures soon,' I promise them.

'When your aunt gets back,' says the woman with the head wrap, giving me a small nod and smile of recognition, 'tell her Ms Beatrice said hello, and that I'll be over soon.'

'Wait a minute,' I squeak. 'How did you know?'

She just smiles, eyes crinkling at the corners. 'Make sure you go out and dance. Young people,' she says, 'should dance every night, while the flesh still permits.'

I scuttle back up to my end of the road, feeling chased, excited and restless. Drop my keys trying to get through the door, almost falling down the basement steps. My mind itches as I upload the fresh pictures to my laptop. I barely register all the brightly-coloured frames and hard shapes. The woman's words have mobilised me for a plan I didn't even know I was forming all day. Longing for action. Humming the theme tune from *M.A.S.H.*

And it doesn't take me long to find him. Reckless Gods has a website, and a quick look on it lets me know that they have a gig tonight at a club called the Knitting Factory.

I've got to find out what's wrong with me. Maybe if I can

figure out why Spanish hasn't called me since the sleepover two weeks ago, it'll shed light on my general lack of appeal.

An hour later I'm strutting down Leonard Street like it's a catwalk, trying to conjure some confidence, some weight, some power.

I'm on time and I'm ready. I've no bag to search at the entrance. All I have in my pockets are banknotes, a Metrocard, keys and my kohl pencil. I pay without seeing the cashier and walk down a plush hallway into the back of a red and black room. The walls are burgundy against the maroon carpet of the stage, which is flanked by jet curtains. The exit signs gleam tomato. I can see neither the beige boy nor his band. Instead a wild-haired compere in a Black Rock Coalition T-shirt is introducing a documentary screening.

'Excuse me . . .' A bald girl with a nose ring looks at me expectantly. I ask her: 'Are Reckless Gods playing here tonight?'

'I don't know, hun, I'm just here for the film . . .'

'Yeah they are,' a friend of hers in space-age eye make-up says. 'I saw it on the flyer. They're awesome.'

About two thousand years later the film ends and the compere announces that the band will be on shortly. I listen to them tuning up. No Spanish. There's a man trying his saxophone, and a tiny guy wielding a hefty double bass with inexplicable ease.

I'm strung high between the awkward layers of sound. The strings and the horn, the dull mournful cry of the bass. Underneath, the tinny pre-recorded music is rendered futile. There is chatter, people drawn tight around candlelit tables.

Where's Spanish? Maybe I got it wrong and there are two bands with the same name. That would be fun. The saxophone spills over the top of the DJ-spun music and oozes down the sides of the room, a disjointed soundtrack to my nerves. My eyes keep twitching toward the door, but it's not him for a solid ten minutes.

Then, suddenly, it is.

And I'm reminded how hard and skinny and weird he is. The rips in his jeans, his cinematic bones, that angry walk. There's something about the injured angle of his shoulders that understands me. And maybe being understood is the closest any of us can ever get to not being alone. He looks neither right nor left on his way past, steps up onstage and drapes a guitar over his slim body.

'I brought in some friends to jam with us,' he says. 'Thanks for another chance to experiment.' All his stern confidence is startling. Attractive. And then he's singing: *Don't fight just let them do it to ya/ Break you open, get into ya/ Like a poison swimming through ya/ Black boy in your funhouse mirror/ Black girl in your funhouse mirror . . .*

He does song after song, thickened by the bass and the sax. The people clap and cheer and feel understood and tired and stretched, and then eventually it's the end and I make my shaky way to the front.

'Hey!' I croak, shaking. 'Why didn't you call me?' This time I'll ask the hard questions. He can say *Because I didn't want to!* and it won't kill me, will it?

'Eden!' he says, shocked. 'Hey!' He leans over and hugs me hard. RJ and Sub nod at me with smiles and I go soft with relief. Eden still. Not just some would-be groupie they don't remember. The only person who isn't smiling is the female standing next to Spanish with bad skin and slightly dopey eyes. I think I've seen her before round the park on a Sunday.

'Why didn't you call me?' I say again, stronger.

'I wanted to but . . .' he trails off. He looks nervously at Bad Skin. Have they fucked before or something? Well I don't care. I don't care if she's his *wife*. I've made it this far. She eyeballs me steadily, a cheap romance novel of a woman hanging off him.

'You wanted to . . . ?' I raise my eyebrows at him in encouragement. 'What?'

'I couldn't find the number.'

'Oh.' I laugh. 'OK.'

Dopey Eyes then decides to put her arm around his waist and interrupt. I can't hear what she's saying, but Spanish hasn't looked away from me once. She rolls her eyes like I'm a run in her stockings.

'Oi! Can't you see that this is a private conversation?'

Oh Lord. *I* said that. I'm gonna get in a fight and get bloody deported. Spanish's eyes flick between us like he can't quite believe what's happening either. But it's too late to back down.

'What?'

'I said. This. Is. A private. Conversation.'

She lets go of Spanish and steps towards me. 'Who the fuck do you think you're talking to?' Squares her bony shoulders.

'I'm *trying* to talk to Spanish.'

She pushes me.

PAK!

It's my fist and her face and it hurts but I know it probably hurt her more 'cause she stumbles back on those ugly heels and my ears ring and my fist throbs and oh my God that felt good but damn. Ouch.

When she tries to rush me, Spanish grabs her from behind and tells her to calm down. 'This bitch just fucking hit me,' she says, eyes glistening. 'She *hit* me! Who the fuck are you anyway? Spanish, let me *go*! Get off me! Hey!' she screams at me. 'If I see you in the streets, it is *over*, bitch! Do you hear me? *Over!*'

She doesn't stop shouting while he half leads, half drags her over to a seated area near the stage and deposits her in the care of a woman in a trilby.

'Come on,' he says, 'let's go before it gets uglier in here,' and I finally uncurl my aching fingers. He throws his guitar on his back and makes various signals at his band mates and at an approaching bouncer. Wordlessly I manoeuvre my way to the exit amongst all the craning necks. His hand is steady on my waist.

When we get outside I can't look at him. The adrenaline is beginning to wear off and I can't believe what I just did. He must think I'm bipolar or on crack or something. He probably brought me out here to call the police. I stare at the pavement cracks and the yellow circles formed by the streetlights. We walk to the corner.

'Eden.'

'Yeah. I know, I know, I'm sorry but she—'

'Eden.'

I look up and he's staring right into me. He almost smiles and I almost do the same.

'It's uh. It's good to see you,' he says. 'But damn, Eden. Damn.'

'I'm sorry,' I repeat.

'Why did you come?'

'Do you need me to tell you? You usually just guess what I'm thinking.'

'Come on,' he says, looking helpless suddenly. 'I need you to be real with me right now.'

'Well, you seemed like. Well, you were so angry at me the other day and I wondered why, you know? What I did. We were so cool and everything I thought we were gonna be friends.'

'Is that all?'

'Spanish. I don't know how you want me to answer that.'

His eyes are gold in the streetlights and he doesn't blink. Then he runs his hand over his face and says: 'Shit. You know what? Me neither.' We stand there for a moment and then he asks me if I'm hungry.

'Starving,' I tell him.

nobody ever wins.

I've been here before.

Spanish and I arrive outside a spot call Joline's, with gingham curtains and a neon sign that reads *Open 24hrs*. It's the curtains I remember. And maybe it was only a place *like* this one. Me and Boy Toy came here once to wait for my mother who was, as usual, running late. I felt so grown up. He told me to meet him at Canal Street station because he wasn't driving that day. He bought me a peanut malted milkshake and chilli cheese fries.

Dominic looked distracted as he sat down. His hair was even longer than usual and matt rather than shiny. His leather-clad foot kept up a nervy tattoo on the linoleum but every time I caught his gaze he would smile at me. He was really trying. I thought he must really have loved my mother to try so hard.

'Good huh?' he said as I took my first sip of the malt.

'Yeah,' I said, wondering what everyone must be thinking of us. He didn't look old enough to be my father. And there was the shade of him, which meant he was unlikely to be my brother. I kept my eyes down, avoiding the questions in people's eyes. I felt a stab of anger at how complicated my mum had made everything.

'So what you been up to this week?' he said, eyes darting every so often to the door. He checked his oversized nineties mobile for the millionth time.

'I met a boy . . .' I stammer. 'I mean, I met Zed, Uncle Paul's son. Zed and me. We went to Madame Tussaud's.'

'Zed and you, huh?' he said and his tone shocked me out of my teenaged sulk. He laughed like he knew how it was for a name to have so much power you stumble on it every time. Tentatively, I laughed too. It was early days, long before I'd touched Zed at all. I was distracted, clumsy and firing with hormones. Just us two sharing a sentence was enough to give me mysterious twinges.

'Yeah, it was cool,' I said. 'Zed got to dress up like Darth Vader.'

'Really?'

'I got some pictures. It was, like, a fake *Star Wars* audition thing.'

I suppose that was the first real conversation he and I ever had. I told him about all the fun we'd had and what we planned to do next. My ever-present urge to say Zed's name would broaden that small moment of empathy into an unexpected friendship. And truth be told, I didn't really care if Boy Toy was being genuine or not as long as he didn't interrupt.

'You guys should come and see the musical I'm starting next month. I'm rehearsing at the moment. You can come meet me at the theatre sometime if you're at a loose end,' he said with that crisp, fragile smile of his. Always he had the air of an abused pet. It amazed me that he cared what *I* thought of him. 'I'll buy you lunch.'

'Thanks,' I said. 'That would be nice. You know Zed?'

'Not really, but his dad brought him over a few times. Katherine and Marie are really close to Paul 'cause they all grew up together back in Saint Lucia but,' he laughed with a touch of bitterness, 'I think the guy's kind of dull, to be honest. It's strange that Zed turned out so creative.'

'He *is* really creative,' I gushed, despite myself.

'I introduced him to some young producers and musicians I know, actually. He'll go far if his parents let him.

His mother wants him to go back and live with her in Atlanta when he's left boarding school, and his dad wants him to go to NYU, so I think it's a little confusing for him right now. I know how he feels; my parents were the same. My dad wanted me to manage his pizzeria – can you believe it? That's as far as his ambition went for his son.' He shakes his head. 'I told Zed I'd be happy to help him pursue his dreams. His poetry is amazing, especially for his age.'

'I know he's a rapper but . . . he writes poetry?'

'You should ask him,' said Dominic with a smile. And then he checked his mobile again. The smile faded. A couple of beats later he said, 'Hey, Eden . . . Did your mother make it down to see you on Tuesday?'

'No,' I said, dumb as an empty plate, seeing nothing, hearing nothing but my own thoughts. 'Was she supposed to come over? That's the day I went out with Zed, I think.'

'Right. OK,' he said with a weird, artificial laugh. I'll always remember it. Always. 'My mistake.'

'What time is she coming?' I asked.

'Soon,' he said.

Then, just as if he'd conjured her, she appeared outside the glass. She waved at us and mouthed an exaggerated 'Sorry!' On her red-painted lips was an only mildly apologetic smile, one that already assumed she'd been forgiven.

'And here she is,' said Dominic.

'So what do you think of us?' Spanish says, nursing a glass of mineral water.

'Reckless Gods?' I reply, dragging myself into the present.

'No. The White House.'

'Ha ha,' I say and he smiles. 'You guys are really original. I dunno. Full of rage and innocence at the same time.'

'All of that, huh?'

'Yep.'

'Sometimes anger is the purest and most innocent emotion going.'

'Anger when it's hot, maybe. Not when it's cold.'

He begins to shred one of my napkins into a little pile on the table. We're at a corner booth. Laminated menu. Fluorescent lights. All we could manage on the walk over was a staccato rhythm of awkward glances and sparse chat about the weather and New York rats the size of Yorkshire terriers.

I look at the hollows in his cheek and fork some lemon meringue pie into my mouth. 'Eat some pie.'

'I'm fasting,' he says defensively. 'Plus what you're eating has no nutritional value whatsoever; it's dead.'

'I'm sure that's not true. Lemons are fruits, right? Plus, you're the one who recommended I get this!'

'Are you enjoying it?'

'Do you see the crumbs all over my face? Of course I am.'

'Well, that was the point. I don't think everyone has to be like me.'

''Cause you're special, right? Not like the rest of us poor fat slobs?'

He shrugs again. I laugh and ask him when the fast is over.

'Tomorrow.'

'Wow. Bet you can't wait, huh?'

'I can wait. I try not to get sensually involved with food.'

'Right . . .' I stop eating for a second. 'So who was the girl? At the Knitting Factory?'

'Ivy? She's a guitarist.'

'Any good?'

'Pretty good. Unspectacular.'

'Why was she eyeballing me? Is she a girlfriend or something?'

'No. I told you I don't do that. She just,' he looks uncomfortable, 'has stuff going on in her head. She has this image built up of me that's not real.'

'You never defined exactly what it was you "didn't do". What are you? Gay?'

'No,' he cuts his eye at me. And then from nowhere he asks me how I know Zed and where I met him.

I look down at the table and up. 'Our families know each other from back in Saint Lucia,' I tell him, slightly less than the truth and as much as I can bear to say. 'How about you?'

'We went to the same high school.'

'But he went to a private boarding school . . .'

'Right.' He looks at me. 'Yeah.'

'Did you get in on a scholarship as well?'

'No.'

Neither of us says anything. The kind of fees charged at a school like that mean he must come from money. He silently dares me to question him further, but then the waitress comes along with that fantastic knack they all have of being able to smell tension. She asks if everything's alright. We say: 'Yeah.' And I decide it's as good a time as any to change the subject.

'So . . . you still haven't told me what exactly it is that you "don't do".'

He drinks some water. 'I'm celibate.'

'No sex for the rock star?'

'Yeah, that's what the word "celibate" is commonly thought to mean.'

I give him a look. 'I've been trying that for a while too.'

'You have?' Spanish flushes slightly pink in the cheeks, gives me a look of suspicion and gut-wrenching hope. To be understood. 'Really?'

'Everything's so fast and convenient and empty,' I tell him, heart beating fast. I take a breath. I never even told Juliet. She wouldn't have been able to help shrinking it. 'There's no sacrifice. It's hard to get a grip on anyone, really. It's hard to feel anything real.'

Spanish nods slowly, his golden eyes harbouring a deep, unknowable glow.

'It's not that I never want love. It's the opposite really. I think I've been celibate because I want love so *much*. It wasn't really a conscious decision. I just got tired of feeling nothing. I need the kind of relationship that—'

'Why would you want any kind of relationship?' he says, looking down at the table. The napkin is now almost as fine as grains of salt. 'Relationships are a war that nobody ever wins. There's a Chinese proverb that says *not caring for anyone in particular is caring for all mankind in general.* Have you ever been in love before?'

I consider lying but: 'Yeah.'

'What did that ever do for you? It make you happy?'

I look down at my pie. Finish it. Tap my fork against the side of the bowl. 'My aunt says,' I tell him slowly, 'that it takes divine strength to be soft when the world is hard.'

He sweeps the pile of torn paper into his hand, making sure he gets every piece. 'Are you finished?' he says.

For a moment I'm confused, then I nod and he calls over the waitress, asks for the bill. When I reach for my bag he says, 'I got this.'

'Thanks,' I say. 'Are you gonna see me home safely?'

He stares at me and finishes his water.

'Sure,' he says.

water.

My seventh or eighth year, I had a thing about digging holes.

I would get down on my knees in our little back garden, in the watery sunshine, take my rusty spade and chip away at the surface of the world until the soil grew moist. Sending up its metallic smell of growth, earthworms and secrets.

When I'd made the hole as promisingly round as I could, I'd go back in the house, through the utility room, into the kitchen. There, my mum would be sitting at the table reading a magazine, *Cosmopolitan* or *Vogue*, drinking a glass of wine, ankles delicately crossed. She'd barely look up.

I'd go to the cupboard where all the miscellaneous kitchen bric-à-brac was, and proceed to take out the black roll of bin-liners, turning it over in my small, dirty hands, searching for a perforation.

My dad might come in then and glance suspiciously at me over the rim of his glasses. He knew about me and my tense little projects.

What's that for? You can't just waste those things, you know! They cost money! Gently he would say this.

Nothing, I would reply, ripping a bag carefully off the roll. I'd scurry outside where it was getting chillier by the hour, and go to work, lining my hole with the plastic bags, which I kept in place with rocks. I'd be so excited. Pushing my sleeves up every five minutes and grinning to myself.

Then I'd go back inside and my mum would be gone from the kitchen, and I would hear her voice in the hallway, laughing conspiratorially over the phone. Perfect opportunity to fill the biggest jug I could find with water, then bring it back and forth to the garden and pour it out into my plastic-lined hole, watching the water catch the light and glisten against the glossy black bin-liners. It made me feel the way I did in church the first time I saw the stained-glass windows.

I imagined the little fish I was going to put in there and the plants I was going to plant around it and how special it would be and that gave me the strength to keep adding layers of plastic, and more rocks, getting dirt on my face, scratching my head, pushing my sleeves up and itching inside my clothes. I'd squat in the dirt and anxiously watch the levels, filling quietly with hope and nerves. Desperate to get beneath the surface of my grim little city back garden, make something beautiful out of something ordinary.

After countless trips to the sink, I would have to admit the truth to myself – one that put me in an inky-black sulk. The soil kept stealing all my water.

I was helpless against it. No matter what I did, my water drained away. Nothing worked. I would chuck my spade in the dirt and go inside, full of childish grief and sudden hunger.

Water was a slippery, beautiful, tricky thing.

in the dark.

Our conversation has dried right down to the crust. We stand in the basement, in the dim lamplight, electrified by a fear that seems bigger than the moment. A man and a woman together on the cusp of something . . . somewhere. It happens all the time, right? It's so common that there are six billion people on the planet, almost all of us made the same way.

I sweep all the assorted debris from the little sofa so he can sit; notepads, magazines, CDs, a bra, a pencil and a novel. Then he perches on it like he's at the edge of a high diving board, looking down into the blue, calculating the odds of him not making it to the water alive. I offer him some to drink. He takes the glass and turns it around and around between his fingers.

'I've never had a girl,' Spanish says eventually, 'track me down and beat up some chick to get to me before.'

'Yeah, well, that's just how we do it in the LDN, rock star.'

'The what?'

'London town. Centre of the universe.'

'I see.'

He beats a rhythm out on the glass, all the music in his head emerging in spurts as a random humming. And then silence. I could cry, looking at the little baby curls at his hairline, the self-protective set of his narrow shoulders, the pale skin on his arms etched with dark tattoos. All it's going to take is for one of us to say something – make one move

– and the space between us will catch alight and burn to ash.

'Seriously though, that Ivy – or whatever her name was – she was just annoying, that's all. I hate to disappoint you.'

'You did track me down, though. I was shocked to see you.'

'Just shocked?'

'Happy,' he says slowly. 'I was happy too, I guess. And a little worried. Why did you come tonight?'

I see right through to the core of him, sitting here. All the tics, the eccentricities, all the moods of him are a clear map I could read blindfolded.

I don't know if I'm going to be able to help myself.

'Why were you worried?'

'Why did you come?'

'I told you that already,' I say, breathless, feeling spun about. 'You didn't call me and I thought you were mad or something. I thought we were gonna be friends.'

'But why did it matter so much?'

'I . . .'

'You know, the first time I met you and we were introduced, I felt something click into place when I heard your name. Eden.'

'Why?'

'The garden . . .' He gives a tense shrug. 'The snake. It doesn't take a genius, right? I knew someone like you would come along.'

'What do you mean?'

'Come here,' he says.

I stare at him. The lamp throws his features into chiaroscuro and the room behind him is completely black. I'm simultaneously magnetised and repulsed.

'Come on. This is gonna happen, right?' he says.

And when he says that, it's like when they switch all the

lights on at the end of a house party and you're scared to look up 'cause you were dancing nasty with someone in the dark but now you're scared to see their face for real in case they're ugly. Or really, really beautiful.

'Come on,' he says again, the command now a request. Fear steals into his face. Mine too, probably.

'I thought you didn't do this.'

'Eden,' he says helplessly.

I go to him because he looks set adrift. I want to re-anchor him, if only for the moment.

He avoids my hug and we kiss clumsily, all tongue and teeth, as if he's never done it before, and he tries to get my clothes off before there's any harmony. We don't both fit comfortably on the tiny sofa, so I lead him to my low, dishevelled bed.

I'm undone by the sensation of his sharp little bones under my fingers. His awkwardness, his quick, jerky release. His forehead shining with sweat.

His eyes are closed, face in my neck. His hair is moist. I'm completely awake, completely myself throughout, though not unmoved.

Afterwards, he lies on his back and closes his eyes, face at war. He pulls me to his chest. He's been waiting for someone like me like some people wait to be diagnosed with cancer.

fast over.

Pick up, pick up, pick up.

'Hello?'

'Hey!'

'Who's this?'

'Juliet,' I say, relieved just to hear the accent. Feels like I've never been so far away. 'It's me, you doughnut.'

'Oh my God! Eden! Mate!' I can hear traffic and loud squeaky brakes in the background. She must be on the bus. 'So good to hear you!'

'What's up?'

'Wow . . . ! Not much going on, bella. You're not missing anything. September's got an identity crisis and thinks it's February. But cool apart from that. Just getting on with it, really. Chasin' boys and bakin' dough. Got your groove back yet?'

'Kind of . . .'

'Oi!' she shouts. 'Call your dad, please! I have to say that before I forget, 'cause he's going mad! Keeps asking me to act as some kind of go-between to bring you two back together. I know he's your dad, but pretty soon I'm gonna have to tell 'im to pee off!'

'I will, I will . . .'

'So are you and Zed swapping liquids yet? I still can't believe you both wound up in the same house by accident.'

'I'm not sure it *was* an accident, knowing my Aunt K. As far as liquid swapping goes, Juliet, you know it ain't basic like that.'

'Nothing basic about liquid exchange. It's how both of us got here and it's pretty bloody magnificent actually. And if you ain't swapping no liquids it's all just a brain strain anyway!'

'I've met someone else.'

It's only when I say it out loud that I realise it's something I've never said before.

'You,' she says, 'Eden Maria Jean-Baptiste, have *met* someone?'

'Stop milking it! But . . . yeah.'

'Migosh! That's immense! Don't waste any time do ya, you MINX!' She laughs and squeals in delight. I imagine the looks she must be getting from other travellers on the bus. 'What's he like?'

'He's . . . well, he's beautiful, Juliet. And strange. He plays lead in a band and he's really smart and profound and we understand each other.'

She sighs. 'I'm so happy to hear that, love. So happy.'

'Thank you.'

'Well, to go from the sublime to the ridiculous, your friend Dwayne poked me online a couple of days ago. He's trying to take me out. I pretty much think he's trying it with everyone at the moment, but it's cool.'

'Ugh! You're not gonna go, are you?'

'Why not? It's a free night out. Plus, me and you are different, you know,' she says. 'Very different. You're always looking for a bloody romantic hero, all windswept and troubled. The less accessible the better. I like 'em quiet, serviceable, and preferably a bit slow.' She raises her voice. 'Driver! Can't you see I rang the bell? Stop!'

'God, I really miss you, Juliet!' I laugh. 'And kebabs.'

'I've got to get off the bus with my bags, so gotta run. Go back to your Heathcliff. Make sure you call me soon though . . .'

'Juliet!'

'Yep?'

'I'm just wondering if . . . I mean. Do you think it's a problem that he's a friend of Zed's?'

Pause. 'Nope. Do for self, bella. That's the first rule.'

the obvious.

'Hey Brandy!' I catch her coming out of her room and she's once again cinched, painted and fragrant. 'The lady is back, huh?'

'Indeed,' she says. 'How you doing?'

'I'm good.'

'Evidently,' she laughs. 'That guy Spanish called for you a couple of times, by the way. What did you do to that boy?'

I shrug, embarrassed, smiling. I've hardly ever been in any kind of relationship long enough for it to go public. I'm not sure what face to wear. He's *mine* now?

'Don't be coy with me, sweetheart!' says Brandy. 'It doesn't suit you!'

'I don't know,' I say, answering truthfully. 'What time did he ring?'

'About an hour ago.'

'Cool, thanks. So where are you off to looking so pretty?'

'Violet fried some chicken for dinner so . . .' she smoothes her hair. 'I'm gonna go help her out with it, seeing as Eko only has five teeth.'

We laugh, standing in the hall. And I can smell it, the scent of fried chicken wafting down the stairs. And a cake, I think. My stomach roars audibly.

'That girl is a kitchen wizard,' I say, with a sheepish laugh. 'It's ridiculous.'

'Why don't you come? She's always cooking too much food anyway.'

Spanish can't hook up tonight, so I'm all alone. The invitation is too good to miss. 'She won't mind, will she?'

'No . . .' says Brandy with a soft smile. 'Of course not.'

'Well, you ain't gotta ask me twice. Lead the way, señorita.'

Upstairs, soul music is playing in the living room. TV on mute. 'Brandy!' says Violet, padding barefoot out of the kitchen. She's bright and fresh in a red tracksuit, her hair covered by the habitual baseball cap. 'And Eden! I guess everybody's in the mood for chicken. Zed's up here too.'

Too late to leave. I take a deep breath. Too late to make excuses.

'I told Eden you were cooking,' says Brandy, 'and honey, she almost tripped running up the steps!'

Violet laughs, pleased. 'Well you know you're always welcome!' she says and leads us through to the living room and the dining table. 'There's enough for everybody.'

Zed is kicking back in the armchair all dressed in blue, legs spread wide. He looks up when we enter the room but doesn't rise and doesn't look surprised to see me. He must have heard my voice in the hall.

'Hey y'all,' he says, an ironic Southern drawl. 'How ya'll doing?'

'Cool,' says Brandy, sounding more like Brandon. She clears her throat.

'Eden?'

'Can't complain,' I say carefully. It feels like high altitude up here with him. The air is thin.

'Alright! You guys ready to eat?' says Violet, speedily adding two plates to the dinner table. 'Stupid question, right?' she laughs. 'Look at your faces. Ya'll *look* hungry . . . especially you, Zed.'

She changes the music from soul to Fela Kuti and we all

take our seats. Violet loads our plates with food and Brandy talks about the weather.

'Getting hotter and hotter, isn't it?'

I steal a glance at Zed and he does look hungry. Hungry, lean and silent sitting there across the table. When his food lands in front of him, he sets into it with determination and doesn't look up from his plate.

'So you're a rapper?' Brandy says to Zed eventually. 'I heard you practising the other day.'

'Yeah, that was me.'

'Sounded like some good shit.'

'Really?' Zed replies, smiling. He rests his fork on the side of the plate. 'What you know about hip-hop, B? You don't seem like the type.'

'I know a lot! I'm into my M.O.P., my Big L, Wu Tang, some Jadakiss, Cam'ron . . .'

'Are you serious?'

'As taxes!'

'That's what's up!' Zed laughs, taking a big bite of potato salad. 'That's what's up.'

Brandy glows. 'Anybody tell you you look a bit like him?'

'Who?'

'Cam'ron!'

Zed turns sideways from the table and doubles over like he's choking. When he emerges, I realise that he's in gales of laughter.

'Ha ha! Cam'ron!' His eyes are narrow with mirth, his cheeks are high and I forgot my camera. This is what happens when I don't have it. I miss things. 'You sayin' I look like *Cam'ron*? That shit is *wild*!'

'It's definitely a compliment,' says Violet, smiling.

'As long as you don't think I rhyme like the dude, we cool,' says Zed, still laughing. And for a few moments we somehow luck into an atmosphere of complete ease.

Fela sings 'Water No Get No Enemy', and we eat our good, hot food.

'Your hair always looks so nice, Eden! You get it done again?' says Violet.

'No, I've actually,' I laugh self-consciously, 'I've been looking up some natural hair tips on the internet. Washing it with conditioner, which stops it from drying out. And then I set it in rods overnight.'

Violet sighs.

'I've been trying to convince Violet to go natural!' says Brandy.

'It's not for everybody, *Brandon*,' she says, a cloud going over her face. Suddenly all the ease is gone. She gets up from the table. 'Anybody want more chicken?'

'Look at you changing the subject again. Damn.' Brandy shakes her head, then turns to entreat us with her big, made-up eyes. 'She doesn't think she's pretty enough to pull off short hair, but she's beautiful. I don't know why she doesn't see it.'

We sit for a moment. Zed concentrates on his near-empty plate. 'You do have a beautiful face, Violet,' I say.

She sighs. 'I asked you people if you want more chicken. Better speak up or I'm gonna send ya'll back to your spot with your stomach growling.'

'No thanks, I'm full,' says Brandy, pushing her plate forward. She's the only one who's barely touched it.

Violet looks irritated and concerned. 'You see that? She buys all these groceries and then doesn't eat anything. You need to eat.'

'I'm fine, seriously.'

'No you're not.' She turns to me. 'Do you know where she's going after this? To do her show at Glitter Bar. And after that, to her customer service job. And after that, she's got classes at Brooklyn College!'

'Wow . . .' I look at Brandy. For the first time, I notice the greyness under the eyes.

Then Zed says, 'Well I ain't contributed anything but . . . if it helps I'm willing to have more chicken.'

The laughter is a bit louder than the joke deserves. Violet goes for more food for me and Zed and when she comes back, she also brings a container of food for Brandy.

'That's for later.'

'Thanks.'

Zed and I get a start on our seconds, racing each other to the finish line.

'Look after you,' says Violet to Brandy, 'that's all, OK? You give so much but you don't really look out for yourself and it's not fair.'

'Alright. But I'm lookin' out for my little homie, that's all. Eko's getting kinda big these days and I don't think baby food is gonna cut it.'

Violet smiles gently. 'So Zed, I still don't know where you fit . . . How you know Umi and Eden?'

He takes a sip of water. 'Aunt K grew up with my dad back in Saint Lucia. So we're almost like family. As for Eden,' he smiles crookedly, 'I'm an old friend. We go way back.'

'Really?' says Brandy, glancing at me.

'Yeah,' says Zed, 'although she seems to be more interested in new friends these days.'

Eko picks that moment to start crying, before looks of bemused curiosity have a chance to settle on Brandy's and Violet's faces. The doting mother rushes off to settle her son back down, and Zed changes the subject back to hip-hop.

When she returns we take our leave for the night and I can't figure out a viable reason why Zed and I should go down separately, but I'm scared to be alone with him. I don't know if he's amused or angry, if he cares or not. I can't see him clearly. I thank Violet and Brandy for the meal, eyes down. Zed does the same, except he jokes with them both, easy, expansive and charming.

'Now that is some crazy shit,' says Zed as we walk back down the stairs.

'What is?' I ask, walking ahead, heavy with food.

'We just crashed a romantic dinner.'

'What . . . Brandy and Violet?'

'Yeah, Brandy and Violet! Are you blind?'

'Come on . . . !'

'Eden,' he says as we land at the base of the steps, 'dress or no dress, your boy is feeling Ms Violet. You should learn to spot the obvious.'

'Wow.'

'So,' he says slowly, stopping outside his bedroom door. 'Spanish not coming around tonight?'

'No.' I swallow. 'Band practice.'

Zed nods. 'Don't get lonely, mama,' he says, closing his door.

wait—

Today I carried Angeline down to the river, Cherry Pepper, only moments from where she was born. She rode with me from town on a transport van that pulsed with Jamaican dancehall music. It made me laugh so much, thinking of how she would have hated it. How she would have complained at every bump and pothole in the road.

I walked through her slow, quiet village trying to see for her, how things had changed. 'We should have come back earlier,' I said to her, and I felt so deeply sorry. How could we have stayed away?

I sat on a rock, cradled by all the thick and singing green, and I spoke until I was empty. I gave her every detail of every injury, sting, scar. I said all the things I wished I could tell her when she was flesh. Fears, dreams and lovers. I retold all the jokes that had made us laugh, spinning loose from pain, restarting. I drew her close to me, Eden. I felt her breath on my neck, and even smelled the pressing oil she would use in her hair when I was a little girl. Then, when my voice had died and all I could hear was the birds and the easy current, slowly I emptied that Bounty Rum bottle over my hands and into the river. Slowly. Angeline running between my fingers, feathering the air, dissolving in the water. The sun turned her into gold. So light. And gone.

We should all be ash. We should all be a sprinkle of ash on the water.

Soon,

Aunt K

black sheep outreach.

Three days after our awkward consummation, I turn up at Spanish's place to find him looking far from serene.

'Shit,' he says, by way of greeting. His face is bloodless, poked around the front door.

'And a good afternoon to you too,' I say. Someone's in there, I can feel it. 'You gonna let me in?'

Of course this was gonna happen. I thought he was different and sincere but that would have contradicted everything I know about the puny, changeable nature of modern love.

He shuffles and grimaces.

'Spanish?' I say. Ready for whatever.

'Yeah. Sure,' he says, pulling open the front door. He scratches his scalp through the big hair and kisses me, hesitantly, on the cheek. 'Uhm. Come on.'

'What's up?'

He doesn't reply.

'Just tell me.'

He sighs. Shakes his head. Looks over my shoulder into the street. 'My . . . uh . . . my mother's visiting,' he says quietly. 'She just got here.'

I stop him, my hand on the cool skin of his forearm. 'Your what?'

'My mother. It's no big deal.' I don't move. 'It's no big deal,' he repeats.

I look down at my clothes, the short shorts and long socks and busted kicks. I can't believe this. I mean. His mother? 'You want me to come back another time? 'Cause—'

'No!' he says in a strong, desperate whisper. 'I want you. I want you here . . . I just. Come on, Eden. She's gonna wonder what the hell's going on down here.'

When we get to his living room, an expertly tanned and painted, platinum-highlighted blonde is sitting there. Cross-legged in modest khaki shorts and an ice white blouse. She looks nothing like her son. Spanish could be drawn entirely in charcoal. She's all polish and gloss.

'Mom,' says Spanish carefully, and she lifts her head and only the crow's feet in the corners of her eyes give her away as forty-plus. 'This is Eden.'

'What a lovely name! Hi Eden!' she replies, springing to her feet, the baby-girl voice slightly incongruous with her quietly aging face. 'I'm Margaret. How are you, my dear?'

'Hi,' I say nervously. 'Fine.'

'I brought over a great Chardonnay. Why don't you get her a glass, James?'

'No – that's alr—' I start.

'It's cool,' he says. 'I'll get you some.'

I sit on one of the random dining chairs – unattached to a table – scattered around Spanish's living room. James. His name is James.

'So is that an accent I detect, Eden?'

'Yeah, I'm from London.'

'Wow!' She raises her eyebrows at Spanish as he comes back into the room, like 'well done'. 'You're a long way from home! Are you on vacation?'

'Well. Sort of. I might be staying for a while.'

'That's great!' she says.

'What part of New York do you live in?' I ask.

'Oh no!' She wrinkles her nose. 'I live in Florida now, but I was in town so I thought I'd stop by for a visit. How do you like it here?'

'Not that different from home – just a little warmer.'

'You can say that again!' she giggles and pretends to faint. 'New York in the summer is hot as steak on a grill!'

I laugh politely. Spanish taps out a quick rhythm on the wall behind him and looks an uncomfortable combination of bored and anxious. She asks him: 'So how's the band?'

'Fine,' he replies.

'Had any gigs lately?'

'Yeah, a few.'

'You all are so talented. You really deserve all the breaks. I've made a scrapbook, you know! All of your press, and your reviews . . .' She eyes him expectantly. 'Corey now has it in his head that you're angry or that you hate him.'

'Then why,' says Spanish, quietly, tapping out that rhythm faster and faster, 'doesn't he call me?'

'Well . . . you know. There's the new baby and I'm sure he's tried. It's just that he—'

'Mom. Not today. I'm sick of getting these messages through you.'

'You're not that easy to get hold of.'

'I've had the same cell number for five years!'

'Yes, but it wouldn't hurt if you got in touch, James.'

'*Five years*, Mom! That's not enough time for him to give me a call if he's so friggin' concerned?'

'I know, I know! But they don't know if you want to speak to them or not. All I'm saying is it might be nice if you opened the lines of communication and got in touch with your brother and sister once in a while, James. They miss you.'

Spanish doesn't answer. He quiets his fingers but remains standing, as though he's waiting for her to leave.

'We all miss you. You don't even come round for the holidays.'

More nothing.

'James?' She fidgets with her outfit.

'Mom,' he says tightly, 'you always try this with me. I'm always the bad guy. They have my number. They have my address. You wanted to come see me and here you are. What the hell else do you want from me?'

I'm starting to wish he had just left me outside, or that he really did just have another chick up here. I sip my wine and examine the dirt under my nails.

'I'm only saying this because we all care about you, James, and you lock us out.'

'Stop lying! You locked *me* out, Mom. You all locked me out! Just like Dad.'

His mother's face crumples. 'You know that's not true!'

'What is this? The black sheep outreach service?'

'Unfair, James.' Fingers clutch around her cold glass. 'Unfair. I'm your mother. I treat you all the same. You're my firstborn!' Her eyes fill with water and I'm panicking. Want to get out of here. 'Don't you ever forget that! I've always supported you! I've always been there.' Her face grows more and more pink, and I realise how much she looks like Spanish after all. She arranges and rearranges the things on the crate-cum-coffee table. 'You're not a black sheep. You're not a stranger. You're my son, my family . . .'

'Mom. Look . . . OK. Just forget I said that. I'm sorry.' Then, with what seems a huge effort of will, Spanish peels himself from his position standing against the wall and goes to her, puts his arms around her. 'Just stop it with the emotional blackmail, OK? I'm gonna do what feels right and that's how it is. There's no point in me coming around just to be fake.'

'We want to see you because we love you.'

'OK Mom.'

'I mean it.'

'OK.'

'Good,' she says, as he releases her. 'There's no pressure . . . We just miss you. Do you understand that?'

'Yeah.'

'Well, don't forget.'

He nods, but he's looking at his toes and then at the clock on the wall.

'Look, Mom,' Spanish says gently, 'do you need me to take you anywhere? 'Cause I've got band practice . . .'

'Of course!' she replies. 'That's no problem. That's OK. My driver's outside. It's fine.'

She hugs and kisses us both like we're being shipped off for active military duty. 'James, I know I keep telling you this, but you really should just save your money instead of paying rent on this place. It was a gift. We don't need it. And we know you're trying to build your music career right now . . .'

'Mom,' Spanish warns. I look at him. An apartment as *a gift*? He doesn't look at me.

'Alright. Alright. I love you. You look really well, son.'

'Thanks.'

'You make sure he comes to see his mom sometime soon,' she says to me. 'You're welcome too. And if you guys wanna come by the hotel for dinner let me know. We're gonna be in town for another couple of weeks . . .'

I glance quickly between them, feeling more like a wife than a sort of unofficial girlfriend thing he's not even sure he wants. My palms sweat. I just met him.

'Yeah. I'll . . . uh,' I say. 'I'll try.'

fragile machinery.

A light tap on the door nudges me out of sleep and I'm saying 'Come in!' before I'm fully awake, just to stop the noise. There are footfalls, and then Zed's voice, catching me before I can fall back under the waves.

'Eden. Come on. Wake up.'

'Mrrrghh?'

'I brought you an icicle. You want it?' The voice, much too close, a hand brushing my hair back. That familiar paralysis. 'Eden. You want it?'

'What,' I say thickly. Body damp, mouth furry, head a purple throb. 'What you doing down here, Zed?'

'Take it or it's gonna melt,' he says and puts it in my hand. The shock of the cold goes right through me. I put it in my mouth without taking it out of the wrapper. Bliss. He gets up. The bed creaks.

'Wait.' I clear my throat. 'What time is it?'

'About twelve thirty.'

'You woke me up at *midnight* to give me an icicle?'

He stands there for a moment and I can barely see him but I can feel him. His presence is heavier than the heat or the darkness. 'I was bored upstairs; I didn't know you were already asleep. It's like an oven up there. I figured down here must be even worse, and I was right. That old broken-down fan ain't doing much.'

I sit up and switch on the lamp. There he is. I bite a hole in the wrapper and the icicle is cola flavour, syrupy-cool. Perfect.

'So what are you doing?' he says, looking down at me.

I suck my teeth. 'Sleeping! What did you think I was doing?'

Zed laughs. I laugh. 'You wanna sit down?'

He hesitates, sits lightly at the foot of the bed. 'Thanks for this,' I say, holding up his little frozen gift.

'No problem.'

'So . . .' I say quietly, but no coherent thought is forthcoming.

He gives me a long look and then says, 'You know, I think New York's been good for you.'

'How so?'

'You seem happier. I don't know . . . more like yourself.'

'You like the Brandy makeover then?' I laugh.

'Yeah, actually. Your hair suits you. I like the way you wear it natural like that. Looks good on you.'

'Thanks.'

'You're welcome.'

'You still seeing that girl?' I ask in a rush of bright confidence.

'No.' Silence. 'The job's keeping me pretty busy.'

'OK.'

'I think my mom is about to blow a fuse any minute though.' He laughs awkwardly. 'She like, "Boy! I did *not* put your ungrateful behind through college so you could serve drinks! You better *use* that education or I'm gonna get old school and slap it back outta your head!"' He snakes his neck back and forth and I laugh and it's so funny I almost pee, like when we were teenaged and he did impressions of the girl who served us at the local burger place. *May I take your aw-dah?* 'She's been convinced my whole life that I'm a genius, and right now she thinks I'm making a mockery of my God-given intelligence.'

'But you're using it,' I tell him, 'in your music.'

'Yeah, well,' he says, thinking. He looks at me. 'She had bigger ideas when I got accepted into the academy. She threw a party,' he leans across the bed. 'But I'd been top of the class all my life and now, suddenly, I had to work damn hard just to avoid being last.'

He shakes his head. I flashback to teenager-hood and how impressed I was by him. All I'd ever known at that point was the local Catholic Girls' Secondary back in Stoke Newington. Baggy opaque tights, big-mouthed girls, harassed teachers and home by four. I was moderately clever and moderately popular. I'd never tried hard at anything before in my life apart from maybe *not* trying and it seemed like most people I knew were exactly the same. Zed was different.

'It was crazy,' he says. 'For the first time I was surrounded by rich people. I thought they wouldn't have any problems, but in some ways the problems they had were worse, you know what I mean? Where I came from, circumstances fucked people up. These kids were all messed up on the inside. Empty, depressed and always looking for new ways to distract themselves. And I was one of those distractions. There were virtually no other black faces in or out of school. At best, I'd have kids come up and ask me what it's like to get shot, or if my family was on welfare. At worst I'd be walking around off campus and have grown men call me a nigger.'

'Are you kidding?' I say, feeling claustrophobic, the way I always feel talking about racism, the *small*ness of it. 'You were a child! Why would they do that?'

'A lot of shit in the world is hard to understand. Hatred is never rational.'

'What about Spanish? He says he went to your school.'

'He did,' Zed looks at me and away, 'but he's a little younger. He came in two years later. He wasn't there for my worst years, when I was trying to figure it all out.'

I shake my head. 'I can't believe that shit happened to you in the *nineties*.'

'Hell yeah,' he laughs. 'God bless America. I got to thinking about all of this meaning contained by my skin. People willing to love me or hate me, accept me or not 'cause of it, you know what I mean? Dudes who'd wanna beat me up on principle, or be like me. Girls – women even – who'd wanna fuck . . .' another quick glance, 'without knowing anything about me. It was crazy, man.'

His skin is so flawless, so even and rich in tone, some-times it's hard to believe he contains all the fragile machinery of life, all those spitting, churning, pounding organs. He could be solid all the way through like a wood carving. I can't imagine him ever getting old. Or dying. Maybe it's not a strange thing that people feel so strongly about skin like his. They look at him and see a distorted likeness. They don't see *in*. He's too beautiful.

'Did Spanish have to deal with all that racial abuse as well?'

'Spanish.' Zed smiles down at my bed sheet. 'Well. I dunno . . . He fit in more. I mean, let's be honest, his look is kind of ambiguous. He could be Latino, or Middle Eastern or even Mediterranean. It wasn't the same for him,' he shrugs. Gives me another long look that makes me nervous – or more nervous – and says, 'Anyway. Somebody threw a brick in the window at my house in boarding school.'

'Zed!'

'It had a piece of paper tied around it that read: *Go back to the projects, homie!* Those motherfuckers. Yep, that shit happened in the nineties.'

'Fuck,' I say. Wishing I wasn't sitting so close to him. Wishing I was closer. He takes a spliff out of his pocket and fiddles with it. Doesn't light it. Puts it back.

'Why did you do that?' he asks me. 'I don't understand you.'

'I don't know,' I tell him.

'I was shook when it happened, I can't lie. I was chilling and then *blam* . . . glass everywhere. Didn't know what the hell was going on. Then I ran to the window and saw your stupid ass. Just standing there. Not even running. Just looking confused and guilty as hell. I just wanna know what you were thinking!'

'I dunno,' I say, 'I dunno.'

He shakes his head, pinching and releasing my cotton bedspread. Pinch, release, pinch, release, between his long fingers.

'I'm sorry,' I tell him. The heat is thick.

'It's so ironic.'

'What?'

'Back when I was in school, they threw that brick because they hated me, or at least thought they did. And you . . .' he trails off.

We sit there for a while. I take my twisted hair out of the hair band and then put it back in again. After a moment I tell him that I'm kind of tired and need to sleep and thanks again for the icicle and maybe we can carry on this conversation tomorrow or whenever. And he says, 'Yeah . . . yeah, sure. I got to be up early for the studio anyway.'

Pops up like toast. Gathers himself. 'I like your T-shirt by the way,' he says. 'Looks familiar.'

The one I stole from him! Crap.

He smiles his crooked smile and leaves before I can apologise or explain.

cigarette in the bowl.

I wake up mid-morning to the poke and tickle of the abandoned icicle wrapper, hiding twisted among the sheets. I
fish it out and there's still a tiny amount of sugary liquid
left in the grooves of plastic. The taste of it still lingers in
my mouth. *Click*. Yet another thing that will always remind
me of Zed.

I swing out of bed and it dawns on me that the house
smells different. There's a tang of cigarette smoke in the air.
Disgusting. I haven't seen Zed light up a cancer stick since
he's been in New York. Plus, he must be late for the studio.
I step into my flip-flops and head up to quiz him on it.
Up the basement steps and out into the hall.

He's not in his room. I walk toward the front of the
house, thinking that he must be in a seriously funny mood
to start in on the fags. But then . . .

The jolt is terrible, like waking up with a cat on your
chest. She's wearing hot-pants and canvas boots and the only
sound is one rubber heel bouncing on the wooden step.

'Max! What the fuck . . . ?'

She starts, almost dropping her cigarette. 'EDEN! You
miserable bitch!' she says, looking me up and down in my
shortie pyjamas. 'What are you bloody doing here?'

'This,' I tell her, 'is my aunt's house.' And I just stand there.

'Oh right!' she says, visibly relaxing. 'That explains it then.
I didn't even know you'd left London. I've been trying to
call you, but it's not like you usually answer my calls anyway.'

'Bloody Max,' I say.

'So where is he, then?' She takes a deep pull on her fag.

I avoid the question. 'How long you been in New York?'

She sits down again and crosses her legs twice around each other. So complacent. She hasn't even asked about my aunt or if the woman minds people turning up unannounced and making her house smell like a pub garden. And how is she doing that with her legs? I have to try that just to see if it's a skinny thing.

'I got in this morning. I'm over here for a couple of go-sees and castings and a shoot starting in a few days. Apparently I've got a good look for the US. I don't know if it's my bag though, personally. The Americans are a bit plastic, you know what I mean?'

'I imagine that everyone in the fashion industry is a bit plastic.'

'Yeah . . . well.' Puff. 'So, you got no idea where Zed is?'

'No,' I lie.

'Well I'm sure he'll turn up soon, hey? I let him know I was coming.'

'How did you get in the house?'

'I checked under the mat.'

'Are you kidding?'

'Nope. I've got a lot going for me, but I can't bloody walk through walls. It's over there on the table. Looks like it might have been there for decades. Maybe your aunt forgot it was even there.' Puff. 'So what've you been up to, Eden? You sort out your mental problems?'

'Fuck off.'

'Dwayne says hello by the way.'

'He alright, is he?'

'Yep. Bit pissed he didn't get a chance to see you before you quit your job, though. Some of the people at work have been asking about you. I told 'em you ran off to join the circus. Hey, you got a drink? I'm boiling.'

I shake my head, looking at her. Are there hidden cameras or something? The hell? And why is it she didn't know I was here? I thought her and Zed were tight as batty and bench. I guess not, then.

'Yeah. Come on.'

In the kitchen I get us each a Coke and tip a desperately needed measure of rum in mine.

'So . . .' says Max with the most pathetically fake nonchalance I've ever seen. 'Zed . . . How's he been?'

'I dunno. OK I suppose.'

She nods, a fragile grin settling on her face. 'So he's been handling the medication OK?'

'What medication?'

'Well I know he's gotta be on tranquillisers or anti-depressants or somefing just to manage being without *moi*!'

That girl he fucked the other week. I don't know. Maybe she counts as an anti-depressant. Max puts out her cigarette in the bowl I use for cereal and goes to light another one.

'Bloody hell!'

'What?'

'It's disgusting how much you smoke.'

'Alright, alright. I'll give your baby pink lungs a break.' She puts it back in the packet.

'Yours must look like a couple of old, nasty teabags. Aren't you scared you're gonna die?'

'Everyone's gonna die, Eden. That's the only thing we know. We're born and then we die and that's it. What difference does it make whether we die aged fifty or eighty-five?'

'It'll matter when you're forty-nine,' I tell her and she shrugs and lights up a new cigarette. I guess the break is over.

The doorbell rings and her blue eyes go massive.

'Zed has a key,' I say, and walk out of the kitchen toward the mystery guest.

'Oh.'

I open the door and Spanish is on the other side of it. I smile reflexively, breathing properly for the first time since I discovered Max sitting in the front room.

'Look at you,' I say. His hair's pulled back into a big, soft, Afro puff. The slicked-back waves all over his head make him look even more like a Latin boy, but I don't say this. His clothes aren't ripped, frayed or faded like usual.

'I went to have breakfast with my mom and step-dad.'

'Bundle of laughs, right?'

'Yep,' he says darkly.

'Well, you're here now. So . . . hello,' I say.

'Hellooo . . .' he mimics in a bad British accent that tickles me. He kisses me in that zealous way he has. 'Damn! Have you been drinking?'

'So who's this then?' says Max, standing in the hall, puffing away.

'None of your bloody business but . . . Spanish, this is Max. Max, Spanish.'

'Heya!' she says.

Spanish gives her a grunt and a nod. After a few seconds she gets the hint and goes back in the kitchen.

'Who's the Barbie?' he says without whispering.

'Zed's girl.'

He raises one eyebrow and gives a cynical laugh. 'His girl?'

I shrug.

'Damn. If she was any whiter, she'd be dead! I guess it must be Christmas all year round for your boy.'

I laugh and he starts singing. 'Riding through the snow . . .'

'That's messed up,' I tell him.

We walk down to the kitchen and Spanish asks if I've got any food.

'Didn't you just eat?'

'Nothing substantial,' he shrugs. 'Plus that was a while ago now.'

Shocking. Seems like his ascetic lifestyle has gone the way of the tape player.

'You want a sandwich?'

'Yeah, cool. Don't know if I'll be able to taste it though. Smells like an ashtray in here,' he says with a nakedly contemptuous look at Max, her cigarette and bowl of ash. She puts it out with a grin.

While I'm slapping on the ham and cheese, he sniffs my drink. 'I can't believe you out here drinking this early in the day!'

'There's barely any rum in there at all,' I tell him. 'You've got a good nose.'

Max looks between us with a smile. 'So this is your new bloke is it?' she says to me.

'Yes,' says Spanish.

'You look pretty together! Spanish,' she says with sudden fervour. 'Have you ever thought of modelling? You've got amazing bones.'

I groan.

'That's what you do with yourself?' Spanish asks, flashing me a look.

'Yeah it is,' she preens.

'I honestly can't think of anything more demeaning or pointless.'

'Um, Max . . .' I intervene, 'Spanish is a musician. He fronts a rock band.'

'Really?' she replies sarcastically, tossing her hair. 'I didn't peg him for the moody artistic type.'

Spanish eats his sandwich. I stare at my rum and Coke and wonder if my drinking it will make me look like a lush. And Max fiddles compulsively with her packet of Marlboros.

'I was gonna have these later but . . .' He's polished off the sandwich in no time flat and now he's taken out a little bag of dry mushrooms. 'No time like the present. I think I need a break from reality right now, anyway, with the morning I've had.'

'Are you sure that's a good idea?' I ask. The past few days with him have been trip-free. I thought I was all the escape he needed. 'I don't think you're in the best mood for it.'

'Wow. The party's started in here, hasn't it?' says Max. 'I can't believe you had a go at me for smoking.'

'Number one,' Spanish holds up an index finger, 'you impose your nasty cigarette funk on everyone around you, while me taking this God's flesh is a *personal* choice and it's got *personal* consequences. Number two: you smoke 'cause you're an addict. I take mushrooms because I want to be involved in a communion with nature and reality.'

'Can I have some then?'

He cuts her a dirty look. I remember him out in the park the first time I saw him, a romantic little hippie with his guitar whom I could imagine saving insects and talking to flowers.

'You're gonna take those now?' I say.

'Tell you what. I won't if you give the sauce a break.'

'What?'

'Eden. It's not even noon yet,' he says. 'You're out of control.'

And he looks accusingly at me and Max, lumping us together. It's so unfair. Ten seconds ago he and I were on the same team and now he's better than both of us.

'Bloody hell! It's just one . . .' I sigh. 'So if I throw the rum down the sink, you'll forgo the "out of body"?'

'Yep.'

'Fine.' So I empty my glass.

'What about the bottle?'

'That's not fair! You didn't have to get rid of the mush-rooms!'

'No problem.' And he chucks the bag at Max.

'Are you serious?' she says, handling it carefully.

'Knock yourself out.'

'But this isn't even mine!' I lie, putting the bottle in the nearest cupboard. 'It's my aunt's!'

'Sorry. Too late. These are mine now,' says Max, stuffing the bag of mushrooms in her handbag.

And then Zed rolls through the door and I get the feeling the four of us together are gonna be a bad taste.

Trick Daddy Mack.

'What are you doing?' I say quietly, right into Spanish's ear. 'Stop it.'

'Tell me you don't like it,' he whispers.

'Not here!'

Spanish and I sit on the sofa in the living room, Max in the armchair, Zed on the floor, some new rap artist on the stereo. Spanish's quick fingers are in my knickers, rubbing me hard in the soft bits while he and Zed argue about music. Only a light print throw keeps my privates private.

'Spanish,' I say, trying to breathe evenly.

I hit him on the arm but he pretends he can't hear me over the music.

'Don't you think it's time,' Spanish says, his voice vibrating through my back and the sensations all rushing together, 'that we stop churning out this minstrel shit? This is why I fucking hate hip-hop these days. It's clown music.'

And his fingers speed up.

'Here we go,' says Zed, puffing on a zoot, 'with your judgemental ass. All people can do is talk about their own experience. Not everybody can be about wearing a fucking knitted hat and rapping about oppression.'

'You sound really stupid right now, man,' Spanish says all calm and furious behind me. 'Own experience? Most of these motherfuckers ain't lived it. They just talk about it. If you really lived it, you don't *want* to talk about it. All they do is play up to a stereotype so they can sell records. And they corrupt an entire generation in the process.'

256

'Spanish!' I say quietly.

He murmurs into my ear, 'We could have been alone, but you didn't want to so . . .'

'. . . Why the hell has a rapper gotta be a role model, anyway?' Zed is saying. 'It's bullshit. Every black man doesn't represent me in the same way that every white man isn't represented by Hannibal Lecter or Pee Wee Herman.'

'You know it's not the same for us! Black art is important . . .' And his fingers really hurt and I want him to stop but my body betrays me. Zed is right there. Right there. Not even three yards away. Damn, that's freaky. 'It's our biggest ideological defence in a culture that's destroying us!'

Tense. Rushing toward the sparks. Spanish still smells of that cologne. Zed's voice is chocolatey. I hit the wall and see nothing. Hear nothing. Release and contract. Flutter down like a feather.

'STOP IT!' I say more loudly than I intend to, eyes closed. I hear Spanish chuckle as he finally does what I say.

'You alright, Eden? It's cool. Just a little discussion,' says Zed.

'Yeah.' I open my eyes and my voice shakes a bit. There's sweat on Zed's dark forehead. 'Yeah. Just . . . well I think you're both right.'

'Whatever you say, dear,' says Spanish. He discreetly slips his hand from under the throw. Pats my shoulder. Then he reaches over to get some tortilla chips from the bowl we're all sharing. 'Want some?'

'No.' I get up, fixing my clothes in the process. I grab the bowl, Spanish stops me, holding it on the table, staring me down.

'I'm gonna get some fresh ones,' I say. 'These ones have been out for ages. They're starting to get soft.'

'They're fine . . .'

'I'm taking them!' I say, and pull the bowl. It goes flying and there are tortillas all over the floor.

'Sorry,' says Spanish, 'let me . . .'

'I'll do it,' I say.

'Eden . . .'

'I'll do it!'

Eventually it gets weird for them to sit in silence, watching me pick the floor clean of snacks, so Spanish tells Zed that black people need to take their art more seriously because we are marginalised as a people. And Zed says that if everybody took responsibility for their own family, then maybe we wouldn't be relying on Trick Daddy Mack to set an example.

'It's not a fucking joke!' yells Spanish. 'I'm so sick of nobody taking responsibility for what's happening in our culture. We have the power to really affect the next generation.'

Zed rolls his eyes and shakes his head. 'Parental responsibility, man . . .'

'Alright,' says Spanish with a sudden, devious smile. 'Alright, my *brother*. If you're so laissez damn faire about the whole situation, why did you leave your crew?'

'Spanish, we ain't gotta talk about that, man . . .'

'It's valid, ain't it? Look, there you were with a damn good deal, thousands of dollars on the table, and you walk. Leave your crew, your management, your label and bounce to Europe. Doesn't make no sense unless your ass had a crisis of conscience.'

'Zed?' I say, confused. 'I thought you said things weren't working out with your crew and that's why you left and came to London?'

'It's 'cause you couldn't live with yourself being a fake-ass gangster! Tell the truth . . .'

Zed looks studiously away from me, his movements caged, frustrated. 'I just wanted to get back to myself, that's all, the best part of me. I was getting lost.' His eyes find me. 'I forgot.'

'Then why,' says Spanish, still on a swell of being right, 'is your material different now? Last year you were rhyming about shanking niggas, shooting niggas, robbing, pimping . . .'

'I wasn't, man!'

'You, ya crew . . . same thing! It's all on the same track, same record! But nowadays you all talking about love and the universe and shit.' Spanish laughs cruelly. 'You're sitting up here saying artists ain't gotta be role models, but you straight up left a lucrative deal with a *major label* because you couldn't sleep at night.'

'You're right. I couldn't,' says Zed. His gaze lights on me and then away.

'Zed . . .' I start, before Max barrels in with, 'Yeah, well I just think it's all a bunch of bollocks! People are people. If we all just got over ourselves, the world would be a better place. We're all mixed anyway. Especially you, Spanish. Yeah, this music is bloody stupid sometimes, but everyone knows that all black guys don't sit around all day in gold chains talking about money and women . . .'

'What the hell do you know, Snow White?' spits Spanish. 'You can afford to think that way because everything is geared towards you. Have you ever had to search stores for products to suit your hair and skin? Or for magazines that represent you? Until you have, you'll never understand!'

Zed looks at the ground. I can see he's not listening anymore.

'Come on! It's bloody modern times, Spanish! You can find whatever you want. Eden, tell your ignorant boyfriend what it's like living in the twenty-first century!'

'I'm ignorant?' Spanish stands up. 'I'm fucking ignorant? You're one of those blind, deaf and dumb white people who'll believe anything just so they can live a guilt-free life!' I grab him by the arm.

'Shut up, Max,' I say, suddenly fed up of her stupid head.

She ruined everything by coming here. 'You don't know what you're talking about! So just butt out of the discussion.'

'What? Just 'cause I'm white?'

'No. 'Cause you're a moron, that's why!'

'What? Are you jealous or somefing?'

'Fuck off.'

'You know what your problem is?' she says. 'You're a bloody fake! Sitting around here with him,' she points at Spanish with her chin, 'when—'

'OK, OK, OK,' says Zed, 'it's getting way too hype in here, man. Just chill the fuck *out*!'

'There are stereotypes about everybody!' Max says with a red spot flowering on each cheek and eyes glistening. 'Everybody gets judged. People think I'm dumb 'cause I'm blonde and skinny and women hate me. They all hate me straight away before I've said anything. They assume I'm a gold digger or stuck up or whatever and they don't even listen . . .'

'Man this is killing my high,' says Zed. 'Max, can you relax, please?'

'I can't believe,' I tell her, 'you'd try and equate the problems of an entire race to you and your petty problems! Give me a break! None of that shit will ever be a barrier to you—'

'Oy! Don't you dare sit there and judge my problems, mate! You've got no bloody idea! All the bloody fucking bookers, they're like, you don't look different enough! You're not edgy enough, exotic enough! You're too fucking fat! ME! *Fat*?'

'SHUT UP, Max!' I say. 'Nobody wants to hear it, OK? Shut your fucking mouth. You are arrogant as hell if you think that everyone's supposed to want you or like you! That's exactly what I was talking about because—'

And then we both gasp and jump up in the air because Zed's thrown half a jug of ice-water on us.

'You prick!' yells Max, wiping her face. I begin laughing and can't stop, every emotion rushing out of me in giggles and snorts. Water runs down my face. My hair is ruined. Zed starts to laugh as well. 'I'm sorry y'all,' he says.

'Eden,' says Spanish. 'We getting outta here, man.'

'You still coming to J'Ouvert with us though, right?' Zed says to me. 'You been talking about it all summer.'

'Yeah, definitely,' I say, despite Spanish's audible disapproval.

'Man, fuck juvay or whatever it's called! Let's go, woman.'

freedom.

'What the hell is wrong with you?' I ask Spanish, struggling to catch up with his quick pace. I've never seen him walk fast before.

'Nothing. I've just been sitting in a hot, un-air-conditioned house in midsummer with a couple of assholes for two or three hours. No big damn deal.'

'I thought you didn't get hot?'

'Have,' he stops, 'you seen me fasting lately?'

I say nothing. He turns back round and starts walking toward the van.

'Where are we going?'

'Shit! I don't know! Just have a coffee or watch a film or whatever it is that people do to kill time between fucking.'

'You're crazy,' I tell him, resigned. I can't go back now anyway. I don't want to. I couldn't breathe. He takes my hand in his, then lets go. Drapes his arm around my shoulder, my neck.

'Crazy about *you*,' he says.

And out here, Brooklyn is getting ready for a party, singing naked in front of the mirror, brushing her hair, glittering. You can feel it. All the radios are singing out with soca, calypso, zouk, cadasse, reggae, bashment. You can feel the carnival coming, feel it in your hips. *J'Ouvert. Dimanche gras.* Fat Sunday, the night before the Labor Day parade. There are more people out on the streets than usual, standing or sitting around in clumps, doing all those things city-dwellers do. Buying and selling, telling jokes, telling lies, suffering, surviving. Tomorrow, summer will be over. Tonight they won't sleep.

Spanish and I jump in the van and go to Fort Greene, a bistro on DeKalb Avenue. We frown and sigh at each other, and hold hands. We order posh burgers with 'pomme-frites' instead of fries.

He stares at me while we wait for the food. 'You are so gorgeous,' he says.

I smile. Who can be mad at that? 'Thank you.'

'All of creation is gorgeous tonight,' he sighs. 'Especially now I'm away from Tweedle-dee and Tweedle-dum back in Flatbush.'

I shake my head and laugh and try not to think about Zed and all that newly disclosed drama about his record deal. I don't understand him.

'You know, I think I'm starting to understand why you take mushrooms,' I say to Spanish. 'Trying to break the world open, right?'

'Yeah. Yeah, I guess.'

'It's like the world is so small these days. And you kind of think, there must be more to it all. You can sense it, but can't see it 'cause we live in a world where we supposedly can explain everything but the truth is, we can't explain *anything*. Not really. You have to try and break the world open a little bit otherwise life is just a parade of commercial breaks and one dumb aimless relationship after another and a job you're doing just for the money.'

'The big "why", huh?' he grins. 'Well, maybe it's hard to be a human, period, but right now it's harder to be a black human because we've bought into so many of the boxes people have made for us.'

'TVs and coffins,' I say as a waiter comes outside to the table with one beefburger for Spanish and a salmon burger for me.

He laughs and takes a bite. 'Exactly! Mmm . . . this is good. Damn, girl! I can't believe you not only got me eating additives, you got me eating *meat*.' He gives me a glance that's half fond and half accusatory. I realise that it's always likely to be that way with him. He's grateful and angry, as if I broke his legs and then bought him a wheelchair.

'I haven't got you doing anything!' I say, wiping ketchup off my fingers. 'You're a grown-up.'

He looks right into me, seeming to pick up on my irritation. 'You're right,' he says. 'You're right.' Then suddenly, 'Eden . . . I'm really sorry about the other day with my mom. It must have been really awkward for you.'

'No, really, don't worry.'

'I just don't get it.' He shakes his head. 'These people who are supposed to be my *family* . . . They got nothing to do with me! You know what I mean? We have nothing to do with each other. It's not like I'm the only mixed kid in the universe, you know?' A thin laugh. 'Damn, it's not unusual. Maybe it's 'cause these people are just plain fucked up.'

'But your mom obviously loves you to pieces, Spanish. She came to see you! She keeps a scrapbook. Not to mention the fact that she bought you the apartment. That doesn't look so fucked up from where I'm standing.'

'It's actually the whole house. The guy downstairs is my tenant.'

I raise my eyebrows.

'It ain't shit though. She's married to this big-shot lawyer guy now and money isn't an issue. Buying that old house in Bed-Stuy was like spending five dollars to him. Now they don't have to feel guilty *and* they made a solid investment.' He's quiet for a moment. 'Do you know how long it's been since I spoke to my real father?'

I wait.

'Seven years, ma.'

'Damn.'

'And even then, I had to track him down. He's never remembered my birthday in his life. He never made it to my high school or college graduation. I only ever really got her to tell me the story one time, about how they met in high school and he kept asking her out until she said yes, then got her pregnant in their senior year. It's really funny how she says that, he got her pregnant. Like she wasn't even there at the time,' he laughs. 'Oldest story ever told. Her family rejected her because she was carrying a little black kid, and apparently my father's family wouldn't really accept her either. So it was tough for them. My dad started dealing drugs, got caught when I was two years old. He went to prison for three years.'

'God.'

'When he came out, he wanted nothing to do with us.'

I clear my throat. 'Why?'

''Cause he'd started studying in jail, joined the Nation of Islam. He told my mother he realised she was a mistake, a product of his ignorance. Yeah, he'd send money now and again when I was growing up, but he stayed away.

'He's remarried now with a black woman and four children – my brothers and sisters – that I've never met. Fuckin' ironic ain't it? I bet I'm the most pro-black child the bastard ever had. I can't remember my parents ever being together. It's like they just made me and then came back to their senses.'

'Spanish,' I say. 'Came back to their senses? Why would you say that? Sometimes shit just doesn't work. It doesn't mean you're a mistake. How can you believe what you believe and say that? Even if they didn't plan you, somebody did. Maybe you even planned yourself.'

When I finally reach over, the tips of my fingers barely

graze his curls and he sighs deeply and once again I feel like he needs earth, an anchor . . . and I want to tell him that I have a problem even holding onto myself most of the time. We eat our food in a companionable silence for a while, watching people walk by.

And then his posture changes completely and I follow his gaze to a group of young men standing by the door to the cafe. 'Pretty, isn't she?' he says to them with cartoonish suddenness. The vibe is instantly sour. His eyebrows are low, his jaw hard.

'Spanish!' All the breath leaves my body.

'Excuse me?' says a man with floppy blond hair. His friends all give each other confused looks and beer-slack grins. 'Are you talking to me?'

'You see something you like, white boy? I asked you a fucking question.'

'I don't know what you're talking about, man.'

'Do,' Spanish enunciates carefully, 'you *see*. Something. You like? What? You thought I didn't see you staring at my girl-friend?'

'Spanish,' I hiss. 'Please . . .'

'Dude, you need to relax,' says another guy in a polo shirt and a cap.

Spanish stands up, shaking my hand off his arm. 'I am relaxed. When I'm not relaxed you gon' fucking know about it. I'm just letting you know I saw your ass.'

'Come on,' says someone else from the group. 'Forget this shit, man. Let's get out of here. There aren't any free tables, anyway.'

'Yeah, that's right,' says Spanish, staring them all down like he can take them by himself. 'Get the fuck out of here.'

I look down at my hands as they file past our table, too embarrassed to look up. I don't until they're several yards away. Faintly I hear them arguing. A hot-head in the group thinks Spanish should have got jumped on.

'Spanish! What the hell was that? I can't believe what just happened . . .'

'They were fucking disrespectful, man! I hate what's happening to Fort Greene nowadays! A bunch of white-bread yuppies just move on into the area and think they run shit! Start looking at black people all crazy . . .'

'I didn't see them look at me! And even if they did, so what? I'm with you, right? We're eating dinner and you lose it because somebody *looked* at me? Why would you act like that? Maybe you really shouldn't eat additives anymore.'

'Maybe you shouldn't wear that dress.'

'You liked this dress earlier.'

'Yeah, well that was different.'

I put down my knife and fork. 'I'm heading back to my aunt's house to get ready for J'Ouvert.'

Spanish shakes his head, sets his jaw ready to say something.

'I'm heading back,' I tell him. 'You can either drive me back, or you can stay here with the yuppies. Your choice.'

splat.

I remember a conversation I had with Dominic one humid
night he came over to my aunt's house, looking for my
mum. We'd grown quite close in the weeks since I'd been
in New York. Dominic bought Zed and I lunch a few times,
helped us cover for a night out at a club and, to top it off,
got Zed some work experience at a recording studio. He
was our favourite adult, and the only one who really knew
how much I loved Zed. I'd never met anyone like him
before.

On that particular night, Zed was out with some of his
guy friends in Harlem and I was bored. I wandered away
from the TV and outside to where he was sitting in the
back yard, wrapping up what seemed like a fairly heated
phone conversation with my mum. He hung up and stared
at the phone like he wanted to smash it, then put it in his
pocket.

The sun was beginning to fade orange and I looked over,
struck by his profile. My mother being with a man like that
made her different somehow. Even less motherly. He was
like the Love Interest in movies, a leading man and not just
The Dad character like my father was.

'Love is strange,' he said.

I didn't want to interrupt straight away because it didn't
feel like he was even speaking to me. But eventually he
swung his face around and smiled at me like he heard all
my hormone-ridden thoughts about Zed and understood.
He had an understanding face. I smiled back and didn't say

anything. I didn't know anything about love apart from the fact I was in it.

'It can drive you crazy if you don't manage it the right way, you know, Eden?' he said. 'It's like you wanna just,' he squinted into the sky, 'freeze this moment that makes you so happy, but you can't. You can't own it because the feeling is a person. And you can't own a person, can you?'

It sounded like a real question. 'No?' I said.

'No,' he confirmed. 'But how do you keep from either walking away or locking them in a room with you for ever? How do you live with so much uncertainty? It's like your heart grows legs, climbs out of your body and goes walking about on its own. In traffic!'

He made a little walking gesture on his knee with two fingers and I laughed, because he was saying all of this with a very light tone. And being a particularly self-obsessed teenager, I was just thinking about me and Zed, and about how, yeah . . .

'That's exactly how it feels.'

'It's just not safe,' he said. 'One day, it's bound to happen . . .'

'What?'

'SPLAT!' he replied.

mollases.

It's a lawless night.

Out in the streets we clot together like blood in a scab, all conflict suspended. The underworld has flooded Flatbush Avenue; an urban purgatory populated by calypso zombies and devils. On one side I hold Zed's hand, in the other Spanish's. One has a light, caressing touch, the other's is tight and steady. Both Max and Spanish have one hand swinging free. There are no more arguments out here. Even if we did argue, we wouldn't be able to hear ourselves over the drums and the steel pan, the shouts of the revellers. The music overwhelms our thoughts, the night infects us. We are surrounded by a parade of the undead, all coasted in layers of coloured mud and flour, as are we. All of us grey. All of us a little like The Woman in the clip frame. The men wear their clothes baggy and hide their faces behind rags, eyes shining in the streetlights. The women wear very little regard-less of their build or age, squeezing into cut-off shorts and bra tops and tanks in army patterns or in the colours of their particular Caribbean flag. They shake and jiggle that flesh; stretch marks, love handles, cellulite and all. They apolo-gise for nothing. They wind their bodies down to the floor in moves that simulate the kind of sex that could make a grown man cry and the kind of hips to make babies pop right out like champagne corks.

We hold tight to each other because if we let go, we don't know if we'd be able to recognise each other anymore. There's a feeling that if you got lost here, you'd be lost for ever.

We dance, we laugh. We drink, all of us, from the same bottle of mineral water. I begin marching in time too, letting my hips roll with the music, overwhelmed by all the noise and all the voices. I shout the words of the songs I know.

J'Ouvert. Daybreak. The youngest descendant of *canboulay* where ex-slaves celebrated the end of their bondage with satire, bacchanal, and masquerade. A dark tide rushing and pooling before the dawn, revelling in their freedom. But there is no sign of the sun yet. A half-naked man emerges amongst the wild crowds, slathered in tar, wearing very convincing horns and wielding a pitchfork. He dances uncontrollably while women dressed as red imps constrain him with chains. *Jab mollasie*. A mollases devil, so finely rendered he might be the real thing pretending to be a man pretending to be a thing. I giggle and scream and clutch at Spanish and Zed, feeling transported.

'This is bloody amazing!' I scream, but can barely hear my own voice. Some hard, fast soca comes over the sound system.

'Come on! Shake that ass, girl!' says Zed in my ear. He's smiling wide, dancing like a true island boy in the hot crush of people. Splashed in green paint and flour, a grinning *jab jab*. 'That's the best you can do? You need some snake oil, baby girl!' And then both of his hands are on my hips, and he is close behind me, breathing on my neck, gyrating, pushing up on me, smelling the way he smells. My hand slips out of Spanish's hand and I whirl about. Anything goes. Anything is permissible here.

I watch Max do her stripper dance all over Spanish, backing up her skinny little bumper. He scoops some mud out of a passing bucket and dumps it in her hair.

'You wanker!' she shouts.

Zed's hands slide up and down my waist, over my hips and my ribs. I try to sing along with the tune but no sound emerges. It's the way it always is when he touches me. He's hard through his trousers.

'Can I keep you?' he says right into my ear, and my heart clangs and turns over like a tired engine. My body is a mass of tingles. I'm singing between the thighs. I'm about to turn round to face him when the first cloud breaks. A few large drops of rain splashing down on our hot faces. It could be tears on his cheeks. A light veil of drizzle sprinkles the crowd. A few rivulets running down over tattooed biceps, between pushed-up bosoms, standing in our hair. Wet bodies push together.

And then, in a single, shuddering moment, the sky empties itself all over us.

Spanish grabs my hand hard and we swear and try to find a way out of the mêlée but everyone running means no one gets anywhere. Soon we're all soaked to the bone and completely clean of flour, make-up, paint or sweat. The crowds knot and heave. Thunder starts and it's louder than the music. Lightning flashes across the dawn-ripe sky and the panic escalates. Being struck by a stray bolt of lightning may not happen often but it's possible and that's enough for most.

'Come on!' says Zed, trying to push through to a kerb where people seem to be moving successfully. His slippery fingers tangling with mine.

'This way!' contradicts Spanish, moving in an opposite direction. The crowds swirl between us and carry me in a third direction.

'Zed!' I yell but my voice is swallowed in all the noise.

'Where's he gone?' screams Max in my ear, and I realise that we've managed to hold onto each other. Soon we can't even remember where we were, and both Spanish and Zed have vanished.

Eventually, after several loud minutes of rain thundering down and running people shouting at each other, we find ourselves shivering, beached on the kerb. It doesn't feel like there was ever a party. A riot, maybe. The streets have regained their edge, the music has faded, rain is still falling.

Max and I begin looking for the guys amidst falling temperatures and ex-revellers who now just look like strangers. Scary ones.

A fight starts amongst some stragglers across the road, one group of men squaring up against another. Far away but not far enough away for comfort we hear a loud POP POP POP.

'Fuck this,' I say, grab her hand and start running.

'Where are we going?' Max shouts, breathing hard, hair and rain in her face.

'Home.'

'Are you mad?'

'Madder . . .' I say, struggling to breathe, 'to stick around here!'

'Eden! Hang about . . .'

'Race you!'

We charge down the dim streets as fast as we can, dodging tired, soggy people. Doesn't feel like much can happen to you when you're running. And we are too fast for the cold. The sight of our mad dash is enough to elicit cheers from groups of men walking home or back to their cars, but they're part of the reason why we're running so we ignore them. We don't stop until my chest burns and my feet are sore. I can't go any further. Max whizzes past me, carried along about three steps by her momentum, and then comes back to stand next to me.

'Oh my God!' she pants, cheeks close to fluorescent pink. 'You have mental issues! I almost . . . I almost died, mate!'

'I think I did!' I croak. 'Is this hell?'

We look into each other's ravaged faces and crack up laughing, hands on our knees, struggling to catch our breath.

'Look,' says Max when she can speak. 'Should we go in there for a minute? Warm up before the rest of our walk home? I think I might have a stroke if I don't sit down!' We're standing in the window glow of what looks to be a little Caribbean takeaway.

'You got any milk?' I ask her, channelling Juliet.

'What?'

'Milk and honey, girl, dinero . . .'

'Oh right! Yeah, come on.'

Inside the joint is decorated in a tropical theme, with a wooden bar painted turquoise and walls hung with seascapes and faded calendars advertising Bounty Rum. It's much warmer than outside; still feels like summer in here. A small, brown-skinned man with freckles and rust-coloured hair greets us when we come in.

'Good morning, ladies,' he says.

'Hey . . .' But then I don't say anything more to him because: 'Oh my God! Aunt K!'

how to act.

'When did you get back?' I say, loud with surprise. What are the odds of catching her like this at five thirty in the morning in a random West Indian takeaway eating a Jamaican pattie? I don't know how to feel. 'What are you doing here?'

Aunt K smiles and finishes chewing. 'A-a!' she laughs. 'You think I'm too old for J'Ouvert?' She doesn't look too old for anything, except maybe foolishness. Her long multi-coloured dress is cinched in the waist with a copper belt. Copper sandals peep out from the hem. Her skin is smooth and shiny, glowing from the sun; her locs tumble free to the middle of her back, snaked with purple.

'Of course not,' I say, shivering, 'I'm just surprised to see you. You didn't say when you were coming back . . . So. Um. Anyway, Aunt K, this is Max.'

Max looks petrified. 'Maxine,' she expands.

'Nice to meet you, Maxine,' smiles Aunt K. 'You guys look like you've been through a couple of civil wars.'

'It was fine,' I say.

'It was great until the storm ruined it!' bubbles Maxine. 'We lost Zed and Spanish. I don't know what happened. It was supposed to be dry today.'

Aunt K snorts, 'These weather people know nothing! They just want you to think they know, which is almost as powerful.' She brushes the crumbs off her hands and takes a sip of her drink. 'Don't worry about the boys. They'll be OK. You girls should have a ginger tea, then I'll give you a ride home. Alright?'

We thank her and gratefully sit down. 'Russell!' she says to the man behind the counter. 'Can we have two ginger teas with lemon, and two slices of carrot cake, please?' Then she turns to us and says, 'I'm having a party at the house tonight, so invite your little friends.'

'Really?' I say, even though I'm quite profoundly partied out.

'Yes really. Ask everyone to come.'

I turn to look out of the window. Across the street, Zed is looking anxiously one way, Spanish the other.

'We're here, you pillocks!' screeches Maxine, rushing outside the cafe. I watch until her performance is mute beyond the glass; she throws her hands in the air a few times and puts her hands on her hips. I wait. I haven't figured how to act yet. I don't know what face to put on. Moments later, she's dragged them into the shop.

'What the hell were you doing, leaving us like that!' she's saying to them as they come through the door. 'We were scared.'

Spanish makes a doomed attempt to straighten up his muddy, wrinkled clothes and frizzed-out curls. 'Doesn't that woman of yours ever shut her big mouth?' says Spanish, coming straight for me.

'Yeah, shut the fuck up, woman,' says Zed angrily. 'I was looking everywhere for you.' And when he says 'you' his eyes are on me. *Can I keep you?*

'Zed,' says Aunt K.

He jumps out of his skin. 'Oh God! Aunt K! Shit! I mean, I'm sorry for my language! Damn!' he gives up and laughs.

Aunt K smiles. 'So you guys made it back to civilisation.'

'Yeah we did! Thank God. You look good, Aunt K. I like your hair.'

'Thanks. Them Lucian girls can twist some locs!'

'Good trip?'

'Very good,' she says. 'It was the right place at the right time. But,' she kisses her teeth, 'what were you doing, Zed, not taking care of these girls here? They came running in this place like hell was chasing them!'

'It was crazy out there . . .'

'Circumstance doesn't make the man! They only reveal him to himself. *As A Man Thinketh* by James Allen,' she snaps. 'Read it! Anyway, let's get back to the house. We have a party to get ready for.'

no sound.

On the subway with Zed from Harlem to Brooklyn, I was still tingling, tingling and sore, and proud because my first time was beautiful and I was in love.

Ten years ago, almost to the day. We walked up the street to Aunt K's house hand in hand. My mother and Dominic were taking me, Zed, Uncle Paul and Aunt K out that night for a meal at a nearby restaurant. We were almost an hour late and breezily unrepentant.

'Eden. Baby girl. You OK?'

Zed put his arm around me. I looked up at him and smiled but suddenly I felt weird. I thought I was just nervous after what had happened, or because we were late, or because we were bound to get in trouble. But maybe I felt a note of discord, the way animals do before a storm.

'Come on,' he said, smiling in that cute, crooked way, pushing me playfully. 'We cool. We can just say we, uh, lost track of time. Playing video games or whatever.'

I pushed him back and returned the grin, but my face was inexplicably tight. Zed went through the door first, using my key. I liked how strong he was, not sheepish at all.

'Hello?' he called up the stairs. There was no answer so we went and sat on the couch. After a moment of silent grimacing, he said: 'Uh-oh. I hope this doesn't mean they went out looking for us.'

Suddenly I noticed my mother's favourite, delicate little gold sandals capsized on the rug. She was there?

'Zed . . .' I pointed. Gave him a puzzled look. A light was flashing on the answering machine and sneakily I checked it, hoping it wasn't a message about us. It was Aunt K, calling to say she'd got held up at work and couldn't make it to dinner.

When I hung up the phone, I noticed a scrap of something poking out from under the couch, between Zed's white Air Jordans. He followed my gaze and looked down, pulled a face halfway between glee and disgust. He took the scrap of fabric between his fingers, a black lacy thong, dropped it like it was an oversized bug. Then I noticed the half-empty glasses on the coffee table, my mother's handbag flung in the corner, overflowing with its ever-present junk. *Oh*, I thought, blushing but also faintly triumphant because I was part of the club now. *Dominic must be here.*

I stood up. Zed had an odd look on his face. I wasn't sure what to do. 'Mum?' I shouted out. Nothing. Something was very wrong. Fair enough, it was all very *nudge nudge wink wink* but the room felt cold. It didn't feel like people had been here recently, stirring each other, wanting each other. The handbag could've sat there for a hundred years.

'Mum?'

They would have heard the door slam shut the way Zed is always banging it. They would have tried some kind of damage control. My mother would have rushed down the stairs, smiling as though we all shared a secret. Her act would be casual but she would have one. I'd seen that look before, that sly sheen in her eye. It said, *What can I do? I can't help it that I'm so damned sexy.*

But there was no sound, and no amused little jog down the stairs. Nothing. A few scenarios flashed through my head. I knew that my mum could be pretty random; maybe her and Dominic had taken off in his car somewhere. Maybe there'd been some kind of emergency and they'd had to leave suddenly.

I walked up the stairs calling out for her. 'Mum?' All the rooms on the second floor were empty. I began smiling, remembering what it was like to be wrapped up in somebody, tangled in somebody. You forget about the world. She probably just didn't hear us come in, that's all. I was just being paranoid. I giggled and felt ill. I really didn't want to catch my mum right in the middle of . . . *Yuck.*

So I called out over and over to warn her I was in the house. And eventually I came to the only door that was closed. I knocked. 'Mum?' I waited. No sound.

purple and gold.

People start arriving at the house at quarter to ten, which is borderline miraculous. It's Labor Day and there must be parties everywhere, but it seems like ours is everybody's first stop. 'Oh hey, Eden!' Zahara says at the door, showing off her pearlies. 'And Spanish?!' At the sight of him, her eyebrows shoot almost all the way into her hairline, which is a long way. 'What's up?'

She introduces us to a few girls at the door, eyeing us all the while. It occurs to me that there have probably been quite a few bets on who was gonna break Spanish of his 'fast'. They give us alcohol and kiss us on both cheeks, commenting on our impressively big hair.

'Y'all could supply weaves to the entire population of Brooklyn!'

We laugh, Spanish and I. But our laughter feels hollow. Ever since we met Aunt K, I've tried to stay close to Spanish but all the time my body knows where Zed is, can sense his every move. I feel off-key, drunk behind the wheel.

Zed says hello and introduces Max, and in the midst of all these brown-shaded girls Max has never looked blonder.

'Hi!' they all say, silkily. *Zed likes white girls?* That old reprise.

'Don't worry,' says Max, popping some gum in her mouth. 'I'm just light-skinned.'

A ripple of tentative laughter flits around the hallway. 'You've been practising that line in your head since this morning, haven't you?' I whisper.

'No!' she replies. Then: 'Yeah. OK. I got it from a film.'

The doorbell rings just as everyone is rooting for something else to say. Zed rushes off to answer it.

'Bleak! Thanks for coming down, man, what's good?'

'What up, what up, what UP! Greetings and well wishes, my people,' he says, walking through into the crowded hall, always loose, always chilled. He hands me a container of food. 'That,' he says, 'is the best curry goat you will ever taste, lady girl.'

'He ain't lyin'!' says Zahara.

Then Zed gathers and leads us up the stairs, and I can't breathe as I'm carried along with the chattering mob right up and up and up to the top floor where I've not been in a decade. Hold firm. Make no sudden moves. The past is the past.

When I get there though, the place is unrecognisable. Aunt K has decorated her living room in purple and gold. Bright silk drapes and fairy lights sweeten the windows. It's a large room, but even so there's barely enough space to turn around. Everybody is here, it seems. Violet, Eko and Baba sit on floor cushions. Arty types lean against the walls wearing head wraps and multi-coloured bead necklaces. There are a couple of baseball cap-wearing teenagers and a woman in a sharp suit and pearls. The only person missing is Brandy.

Aunt K is the fairest of them all in a long, form-fitting, burgundy dress, her locs twisted and sculpted into a crown. She wields her trumpet, and on the dot of ten she plays a haunting solo, 'God Bless The Child'.

I search for Zed's face and find it, and retreat. Spanish slips his hand into mine and squeezes it. 'Why do the beautiful things hurt so much?' he asks quietly, as Aunt K reaches into every soul with her playing, drawing out the quiet. Even Eko doesn't make a sound. When it's finished, applause swells to fill the room and Spanish puts an arm around me. 'Did you say there was a roof terrace?' he asks.

'Yeah, but I haven't been up there in a long time . . .'

'Let's go,' he says, leading me by the hand.

It's a night on the brink, almost autumn and dizzy with stars, city winking at me from below. The roof is split onto two levels and surrounded by reassuringly solid railings. Pots of plants and flowers line the periphery. Lanterns brighten the darkness. I walk to the furthest corner, where the party is a wraith of a thing and I can barely hear Aunt K's trumpet or the drums or the cheers and I can concentrate on taking in oxygen. Before I've taken in much, Spanish is snaking an arm around my tight shoulders, pulling me against his side. 'Hey, you OK?'

'Yeah,' I answer, although I'm not sure if it's true.

Spanish asks me if I'm cold and I say no and he says, 'Eden . . . I . . . I just wanna say how glad I am that I met you. You throw,' he hesitates, 'you throw my world open. Everything just feels fresh for the first time in a while and I thought I had it figured out,' he says, looking down at the view instead of at me. 'So I'm sorry about how I've been acting but if you haven't been able to tell, I got issues. I mean, my *issues* got issues,' he laughs awkwardly, 'you know what I'm saying? But I'm working on them, you know? For you . . .'

I can't think of anything better to say than, 'It's cool.'

'I just want to stay in your life, mama. All that time I thought I was just tired of it all, really I was waiting for you . . .'

'Well, looka here!' shouts Mohican Joe. 'Spanish done left the monastery!'

Spanish jumps around. 'God! You asshole.'

'What's happening?'

'I'm 'bout to knock you out, rooster head, that's what! Need to quit fuckin' sneaking up on people, man!'

'Chill, chill. Just thought I'd come over and say what's up. Damn.' Spanish shakes his head and laughs. Mohican Joe says, 'So what's up?'

'Your hair, man! That's what's up.'

'Fool,' Mohican Joe says to Spanish, then he turns to me and says, 'Hey, Trouble.'

I stick my tongue out at him, glad of the interruption. 'How's you?'

'Not as good as Spanish, obviously.'

In no time we're surrounded by guests as they spill out onto the roof. Someone brings a crate of beer and someone else starts setting up some decks and speakers. Bleak, Zahara and Nami are here, as well as Zed and Max. Everyone is drinking and chatting and laughing, except Max, who doesn't seem to know what to do with all the attention Zed is getting and all the attention he's not giving her. Spanish gets a chair and draws me into his lap and there, despite my noisy mind, I feel safe. People talk to him about his music and his politics and they give me soft smiles, like I'm part of something wonderful. Zed draws up a chair and Max tries to sit in his lap too, but he leaps to his feet. 'It's cool,' he tells her. 'You take the chair.'

Then Zahara asks Spanish how he got his name, since he can't speak a word of the language. 'It's not important,' he says.

'Come on, what's the big secret? Just tell me.'

'Maybe you should ask Zed why they call me Spanish.'

'Zed?'

Zed grins. 'It's not complicated. I mean, look at the guy. He looks like one taco-eating motherfucker. It was back in school. I was a couple years older than him and he kind of looked up to me. Started following me around . . .'

'I didn't follow your ass around!'

'Come on. I saw my shadow less often. Anyway he was this chubby kid—'

'Damn, player! You gotta expose me like that?'

'Chubby?' I say.

'When I say chubby, I'm being kind, alright? Suck it up, Spanish. You want me to tell the story or not?'

'You wanna dance?' Max asks Zed. The decks are ready and there's a DJ playing an odd mix of seventies funk, eighties cheese and assorted hip-hop and reggae.

'Not right now,' he says with barely a glance. 'So anyway . . .'

'Come on, I'm in the mood.'

'No!'

Max looks grim. 'Hey, Spanish! How many of those mush-rooms you gave me are gonna give me a good time?'

'I'd just take all of them and fly,' he shrugs. Max walks off and Zed carries on his story.

'So he was just about getting into all of this black and proud shit. And it was like I was the only black guy he'd ever met, so he was all excited. Started talking about how we all gotta stick together. This kid all pale with his little curly hair. I was like, you ain't black! You are *Spanish*, chico. And all of the rest of the kids started calling him that.'

'Amazing, isn't it?' Spanish's hand tightens around my arm. 'The only other black guy in school is the one who stereotyped my ass.'

'Whatever, man. Would you prefer "James"? Anyway, you're the one who started everyone off calling me Zulu.'

'Only after the "Spanish" thing started. Besides, your name didn't hurt you much.'

'I made it my own.' Zed shrugs. 'I don't waste my time fighting the world on everything. But "Zulu"? Talk about "perceived skin colour"! First it got shortened to Zoo, then

Zee, then this rich little British kid from school called me Zed once and that was that. A nickname for life.'

'For both of us,' adds Spanish. The recounting of this story has done nothing for his mood and I'm starting to feel not great about everything again. All this history between them. It's freakish.

'Wow . . . I never knew that!' says Nami, turning up from nowhere and inserting herself into the conversation. She's standing next to Zed, flicking her yak hair and pulling at the super-tight hot-pants she's wearing. 'I thought Zed was your real name.'

'No, it's Aaron,' I say a bit more loudly than intended, but she doesn't even look at me. She's started off with her 'Damn, you look good!' speech again. The slapper.

'Eden?'

'What?'

'Eden, I just asked you,' says Bleak patiently, 'if Zed or Spanish played you any of their collaborations that they recorded?'

'No,' I tell him.

'You wanna dance?' Nami asks Zed, and he says, 'Cool.'

She leads him a short distance away and they start dancing and grinding it up to an old nineties dancehall tune. She's tack personified in her cheap glam look, dropping her fast behind and shaking it. I wish Aunt K would come up and see this. She'd probably throw her over the railings.

'Girl, it's bananas! I need to give you a copy of Zed's new EP. The joints are ridiculous, ma. Completely different. I've never seen him write so deep. He's always been a clever writer, but lately his material has profundity, you know what I'm saying? And a lot of heart.'

'Really? Good for him.' I want to go back down to the basement. It's too noisy, much too noisy up here. Zed's hands are on Nami's hips.

'Well you're gonna hear some of it later anyway . . .'

'What do you mean?'

Then Brandy sweeps onto the roof and shouts, 'Boss lady wants all the musicians downstairs, so ya'll better shake it fast!' She looks at me. 'You have on the prom dress!' She claps. 'You are working it, girl! Wow.'

'Thank you. Hey, Brandy!'

'Yeah?'

'How come you weren't around earlier? You missed Aunt K on her trumpet.'

Spanish makes his way downstairs with a kiss for my forehead.

Brandy says, 'I was just summoning my courage, girl. Summoning my courage.'

'For what?'

'Because tonight my life is gonna change, Eden.' She smiles, exhales, and pats her hair. 'I'm gonna ask Violet to marry me.'

I gasp. 'Really?'

'Really . . . I should have done it before. She was giving me all the signs, saying she wanted us to tell everyone we were together, start thinking about our future. But I was too scared. I mean, I didn't know what I had to offer a woman like Violet. I only want to be with her, but it's never been simple for me and mostly I don't even know if I want to be in panties or boxer shorts. What kind of stability is that? But then I got this letter from your Aunt K in Saint Lucia. She didn't say anything. She was just writing about her trip and all, but suddenly I just knew: it was enough for Violet and me to want to be together. We'll sort it out.'

'Oh my God!' I give her a long hug, like a sister. 'That's amazing, Brandy. Good luck. Who cares about the surface, anyway? It's so rare to find somebody you fit with and have it stick. I wish you the best!'

287

'Thanks,' she says. Beaming, happy, brand new. 'You seen her new hair?'

'Yeah,' I smile. 'It's wonderful!'

'Those cheekbones of hers were *born* for a boycut!' says Brandy with a theatrical roll of the eyes, and then a wink.

Zed catches me in the hallway. 'Hey,' he says, easing himself off the wall, like he's been waiting. 'I never got a chance to say how good you look in that dress. It really suits you.'

'Cool,' I say and push past. I can hear Aunt K introducing Violet up to the mic in the other room.

'Damn,' he says, hands in the air, 'is that how we repay compliments these days?'

'Whatever.'

'Eden,' he touches my shoulder, 'come on, "thanks" would be nice.' He ventures an awkward laugh. I stare at him, with neither the feeling nor the inclination to laugh in return. 'Seriously, what's going on with you?'

'It doesn't matter, Zed.'

'It does! One minute we're cool and the next you act like you hate me. I don't know which Eden I'm gonna be dealing with from one minute to the next. I don't even know how to act with you.'

'Well maybe you'll never learn, then.'

'What the hell is that s'posed to mean?'

'Listen, mate,' I say to him, snapping suddenly, feeling dizzy and finished. I bustle him halfway up the empty stairs to the roof. 'I can't play this game anymore,' I tell him, then drag him up further, almost to the top. 'I'm in love with you. I've been in love with you since I was fifteen years old, and I've never gotten over it. I haven't,' I choke, 'I haven't been able to *move* because of you! I'm sick of pretending like that's not how I feel. And I'm sick of you parading other women in front of me like I'm made of rock! It's not bloody fair!' I say. 'It *hurts!*' I wipe my eyes. 'Max was my friend, Zed. You didn't see anything wrong with that? I don't care how long it's been. How could you do that to me? I've had enough. You're gonna either have some fucking respect for me or stay the fuck out of my life!'

'Eden . . .' Zed just stands there, outlined by the sky. Violet's voice cracks but she carries on, accompanied by only a piano.

'Act *human* with me, that's all,' I say, buoyed by the music from the other room, bobbing on the water. Hollow. 'Be my friend.'

'I've never,' he rubs his face, 'I've never been out to try and hurt you. That's never been my intention . . .'

'But you do. You do it all the time! And I know you don't feel the same way I do but it doesn't mean you have to be so cruel, Zed. Sometimes I feel like my heart just can't take anymore. I just—'

'Zed? You up there, man? Been looking all over for your ass. Come on. We out to get in that jam session after Violet. You too, Eden!'

'What the hell have I got to do with it?' I manage.

'You got one of our skits, girl. Whatchoo think? We give them shits away for free?'

'Bleak, I'm not a performer,' I say, but he's started walking off. Zed gives me a helpless, loaded look and follows. He shakes his head as he walks.

In the living room the band plays lazy, waiting for us. All minor chords, all murky drum patterns, double bass intertwining with low chatter. The room is drunk and we've eaten all the chicken. A big black cake full of dried fruits and rum awaits, dominating the table in the corner. Shoulder straps hang awry. Shirts are half-unbuttoned, hats off, shoes off. Eko sleeps on his mother's chest with his mouth open. He's had music since the womb. Violet does look gorgeous in her short hair, satin dress, and broad smile.

'I'm not a performer,' I say again, standing near the musicians, near Spanish tuning up his guitar. The music is loudest in my head, squeaks and riffs and rippling melodies. I feel so confused and so strong. I can love him and walk away. I can choose me.

'Everybody's a performer,' says Spanish, his voice languid with drink.

'Huh?'

'Everybody,' he stops fiddling with the strings, 'is a performer. It's a decision, you know what I mean? It's a decision as much as it is a talent. You just gotta decide. Wait till I give you the cue and then do what comes into your head.'

'You ready?' Zed says to him tightly, walking up. I've never seen him nervous like this. They start a song I've heard before in London. But this time he's different, rhymes slightly off-beat and with a sense of irony. No two-step. No showmanship. Only his neck and his hands are mobile, as though he's trying to shape his sounds in the air after they've left his mouth. Everyone can see the places where he's broken, places he won't even show me. And his talent is just like cramps, to me. It's like walking past a gorgeously fragrant restaurant when you're hungry and penniless. You can see them eating through the window. The expectant forks and smudged wine glasses. You can see the crumbs on their lips. You can see the steam rising from the dishes. He's everything I can't afford—

'Poem!' yells Zed into the mic halfway through a verse. Everybody looks at him. The band keeps playing. 'Shut up!' he tells them and they obey.

'Hey, what we doing here, man?' Spanish asks quietly.

'You'll see,' says Zed. Then he turns to the room.

'This is a new song,' he says, with a nervous laugh. 'It's for everybody in particular and somebody particular in general.' I shiver. He paces, unrestrained and jerky, changing the energy of the room, buttoning it up. Waking up Eko. Violet leaves with her son before his complaining escalates to full-blown opera. I notice Brandy follow her out. Zed takes a few breaths and pulls his hood up—

'Mama if I climb inside myself,' he begins, 'can I take you with me?'

Before he's spoken his second line, I draw my cam like a sword and *click click click* his mouth – his hands – his eyes – his mic – his smile – his frown – his artful silences and I let him and the clicker resume their powerful romance . . . but me? With a great and unanticipated shift in myself as powerful as the grinding of tectonic plates – I *let go*. And breathe.

Then, before I have a chance to prove Spanish wrong about my skills as a performer, Baba rushes into the room and shouts, 'Who the white girl belong to?'

problem.

'She in that back room!' says Baba. 'I found her trying to eat the window blinds!'

'Shit,' says Spanish. 'The fool must have dosed the whole bag. I thought she knew about that kind of shit! It was over nine grams in there . . .'

'She gonna be alright, man?' asks Zed, as we all rush towards the door, from which comes the sound of Max cackling.

'Yeah. She just gonna be a little cracked for a while, but it's not like she can OD.'

The back room. We're standing outside it.

'Eden, you OK?'

'Yep.'

It's just a room. It has no creative power. Then is *then* and now is *now* and never the twain shall meet, right? No problem.

Zed pushes the door open and it's dark so I switch on the light and . . .

Wait.

I can't stop screaming.

'Eden! Eden!'

I'm trying to find the doorknob behind me but my fist keeps closing on air and—

a minute.

Blood.

Everywhere.

So much red I shorted like a faulty wire. I couldn't compute. My mother was still tangled in the sheets and so was Paul. Zed's father. First thing I thought despite all the red was, *What's Paul doing in bed with my mother?* She was on top of him, head on his chest and a big hole in her side. Her hair still looked great. The sheets were ruined. Paul's arms looked like they'd tried to come around her, but had weakened. Her eyes were closed. His were open. The curtains were the only thing that moved.

'Eden!'

Zed had still been downstairs, and I could hear the TV. I didn't answer. I didn't step into the room or back out into the hallway.

I heard Zed charging up the stairs. 'The phone's ringing,' he said. 'It's so weird . . . What's wrong?'

Little sounds came out of my mouth. When Zed came to stand beside me, he did all the screaming. All of this happened in the space of a minute or so.

Then he pulled me out of the doorway and against the wall. He was breathing hard and shivering. 'They've been shot.'

'I know.'

'Who shot them? Somebody shot them, Eden.'

'I don't know.'

'Who shot them?'

We could hear the kids playing next door and the TV downstairs. We went to the kitchen and I called 911. They told us to leave the house, in case it was dangerous, and that they were sending someone right away. On the way out I noticed Dominic sitting in the back yard on a lawn chair, staring into space. He still clutched the gun in his right hand. I grabbed Zed's hand and we ran.

I didn't tell him about Dominic until we were across the street and we'd seen the police cars come around the corner.

Then we heard that last POP! and we knew that he was gone too.

flame shakes.

'Eden . . . Eden, can you hear me?' Zed's voice pushing through the blissful dark. I try to scramble up from the bed and instead fall to the floor. We collide as he draws me carefully to my feet. 'You fainted! It's just wine she spilled down her dress, alright? She's OK, just in a trance. It's red wine. Calm down, alright?'

Look around. Max is laying in all the red, smiling. 'You're so many colours, Eden,' she says very slowly. 'I ever tell you?' Then she closes her eyes.

'It's alright,' I say, sitting down heavily on the floor. 'It's just a bed. It's just a bed.'

He puts his arms around me and I crumple and fold and my head is a solid ache and my face is covered with water.

'It's OK, Eden. It's OK. Aunt K has taken Spanish to the roof to cool down. The others are giving us some space. Just relax.'

I didn't scream when it happened. I didn't cry. But she was dead. Stolen before I knew her properly or before I'd forgiven her for leaving and before I asked her why she didn't love me and before we went to Mexico like she promised or ice-skating or she'd taught me to speak Creole or . . .

'Talk to me,' Zed says.

I look at him. 'You know it all,' I say. Nervously he takes a spliff from behind his ear and lights it. And in the midst of all the tension and dark memories, Max lets rip a deafening snore.

'Bloody hell!' I say, and we laugh manically until her snores settle down to normal.

'This is the room,' he says eventually, blowing out a long plume of smoke.

I notice for the first time that he's shaking. The flame shakes, the spliff shakes, his lips shake. His face is slick.

'Zed,' I say. 'Zed?'

'I do know it all.' He shakes his head. 'How do you go on in life and see anything the same, when something like this could happen to regular people, Eden?' Puff. 'How can you ever feel safe? I still have nightmares about their faces. About Dominic . . . It fucks my head up, you know? That he was human, like that. Not Satan. Just a *guy* who would put insects outside instead of killing them.'

'Yeah, I remember that too.'

A whoop goes up outside. The party is still going on while we sit here. Feels like the whole world should stop, but it never does.

'He was the first person who ever took an interest in me, what I really wanted to do with my life. I grieved for him. But how can I feel grief after what he did? He took my father . . .' His voice catches. 'He took your mother.'

'I know,' I tell him. I grip him and he grips me and we're like a knot pulled tight as it can go. All my muscles hurt, especially my heart. I can't stop crying. 'I know.'

He takes my face in both of his hands and I'm drumming in the chest and strange in the abdomen like every time. 'Did you mean it?' he asks, breathing off-time.

'What?'

'When you said you still love me?'

It's so quiet. Neither of us moves. Can't hear anything but my blood. This is how it would feel seconds before the apocalypse. Kissing him would be the end. What could come after that? What world would I be born into? His mouth.

Seconds pass and each one is long enough that a civilisation could rise, fall and crumble to dust.

'It's like my name,' I tell him. I clear my throat. 'It's who I am. I love you for ever.' He closes his eyes for a moment. 'How . . .' I ask him. 'How do you feel about me?'

'You already know you're the best part of me. The purest. I reached a point in my life where I barely recognised myself anymore. I didn't know where I belonged. I woke up from dreaming one night and I knew I couldn't act like you weren't *home* anymore, you know? I was lost. And then when I saw you, the feelings were even stronger than when we were kids, but there was all this distance between us. I just wanted to be close. I damn near drove my bike into a brick wall trying to figure what had happened to me and you,' he laughs. 'It's never gone away.' He smoothes my hair back from my forehead, kisses me there. 'I can't be a coward anymore.'

'Don't,' I manage. 'Don't be a coward.' My chest hurts. And he reaches down, his warmth closer and closer and then his mouth so soft on mine and the love is too thick. I must be dying. And his hands under my clothes and his body under my hands and salt on his face and the taste in his mouth is exactly the same as the first time.

'You want me?' he says quietly, lips on my neck. I fizz right to the ends of my fingers and toes. 'Tell me.'

'We can't . . . Max is here . . .'

'Tell me,' he repeats, running his hands under my dress, up the insides of my thighs. 'I don't care. I don't want to think. I just want to be with you.'

'Max . . .'

'Is asleep.'

'Don't do this unless you love me, Zed,' I tell him. 'I won't survive.'

'I wish there were new words I could say.' He takes my face in his hands again. 'I'll make new ones up for you.'

I laugh softly, dying in tiny increments, feeling time move us along, always toward each other. 'You are so bloody corny.'

'That's what you do to me, girl,' he says. 'You wanna see my room?'

'You fool!'

'You wanna hear my poetry? I got some poetry for you.'

He turns off the lamp and we sink down to the floor, burning and sweating, slotting together in the dark. This will be a new room.

We ignore the footsteps out in the hallway, and then there's a knock at the door.

cold poses.

And what could we do except put on our dusty black clothes and try to forget that we were red inside too? And that it only took one moment to find out. What could we do except read assurances from the God Book, leak our salty colourlessness. What could we do but make tables full of tuna sandwiches?

Aunt K locked herself away in her bedroom and wouldn't come out. Zed's mum flew in from Atlanta and my dad came from London, and we all camped out on the ground floor until the funerals. Zed and I, living in the same house. Sun-up and sun-down and the radio and the bodega for Almond Joys and Fritos. I don't know how the world kept going like it did except that what happened was so strange and vicious and hard to take it didn't feel like it had anything to do with everyday life anywhere.

A double murder in Brooklyn.

The incident was covered on the local and national news. Dominic is what made the tragedy primetime delicious; a hunky actor arrested for the murder of his wife and her lover. It was so Hollywood. It was just like one of the dumb storylines from a soap opera. It didn't sound like a real thing that happened. Not to any of us, left flopping about in the aftermath.

We'd watch the news with them on it. Frozen and pretty in their post-crime sympathy photos. Marie and Paul. They were great for this sort of thing. People were captivated for that thirty seconds it was primetime. Pretty people like that shouldn't die. Everyone was waiting for the credits to roll and for these straight-toothed actors to jump up from their cold poses. Including us.

I kept replaying the last words I ever exchanged with my mother. They seemed so senseless now she was gone. A couple days before it happened, she'd come over from her apartment to eat breakfast with us (in a fit of guilt, I thought, over how little time she'd spent with me) and to bring me some cash.

When I was just about ready to go out the door she said, 'I don't really like that shade of yellow on you, Eden. You ought to wear richer colours with your skin tone.'

And even though it irritated me, I thought she might be right and I wanted to look good for Zed. So I rushed up the stairs to change into a pea green T-shirt, but then couldn't choose between the pea green and a hot pink vest that I had. By the time I made a decision and came back down the stairs, my mother had gone off to some audition or other. So those were her last words.

'You ought to wear richer colours with your skin tone.'

And my last words had been, 'Oh bloody hell, Mum!'

Imagine.

In the dark, upturned like a stone, I found myself scrolling through all our most recent conversations to the last thing that sounded truly significant. I wanted to remember that too. I didn't want it all to fade except for that statement about yellow, and her plastic-y dead face.

I picked official last words. And this was something she'd said to me a couple of weeks before, when we'd been out shopping for her favourite lipstick in Macy's. A deep fleshy-toned matt. She pouted in the mirror and she smiled at me. She let me try some on too. They had an oldie, 'The Boys of Summer', playing on the store's sound system.

'Try this on!' she said and wiped the other one off gently

with tissue and make-up remover. She handed me a noisy red. I looked at her suspiciously. 'Go on!'

'OK.' I put it on and watched my lips become a serious primary. I looked totally different.

'See, look at you!' she said. 'Pretty as a film star!'

And she'd never said anything like that to me before. I'd always been too awkward and too coarse for her. 'I love it . . . It's so bright though . . .' I said.

'Here's an important life lesson, sweetheart: don't fade and don't apologise. Women hold the key to men's souls. They only know themselves through us. They're gonna do everything they can to hide that fact, but it's the truth.'

And for once, I felt like she was really speaking to *me*.

She let me keep that Technicolor lipstick on while we went for lunch and I felt so vivid in my adolescent body and lip paint.

I thought and re-thought that memory until it was tight and every minute was in its place. I tried to pull it over the other stuff like a blanket, but failed. I was too sad, and too angry and cheated. But maybe now I can finally appreciate that last hug from her, a gift from one generation to the next—

twins, remember?

'Eden?' Knock. Knock. Knock.

'Uh oh,' says Zed. 'Oh God.'

Then a crash as the door is thrown open.

Spanish blocks the doorway, light pouring in from behind him. And somewhere deep down I'm laughing in disbelief. A black laugh. This can't be happening. It's the same room. I imagine what Spanish sees, Zed and I dishevelled and intertwined at the limbs, half-dressed. And is that the face Dominic wore? My whole body tingles and my mind is one single putrid shade. Guilt. Is this how my mother felt?

'I'm sorry, man,' starts Zed and gets up off the floor. Spanish's mouth is hard, turned down at the corners. 'I didn't mean for things to . . . Look, I love her . . .'

Then everything speeds up and I'm trying to reach Spanish because – *Pak!* – Zed is on the ground and Spanish is on top and I can feel the sound of it—

Pak! Pak! Pak!

The pain of his fist smashing into Zed's cheek. Over and over. I'm screaming 'Help!'

I jump on Spanish's back, biting, pulling, twisting, trying to get him off. His rage is massive. Every tendon in his body is taut. 'Stop it!' Zed can barely get his arms up. I sink inside, hearing the sound. *PAK! PAK! PAK!*

In desperation I scratch Spanish's arms, bite him hard on the neck. I slap him with all the power I can muster. 'HELP!'

Finally, Aunt K sweeps into the room followed by Baba.

'What the hell is going on in my house?' she yells. 'Stop that right now!'

And Zed starts getting in some punches and they hit the floor and roll and they don't listen to me or Aunt K screaming for them to stop. They don't listen until Mohican Joe and Bleak rush in and pull them apart. Spanish springs up from the floor. His T-shirt hangs in flaps off his narrow chest.

'Spanish . . .'

'Don't speak,' he chokes out, breathing hard, tears pouring down his face. 'Don't fucking speak. Eden . . .' He shakes his head. 'I came back to . . . I can't believe this. You're gonna choose him? He doesn't love you. He's using you, just like Max.'

'I can fucking speak for myself!' says Zed finally.

'Yeah, but it might be healthier for you if you shut your mouth! You don't think you've said enough? You wanna get beat down again, nigga?'

'You are the only nigger in this house, nigga! Are you happy? That's what you've always wanted, isn't it?'

Spanish's face colours deeply with anger. I think he's going to swing another punch, but he doesn't. He goes still. He looks at me. 'For you, Eden,' he says to me. 'For you, I'm gonna leave before I do something stupid.' He throws his hands up half-heartedly. 'I saw this coming. You and me . . . we're like twins, remember? I can't compete with your first.'

'Spanish!'

'What? You think I didn't know?' He gives a laugh as black as the inside of my head. 'Everything shows on your face, Eden. Do what you gotta do. If it all goes wrong, you know where to find me.'

Then he pushes through all the people piling up at the doorway behind him and is gone.

the big magic.

A few nights after we found them, Grandma came back from her holiday in Saint Lucia early. I remember dreading it. Her coming back would concentrate the whole experience and make it into a finished incident, rather than some odd trip I might snap out of. When she arrived in the house with her bags, tears and big Caribbean grief it all seemed irreversible and real.

I hadn't seen her for years. I stood dutifully in the hall and kissed her loose cheeks. She was still bird-boned and petite under all the wrinkles, a baked-in bronze. She looked like my mother. But my mother would never be old now.

Before and after the funerals, Granny would just sit in the dusty living room staring at the TV screen, whether the TV was on or not, whether it was the news or not. Back and forth in her rocking chair, drinking strong rum.

Sometimes I would sit with her and she would tell me stories about my mother. 'My Marie,' she'd chuckle in her fake teeth. 'Wow! She always had her own mind! And she was so beautiful! Nice face, nice complexion! Everyone wanted to marry your mother, you know. Everyone. I can't believe that she was the one to go. Why she have to go, oh lord? Why *she* have to go?'

And sometimes, I'd feel a bit uncomfortable when she said that, like maybe she wished that Aunt K had gone instead. Or me. Or anybody else but her perfect Marie. And then I'd feel stupid and selfish for being so insecure.

But Zed was so good with her; he would always get her

to smile. He could get away with anything with her. She would say, 'You remind me of my grandfather! So tall, handsome and black. Black just like you, boy!'

And he would smile at her. That special smile he has, despite all the pain he was feeling. He was sleeping on the couch in the living room. And although we were never together again, the way we'd been together, it felt just the same being near him. My heart drumming relentlessly. Mouth dry as dust.

Only difference was, before the murder he'd seemed like the most dangerous thing in my life. Afterward, he seemed like the safest.

'Aunt K?' I knock on her bedroom door. 'Aunt K?'

It's about four in the morning. The party is over, everyone has gone home and dawn is creeping into the sky. I've left Zed asleep in the basement.

'Come in,' she says. Her voice is tired. I push into the room and she's sitting on the floor in a purple robe, illuminated by candles. Max is lying asleep in her bed.

'I hope I'm not disturbing you.'

'No. Come sit down. Your friend's snoring so loud I don't think a bomb could disturb me more.'

Tentatively I laugh, go in and perch on a stool. The room is richly coloured and antique, heady with sandalwood.

'I'm sorry for spoiling your party, Aunt K. I haven't been a very good house guest.'

'No, you haven't,' she smiles. 'But I don't need my guests to be good, Cherry Pepper, I need them to be honest.'

I nod.

'This house has seen so much pain,' she says. 'And now I want it to be a place of healing. It has healed me, it seems to be healing you and, you never know, it might just heal Spanish. That's a powerful young man. He's going to do a

305

lot, especially now you seem to have given him back his free time,' she says wryly. 'I need to try and get him involved in the community.'

'Healed you how, Aunt K?' I ask, trying not to think about me and Spanish and pain and time.

'I need to tell you something,' she says, her gaze piercing. 'It was me.' She takes a slow breath. 'It was me who told Dominic that Marie was having an affair. Dominic came to my office with his suspicions, and I told him they were true. Then I let him storm off in a fury.'

I don't move.

'For the past ten years,' Aunt K continues, 'I've felt responsible for Marie's death. I've tried everything to shake the guilt – drugs, counselling – but finally I've realised it won't go away. I've just got to live with it and give my life to others. Trust in the big magic.'

'But why,' I say, 'why did you tell him?'

'A lot of reasons. Because I was jealous of your mother. Because I was self-righteous and moralistic. But the most painful one is also the most obvious, Cherry Pepper. I was in love with Paul. So long I carried those feelings and then as soon as Marie grew into womanhood, he wanted her. And when she left, I wasn't even his second choice. We both moved to the States where he met Zed's mom, Grace, and settled down. And I just gave up. Got fat. Got old. Did nothing but work. When I bought this house I sent for my mother to come and live with me.'

Tears stood in her eyes. 'Paul and Grace eventually got divorced, but by then I didn't even see myself as a romantic interest. I'd resigned myself to being Paul's friend. Sure I went out with a few guys, but always half-heartedly. If Paul couldn't see me as beautiful, then I wasn't.

'As much as I loved my sister, when she moved over to New York was probably when I reached my lowest point.

I couldn't help but compare us. She was my younger sister, but it felt like she could've been my daughter. Her life was so shiny and fresh. I'd been locked in the same job for years and spent all my evenings watching TV with an old woman.

'And then there was that summer . . . I knew, Eden! I knew that she and Paul were seeing each other again. I watched it all unfold before my eyes and did nothing. The truth is that I . . . I wanted for Marie to have a fall from grace. Nothing like what happened . . . but just one time when she'd be brought low like I'd been.'

'Oh my God . . . Aunt K.' Everything in my mind shifts around, all the links between people, all the things that didn't make sense before that suddenly do. And I know it will be ages before I really know how I feel about it all. 'I had no idea.'

'So they died because of me.'

'Dominic did it, Aunt K. He's the only one.' Her gaze is moist with gratitude. 'He already had his suspicions. He even tried to ask me about it. It was just. It had to be the way it was, didn't it?'

She nods.

'My dad knows what you did, doesn't he, Aunt K? That's what he's got against you.'

'He guessed right away. Said he'd never speak to me again. But that's changing now, Eden. Since you came here, he and I have been corresponding. It's time we put aside our differences. They've done you a lot of harm.'

I reach out and touch her hand.

'There's no way you could have known what Dominic was going to do. No way . . .'

She nods, wiping her face. 'Yep, but I acted out of bitterness. Never let a force so negative take over your life.'

'It's hard not to be bitter about Marie,' I say.

'Your mother did the things she did because she was in love with life. And she never stopped loving you, Cherry Pepper.'

At that moment Max wakes up.

'Bloody hell,' she says. 'That was some fucked-up dream.'

right now.

Light-footed I am, walking toward Brooklyn Avenue. Blue skies are uninterrupted block after block, 'The Boys of Summer' on my MP3 player. And 'I Can't Stay Away From You'. And 'Wuthering Heights'. If I weren't walking, I would dance. I would throw my body around the way I did when I was small, with no fear of table edges or walls or teetering ornaments. The way I did with her. I arrive outside the double gates of Holy Cross cemetery and stare at the sign. She was laid to rest here, in the foreign soil of her favourite city. I haven't been here since the first time. A few people wander in quietly, alone or in groups but I don't steal any pictures. Instead I switch off my music and dig for my earliest memory; Ridley market on a Saturday morning, all those years and moments and miles away, emerging now as a jewel in my eye. The smell of her. The green and blue print on her long gypsy dress. Her red-painted nails. The sky seemed so far away, and only slightly closer was her face up there, curls loose and shiny about her cheeks. Smiling at me.

A young autumn breeze sings amongst the maples and the air is fresh with the scent of cut grass and flowers. Tombstones stretch away and away, glittering in that early-morning sun. I make it to my mother's name almost without searching: *Veronica Marie Boccelli*. Run my hand over the cool stone. Aunt K reminded me that she is not this grave; she is not the dust and the bones. She stands over me in the mirror smoothing out my wrinkles. She picks lint out of my hair. She blows a breeze across my forehead on hot nights; she keeps watch over my dreams. She's still my mother.

The grass is soft on my knees as I sink down to the earth. The sun is kind to my skin.

'Hi Mum,' I say, and smile. I haven't said those words in so long they fall out of my mouth with an awkward, baby-like joy, and never before with such conviction that she can hear me. Not even when she was alive. She would love this dress I have on. She would love the shade of red on my lips.

In my knapsack are scores of prints that I lay out, a tapestry on the grass. I talk her through all my enthusiasms and madnesses, I tell her all about Old Chanders and Dad and how they're coming over to New York to celebrate their engagement. I tell her about Juliet and The Woman Who Got Away. I tell her all my fears, dreams and lovers. My tears are absolutely painless.

'I wanted to show you these. I'm a photographer, Mum! An arty chick just like you,' I tell her, feeling somehow like she's seen it all already. She lurks somewhere in my clicker's heart, racing for experience and new colours even beyond her passing. She's that part of me.

A long shadow falls over the grass.

'Aunt K said she thought you'd be here.'

Look round and there he is, twinkling like a silver coin in amongst the coppers. 'Zed!' Sporting a blue-black eye and a red T-shirt, hair growing in thick on his face and scalp. My Aaron. My Zulu, Zoo, Zee, Zed. 'Where have you been?'

'I didn't want to interrupt,' he says, hiking up his sagging jeans, putting his hands in his pockets. 'I'm sorry. I just wanted—' Pause. 'I just wanted to see you.'

'It's OK,' I say lightly, breathless like I always am when

I see him, but without the fear. Flying instead of falling. 'Where have you been?'

'I took Max to Manhattan, some friends she's got in Soho,' he says and laughs. 'She's got a message for you. She said –' he puts on her rough cockney voice and mimes tossing long, blonde hair – 'Tell that miserable cow she can have you! I don't know why she didn't just bloody tell me she fancied you in the first place! It's not like I didn't guess! I only wanted you for summer, anyway. I am *way* too pretty for you! And she knows I really only like boys from Shoreditch!'

I shake my head and laugh, and it doesn't feel bad at all to laugh here, by my mother's grave. That curtain between life and death is, after all, just a curtain. She's laughing too.

'And I called Spanish,' he says, looking down. 'He didn't answer any of my calls but not long ago he sent me a text message. Said he's gonna go look for his father. Aunt K said he'll be alright. She said everything had to happen just like this. For all of us.'

I nod. 'She knows all, she sees all, huh?'

'Indeed she does,' he says, hanging back still, waiting for an invitation. Silently I give him my open palm. He doesn't move. 'Come on,' I tell him. And after a few moments he does. Our hands are dark brown and light brown, each more vivid for being intertwined. 'I know why you threw that brick,' he says.

'Why?'

'Because I'm an asshole.'

I laugh. 'Yeah. And because I was lonely and tired and spiteful. And because I'd rather you hated me than just didn't care. I wanted you to feel something.'

He closes his eyes. 'You gonna come with me to see *my* father,' he says so quiet and thick I barely hear him, 'some-time?'

'Whatever you ask, you already got it.'

He snakes his arms around me and his hug is the realest thing I've ever felt, snapping me right up against the moment. 'I get all twisted up wondering how things would have been if my dad was alive, and your mom,' he says, voice muffled by my hair. 'What would have happened with us if they'd gotten serious. We couldn't have been together. It seems wrong to . . .' he drags the words from down deep, 'to benefit from their death in any way at all.'

'You heard Aunt K. This could only be how it is, Zed. Maybe we're living their dream.'

He squeezes me and pulls back slightly so he can look at me, letting the possibility sink in. 'Maybe,' he says, and then reaches over and fingers all my prints. 'I love these.'

'Thank you.'

'Where's your camera?'

I take it out of my bag and hand it to him. The clicker gleams silently and is just a piece of technology today. It's asleep. He stretches out his long, dark arm and takes a picture of us.

'Put that with the rest,' he says.

acknowledgements

Isaiah! Everything for you, little one. Stephanie Cabot (and everyone else at The Gernert Company) thanks for your guidance and support from the end of my teens up to the present! Rebecca 'Midwife of the Soul' Carter, you have taught me so much! Poppy (+1) Hampson, Claire Morrison, Lisa Gooding and everyone else at Chatto, thanks for your patience and enthusiasm. The Arts Council, and more specifically Charles Beckett, thanks for giving me a real start on this thing. My wonderful family: Mum, Dad and 'Graunty'; my three departed grandparents and Papa, who remains; my gorgeous brothers, Marlon, Jermaine and Malcolm, and their own families (I love you Tia!); and the rest of my massive tribe (including super-fly Emma Robinson), thanks for your abiding love and fanatical cheerleading! Mary Valmont, Leon and Valerie, thanks for giving me shelter and wisdom in Brooklyn. Friends, muses, mentors and confidantes – Clara Mintah, Kelly Foster, Rich Blk, Ms Mimi Fresh and Nayak, Priscilla Joseph (Lucian girls RULE), shortMAN, Caroline Morgan and the little ones, John A., Karee and Kemi, Bris Carclay, McGavin James, Matthew 'Face' Lawrence and lovely Mumma Sandra – thanks for your hospitality and kindness. Simone Stewart and Ms Loseca Austral, Street Journo (thanks for reading!), Courttia Newland, Kim Trusty, The Bard, Diran Adebayo, Karen McCarthy, Patrick Neate, Eric Jerome Dickey, Ty, Cody ChestnuTT, Soweto Kinch, Kn0wn, One Taste et al, Paul Stiell, the entire contingent of London artistes, writers and thinkers, expecially the Free-Write Wednesday crew, Uprock and Amplified, thanks for giving me somewhere to go dance, and all the other wonderful people who have offered advice, a meal, a joke, or a willing ear during this lengthy process, you like, totally rock dudes. You know what? Just everyone, yeah? All 6 billion and change. Especially you, who's reading this right now. And Michael Bhim, my dear, you are just in time. (Oops! Is that a cliché? Ha ha!)

Peas,

Gem xo